Funerals and Obituaries Series

dead and GONE

jennifer rebecca

Dead and Gone

Copyright © 2019 Jennifer Rebecca

Cover Design by
Alyssa Garcia
www.uplifting-designs.com

Photographer:
Reggie Deanching
www.rplusmphoto.com

Model:
BT Urruela
www.bturruela.com

Editing by
Bethany Pennypacker
Outthink Editing

For more information about Jennifer Rebecca & her books, visit:
www.jenniferrebeccaauthor.com

ABOUT THE BOOK

You ever have an out-of-body experience? Like one of those moments where you're standing on a street corner watching yourself do something monumentally stupid? Something you know you shouldn't do but you just can't help yourself?

Three weeks ago, Trent and I were deep into the honeymoon stage of love, and I swore I wouldn't be the first one to rock the boat—Lord knows with our two Irish tempers it would happen soon enough—so when he made me promise to keep my nose and our grandmothers out of his investigation, I did.

It didn't hurt that his head was buried between my legs at the time either. But then Daisy showed up, begging for help, and what kind of bestie would I be if I shut the door in her face? That's right, a shitty one. So I packed up our grandmothers and their go-go boots, G-strings, and pasties to get to the bottom of things. Only problem is if Trent catches us, I'll be dead meat, folks.

My name is Shelby Whitmore, Funeral and Obituaries columnist for the *San Diego Metro News* and most likely to be single again if I survive this shit. But hey, at least I'm still a hit with the blue hairs . . .

DEDICATION

For my very favorite hookers: Alyssa, Stacy, and Christina.

Thank you from the bottom of my heart for your unending friendships. Thank you for your kindness and your love of life, of books, and all those around you. For the light that you all bring to everyone around you, including me.

Don't ever let anyone dull your sparkle, because it could light the world over.

prologue

FATAL ATTRACTION

I'm dead meat. Literally. Dead. Meat.

Last month, when Trent and I started up for real after all of our false starts at the beginning of our relationship I promised him I wouldn't do anything crazy. I wouldn't go off half-cocked. And most importantly, I wouldn't follow our grandmothers down the crazy-assed rabbit hole of Granny Grabbers and Dangerous Dames.

"You're not police officers," he had said.

And I agreed. We're not.

Trent also might have coerced me into agreeing with him in the most despicable ways. One minute my legs were wrapped around his neck, my eyes were rolled back in my head, and I was one more "Oh, yes!" away from the promised land.

"Shell," he said to me in between licks and kisses. "Promise me you won't do anything crazy." He kissed me again and again.

"Yes." I ignored him as I rocked against his mouth, moving closer and closer.

"Promise," he commanded as I spiraled the edge.

"Yes!" I cried.

"You promise?" he asked me again, but I was too far gone.

"Sweet petunia, yes!"

"I'm so glad we agree. You have no idea how happy this makes me, Shelby." Trent smiled as he slithered up my body like the snake that he was.

Although, I had an idea how happy my climax had made him, as it was currently poking me in the thigh. Before I had a chance to catch my breath or even question what, exactly, Trent and I agreed on, he slid all the way inside me, to the hilt, and my eyes rolled back in my head.

As it turned out, we had allegedly agreed that I wouldn't go on any more capers with my friend Daisy, the retired hooker, and our grandmothers. Sophia was out; she was at some big, fancy figure-skating competition in Chicago.

I still agreed. Because, what kind of trouble could two widowed senior citizens, a retired hooker, and an obituaries columnist for the local paper get into? I mean, really. Lightning doesn't strike twice. It doesn't, right?

And Trent and I had worked out some kinks. He

yelled less. I pretended to listen more. And when I didn't, he used his handsome mouth in better ways than yelling, if you catch my drift. We were officially in the love bubble. The honeymoon stage. I wasn't ready to rock the boat for just anything all willy-nilly.

But Daisy, my sweet, fabulous, eccentrically dressed best friend, had a problem. Several of her . . . um . . . *colleagues* from the old days were missing. Like, really missing, not shacked up with a john. And she was worried. Yes, Daisy had a problem and she came to me for help . . . advice . . . I don't really know what. All I know is that that led me to today, as I sit, handcuffed to the pipes of a bathroom sink in a filthy motel just this side of Mexico, dressed like a cheap hooker. Yep, I'm in trouble, folks. Just like I said . . . Dead. Meat. My name is Shelby Whitmore, Funeral and Obituaries columnist for the *San Diego Metro News* and most likely to be single again if I survive this shit. I guess I should start at the beginning . . .

chapter ONE

THE CARPET AND THE CURTAINS

One week earlier . . .

"**W**ould you look at this up in here?" I hear my friend Daisy's voice ring out in the quiet restaurant over the low mood music. "This is some *Lady and the Tramp* shit up in here."

Trent and I having been fully committed to life in the love bubble after Sophia's brush with fame and are dining in a ridiculously expensive Italian restaurant in La Jolla.

Six months ago, Sophia was new to our social group and was firmly trying to remain a fringe friend when she discovered the body of her friend shot between the eyes and riding around an ice rink on a Zamboni. If someone were to ask me, I would say that's a pretty cold way to go. Anyway, after that she needed our help, and now she's part of our inner circle, the Dangerous Dames.

That was also the last time the grannies—mine

and Trent's both—had been involved in uncovering a crime ring. I'd like to say that lightning doesn't strike twice and all that shit, but . . . Needless to say, Trent has been a little nervous around them. He's been keeping us all on a short leash, and, truth be told, I haven't minded one bit. Now, that's probably because he keeps my cage gilded with fantastic orgasms from his magical penis, but I could be wrong.

I'm not, but I could be. It's bound to happen sometime.

So here Trent and I are, sitting at an exclusive table for two overlooking the ocean while we feed each other bites of rich lasagna (mine) and penne carbonara (Trent's). Somehow, when Trent feeds me food, he makes it seem like sex.

It might be because he turns to me and says, "You lick a fork like you lick a cock, and now I'm hard under this tablecloth."

I look up at him and wink my eye saucily as I lick the tines of my fork one more time.

So it's safe to say things were progressing in a certain direction for the evening when Daisy and Officer Jones showed up.

"Move over, Detective Hot Pants, and me and Jonesy will show you how it's done," Daisy shouts before yelling into the restaurant. "We need two more chairs here and some spaghetti STAT! I need to *Lady and the Tramp* make out with my man here."

Trent and I just sit here a little shell-shocked. Although, after knowing Daisy for over a year now, I think it's safe to say that nothing where she is concerned should surprise us anymore, so I just shrug it off and down my glass of pinot grigio like it's my job.

The maître d' hustles in with two more chairs and a look of apology to Trent, one that also says he's not getting the Benjamin he promised this guy on the way in when asking for a very secluded table with a romantic vibe and a view of the ocean. So far all we got was the ocean, and we could get that by staying home and watching *Finding Nemo* on TV.

I have to bite my lip to keep from laughing. Poor Trent looks so disgruntled. I'll have to make it up to him later. And by later, I mean as soon as we walk through the front door. I have consumed enough wine that it is guaranteed to be a fun time had by all. Maybe I'll even show him the new moves I learned from my new stripper aerobics DVD.

I nod to myself, thinking that that stripper aerobics DVD was the best nine dollars and ninety-nine cents I ever bought off of an infomercial in the middle of the night, as a waiter brings over a mountain of spaghetti, heaping with meatballs, precariously balanced on a plate and sets it down between Daisy and Jones.

"Let's show them how it's done, Jonesy!" she croons.

"Sure thing, baby," Jones says with no lack of self-confidence or male prowess.

It's like passing a car wreck on the interstate. You just slow down as you pass by, like every other rubbernecker out there, to take a look at the carnage. And, oh boy, is there carnage.

Both Daisy and Jones scoop up several strands of pasta with their forks, not bothering to twirl the noodles as one does with spaghetti. Instead they suck the ends into their mouths and then start hoovering toward each other in a very carnal version of the beloved and aforementioned children's movie. When they meet in the middle, they are a mess of teeth and tongues and red sauce.

"Best spaghetti I've ever had," Jones says when they break apart to come up for air.

"You got that right, Jonesy," Daisy agrees.

And then Jones spears a massive meatball on the end of his fork and dangles it over Daisy's lips from above. I feel a resurgence of my lasagna and a bit of jealousy as Daisy's tongue darts out to master Jones's ball. Girlfriend has some skills I may not ever possess.

I wonder if I should have the gals over to my place one night and have Daisy teach us all some new skills. It'll probably be awkward with my granny and Marla there, but it would hurt their feelings to be left out, and I can't have that on my conscience.

I look to Trent out of my peripheral vision and see that his eyes have glazed over a bit. Yep, we definitely need to have a girls' night. It'll be like a master class on blow jobs. This may be the three glasses of wine talking, but I think this is a spectacular idea.

"Maybe we should get out of here and give them a little privacy," Trent tells me.

"Yeah, that's a good idea," I say, tipping my head to the side to watch them from a better angle.

"Check, please," Trent says out loud.

The waiter brings Trent the check, and he tosses in more than enough cash to cover our dinners, theirs, and a heavy tip for the inconvenience before grabbing my hand and leading me out to the valet to claim his SUV

I snuggle into Trent's side while we wait for the kid working valet to bring the car around. Wine makes me extra cuddly. I let my hands do a little wandering as I trace a fingernail around his back in circles and curlicues.

Eventually my hand and I get a little bored, and I let it wander down to cup a handful of Trent's backside. He has a spectacular ass, and I like to worship at its altar. I think that I may bite it tonight. It's very bitable.

"Eeep!" he squeals like a girl when I pinch one of his cheeks.

"Jesus, Shell," he rumbles in my ear.

"What?" I ask as I look up into his handsome face with my eyes wide and drunkenly innocent.

"Nothing," he says with a chuckle as the car pulls up.

Trent opens my door for me and I climb inside, buckling my seat belt as he shuts the door behind me. He meets the valet kid around the curb and offers him a tip in exchange for the keys before climbing into the driver's seat and heading toward the interstate to take us back to his house.

"What are you thinking about?" he asks me once we're safely cruising up the I-15 toward Escondido.

"I was thinking that I need a master class in blow jobs," I answer before I can censor my mouth.

"Really?" He chokes out a laugh.

"Yeah." I shrug my shoulder. "I feel that my education is sorely lacking at the moment."

"Well, I, for one, think your education in the subject is just fine."

"Yeah?" I say, having a brilliant idea. I unbuckle my seat belt and lean across the center console. "Maybe I should practice a little more."

I trace a fingertip up and down the ridge in his slacks before deciding to undo his pants and pull his cock free.

"Shelby?" he asks as I stroke his length in my fist.

"Shh," I tell him. "I'm practicing."

"Oh God," he moans when I lean forward and suck the tip into my mouth.

I twirl my tongue around the tip again and again. Trent shifts in his seat as he speeds up the highway. I love the way he shifts his hips around in his seat and the girly little whimpers he makes. It turns me on.

But it's when I dip my hand down into his pants and cup his balls that Trent yelps and takes a sharp right onto the off-ramp from the highway. I flop back and forth across the center console of Trent's SUV like a drunken monkey—mostly because I am right now— and the movement makes me bob up and down his hard length with rapid momentum.

Trent takes another sharp turn onto the road that leads to his Spanish-style home in the northern hills of Escondido. Unfortunately, the city is doing some heavy road construction in this area and there are a lot of potholes and torn-up places that haven't been smoothed over yet. The effect is me braced on my belly over the center console while Trent and the road try to buck me off like an eight-second ride on a bull with an ominous name, like The Devil's Cock Block. I don't know if that's something the PBR would name a bull, but it would sure as shit scare me! The only things I have to hold on to as I flop around inside the vehicle while we travel up this highway to hell at a high rate of speed just so happens to be Trent's balls.

This only makes his foot press down harder on the accelerator while trying to buck me off.

Here in California, a simple roadwork job can take anywhere from six months to ten years. It's a crapshoot as to how long it will take. Uncle Sal, Granny, and I usually take part in a pool when the paper announces the start of a new job. Here's another *job* I won't be diving into for another ten years. That is, if I survive this one. The current outlook is not so good.

Trent reaches the crest of the hill and rounds the corner, pulling right into the driveway. He manages to slam on the brakes and stop just mere inches before he would have plowed right through the closed garage door. I let go of my hold on him when the car stops, and I fall into a heap of cute drunk girl on the floorboards.

"Jesus, Shelby!" Trent practically shouts. "Are you all right?"

"Sure," I answer. "Look! I stuck the dismount! Now help me out; I might be stuck."

Trent looks at me like he's trying to hold back a laugh. "It looks like it was your ass that stuck the dismount, Shell."

"You better not be calling my ass fat!" I snap.

"I wouldn't dare, baby," he rumbles in that deep, sexy voice of his that checks all of my boxes. "I'm going to bite that beautiful ass as soon as I get you out of this car and into my house, and then I'm going to show you what else I'd like to do to that ass."

"I don't think I'm drunk enough for anal," I tell

him honestly.

Trent throws his head back and laughs. "Trust me, baby, when I fuck that ass, it won't be because I spring it on you last-minute. That's how accidents happen."

"You can't get pregnant from your ass," I blurt out before slapping a hand over my wayward mouth. Damn you, delicious bottle of wine!

"No, but you can shit on my floor."

"I don't want that," I say, shaking my drunk head furiously.

"I don't want that either."

Trent refastens his pants and unbuckles his seat belt. He pushes open his door. The SUV rocks when he throws it closed, and I'm jostled back and forth on the floorboards. I'm still drunk enough that I don't really care. When he pulls open my passenger door, I am greeted with an impressive tent in his pants that could put my eye out like that kid in *A Christmas Story.* I never did get through that movie. I know everyone and their mother loves it, but I always thought it was kind of stupid and I felt bad for the kid with the glasses. That thought makes me giggle.

"I know you aren't laughing at the state you've left me in, now are you, Shelby?" Trent asks as he pulls me up from the floorboards.

I kind of am, but I don't want to tell him that, so I say the first thing that pops into my head. Unfortunately, it was a bigger mistake than telling him I was kind of, sort of laughing at his giant erection.

"I was thinking about anal," I answer, slapping my hand back over my mouth. I really need to stop talking.

"Well, that sounds like something I can help you

with."

Oh, shit!

Trent tosses me over his shoulder and I let out an "Eep!" I watch as he kicks the passenger door closed with his foot braced on the door. My view from this vantage point awards me with the spectacular view of his ass as the muscles play through his movements.

I bounce and jiggle as Trent stalks up the steps that lead to the front door of his home. My boobs nearly break free of their confines of black lace that lies hidden under the scoop neck of my LBD, because gravity is a real bitch when you possess anything bigger than a full C cup.

Trent does not breathe heavily or even break a sweat as he holds me over his shoulder with one hand while he pulls his keys from his pocket and unlocks the front door. He shuts the door behind us and lets me slither down his body until my heels touch the Spanish tile floor of the entryway. The look in his eyes both terrifies me a little and heats my whole body up from the inside out.

"So you want to play, cupcake?" he growls.

"Well . . . ," I start. "It had seemed like a good idea at the time."

Trent's muscular arms wrap around me, pulling me into his body. His hard length presses into the softness of my belly, and I feel like I'm either sinking into quicksand or turning into a pile of chocolate pudding, starting with my toes and moving upward.

"It still does to me," he says before crashing his lips down onto mine.

I hold on to his shirt for balance while Trent kisses

the daylights out of me. He licks into my mouth, and he rubs his hands up and down my back.

When he breaks his mouth away from mine, Trent turns me around. My breath seizes in my lungs as he pulls the zipper down on the back of my little black dress. The teeth rasp in the silent room. He pushes the straps down my shoulders one at a time—first the left, then the right. My dress falls to the floor in a pool at my feet, and I stand there, in the middle of the entryway, in nothing but my strappy heels and matching black lace bra and panty set.

"You're so fucking beautiful," he says as he rakes his eyes down my body and then back up again.

Trent walks me backward toward the sofa in the living room. It's almost like a dance we're doing—a tango of naked people and orgasms. I stop when my booty hits the arm of the sofa and brace myself with a hand on either side of my hips. Trent keeps moving forward until his hips are cradled against mine and I am leaning back a bit to accommodate his crowding me in.

He reaches around me and slides his hand up my spine until he reaches the clasp on my bra, unhooking it without even trying. I raise a silent eyebrow in question. Trent always seems to be well versed in the seduction of women. We both know he is way more practiced than I am. Trent pulls the lace away from my body before letting it flutter to the floor.

He kisses me again and it steals the breath from my lungs. I reach for the buttons on the front of his dress shirt and manage to unbutton several down from the collar before he grabs my hands in his, stilling my actions.

"No," he says as he steps back from me just enough to separate our bodies. "You got to tease me in the car. Now I get to tease you."

Trent turns me around so that I am facing the sofa. He places a palm on the spot between my shoulder blades and tips me forward. I lean on my forearms with my hips over the arm of the sofa and my legs stretched down to touch the floor.

Trent peels my panties down my legs, and I watch from over my shoulder as he tucks them into the front pocket of his gray slacks. He kicks my legs wide like he would searching a perp, and I have to bite my bottom lip to keep from squealing.

He drops to his knees between my stiletto-clad feet and buries his face between my legs. I gasp as he licks and bites. I squirm against the sofa cushions, the leather fabric, worn rough in some places, abrading my nipples as I do, which only serves to heighten my arousal.

"Trent," I whimper as he spears my pussy with his tongue.

"That's it, cupcake," he says between licks and kisses.

"Please," I beg. "I need more." And I do. I need it all, and right fucking now.

He chuckles as he pushes to his feet, and I moan as I hear the clank of his belt buckle echo through the living room. The sawing of my breath in and out of my lungs is the only other sound. I try to slow my racing heart, but it's no use. The anticipation is killing me. I hear the foil wrapper of a condom crinkle before Trent nudges my opening with the tip of his cock and then

. . .

Britney sings "Baby One More Time" from his pants pocket. I snicker. If someone were to ask Trent about his ringtone, he would tell them he lost a bet. But that's a load of crap. Homeboy loves him some old-school Britney, before the kids and the umbrella.

"You have got to be kidding me," he growls.

"What?" I ask as he pulls his phone from his pocket.

"Foyle," he barks. "You better be kidding me right now . . . okay."

"Trent?" I ask hesitantly, still flopped over the arm of the sofa.

"Roger that," he says. "I'll be right there." That can't be good.

Trent ends the call and pockets his phone. He pulls the condom off his cock and does up his pants. It's then that I realize nothing about tonight is going to go as planned. Goddammit.

"I caught a case, cupcake," he says, placing a kiss behind my ear. "I gotta go."

"Right now?" I snap, feeling a little on edge and a lot unfinished.

"Yeah." I feel his smile stretch across the skin of my neck. "Trust me, this hurts me more than it hurts you."

"I'm not sure I'll ever trust you again, you ass," I snap. "Can't it wait, like, five, maybe ten, minutes?" I know I'm being unreasonable, but in my inebriated and highly aroused state, I don't care at all. I want my orgasm and I want it now.

It's then that I have the bright idea to finish myself

off while he's gone. I mean, let's face it, life with a homicide detective is unpredictable at best. Who knows when Trent will be home, and I'm in no condition to drive, not to mention he already dropped off Missy, my cat, here earlier, as he was planning to spend the weekend with us in the love bubble.

He must see the determined look in my eyes because he narrows his own on me before issuing a bullshit demand.

"Don't you dare touch yourself while I'm gone," he says, and I feel my jaw drop open. How could he tell? "Go take a shower and curl into bed with Missy. I'll be home when I can."

"You're not the boss of me," I snap as I push up from the sofa, noticing that I am completely naked and he is completely dressed. This seems to be pretty telling in the story of Shelby and Trent. I can't help but sigh.

"You're right. I'm not the boss of you," he says as he stalks toward me. "But I am the owner of all of your orgasms."

"Ha!" I laugh. "Hardly."

"If you touch yourself, I'll know," he tells me ominously.

"And if I do?"

"I'll spank that ass, and then I'll give you a real orgasm, not the empty one you'd get now when you're drunk and pissed as hell."

I sigh again. He's probably right. Then Trent kisses the daylights out of me for the second time tonight, effectively scrambling the last of the brain cells that the bottle of wine I had consumed at dinner left me with.

And then, when he lets me go and I slump against the sofa, he turns on his heel and walks out the door, leaving me standing here wondering—not for the first time in the history of our relationship—what the hell just happened?

And also not for the first time in our relationship, I am left high and not so dry when I am not wearing any pants.

Well, not that I'm completely sure what took his rod and reel away from my red snapper bay, but it looks like Trent isn't coming back anytime soon. I might as well throw on some sweats and find some way to resurrect my evening.

So here's where I am at a crossroads. I can toss on some comfy clothes and dig out the carton of mint chocolate chip I hid in the back of the freezer, pray that Trent hasn't found it yet, and drown my sorrows, or I can pop open another bottle of wine and ride this drunk train straight into the party-of-one station.

Trent thinks he can tell me not to close out the game on my own . . . I think not!

Yep, that sounds good, I think as I look around and take stock of my still-naked body standing by the arm of the sofa right where that miserable bastard left me. I'll just run down the hall and put on some clothes.

Suddenly a shiver racks my spine. As Granny would say, "Someone must have stepped on my grave." I mumble the words again as I step toward the hallway that leads to the master bedroom at the back of the house. I'm just going to steal one of Trent's shirts to sleep in. Pants just seem too complicated to contend with right now, not to mention I am feeling a little eager to get down to my party for one after the way Trent revved me up.

I have just reached the mouth of the hallway when the front door swings open and the tall and thick frames of Daisy and Jones spill into the room. Jones takes one look at my cat, Missy, and shrieks. Now, Missy isn't the prettiest of cats, but she's mine, so I would be a little offended if Missy hadn't shouted a meow right back before taking off down the hall.

"Emergency!" Daisy shouts. "*Eeee*-MER-*gency*!"

"Jesus Christ!" Jones squeals like a little girl and not a giant, 240-pound man. "What the fuck is that?"

"That's my cat, Missy," I say in a haughty voice.

"Girl, that ain't no cat."

"Would you two shut it!" Daisy shouts. "This here is an emergency!"

"Let me just go and get dressed," I say as I throw a thumb over my shoulder to indicate the bedroom down the hall where some clothes are waiting for me.

It's then that I remember I am stark naked. I'm as naked as the day I was born, in front of one of my best friends and her on-again, off-again boyfriend. Based on what I saw at dinner, they are decidedly on.

I let out an "Eep!" and cross my arms over the front of my body, trying to cover all of the high points—and some low ones too.

"Quit that!" she barks, and I jump again. "We don't have time for your shenanigans. Christina is missing!"

"Who is Christina?" I ask.

"Christina is one of my best girls from the hood," Daisy explains. "She's one of my friends."

"Really?" I question. "If she's such a good friend,

how come I've never met her before?"

"Because she works nights . . . ," Daisy explains with a pointed look and a weird head nod. Really, what the hell is she doing with her head? Is it Morse code? I'm not sure. I squint, trying to decipher if there is a series of dots and dashes in her head-shaking, but really, I'm too drunk to make anything out. I will overanalyze this later when I'm sober and less naked.

"I don't understand," I hedge. Jones makes a weird choking noise that appears to be coming from the back of his throat. "Well?" I ask, holding my arms wide in my frustration and forgetting that I was covering my breasts, letting them swing free again.

Jones is choking in earnest now.

"Stop that!" she snaps, making him erupt into roaring laughter. I'm not quite sure I understand his hilarity.

"Is he okay?" I ask distractedly.

"Would you two please pay attention!" Daisy barks, making Jones laugh even harder, and I'm not sure if he can breathe fully.

"Are you sure he's okay?"

"He's fine!" Daisy yells.

"Maybe I should just go . . ." I point at the hall again before waving my hand up and down in front of my naked body. Again. "You know."

"No!" she shouts. "Aren't you listening to me? Listen to the words that are coming out of my mouth. Christina is gone. G-o-n-e. *Gone!*"

For a hot minute, she reminds me of the video of that little baby yelling at his mom, and all I can hear is him shouting, "Linda. Linda, listen. You're not listening to me!" And I really want to laugh. And then she bursts into noisy sobs, and Jones and I jump into action, herding her toward the sofa.

We slowly shuffle in our awkward huddle over to the sofa, where Daisy flops down unceremoniously. Jones and I follow her down, one of us on either side of her.

"I just don't know what I'll do if we don't find her!" she wails.

"Where would she have gone?" I ask.

"I don't know!" she cries harder. "And we all know I know everything!"

"Well, I don't know about that," I mumble.

"I heard that!" she snaps. "If I say she's gone, she's gone!"

"Okay," I agree quickly.

"*Christinaaaaa*!" she wails. It's getting a little too *Streetcar Named Desire* for me in here.

"I told you, baby," Jones says as he wades into the conversation. "I bet she's just with a john."

"I done told you I already talked to Alyssa," she explains while shooting Jones the stink eye.

"And who is Alyssa?" I ask, feeling even more confused than before.

"She's my girl!" Daisy says brightly between theatrical sobs. "She's the head ho."

"Oh, okay," I say. "She's the head ho . . . *the head what*?"

"She's the head ho, the boss, the head honcho, the big cheese," Daisy lists off for me.

"She's a madam," Jones says.

"*Ohhhh*," I say with my eyes wide. I totally get it

now. "And Alyssa says she's not with a . . . with a . . ." I struggle to get the words out.

"With a john!" she shouts.

"Yeah, that." I take a deep breath. "And does Christina ever take clients off of Alyssa's books?"

Daisy shoots me the *Are you stupid?* look. "No one takes clients off of Alyssa's books and lives to tell about it."

The look Daisy gives me sends a shudder up my spine. I get the feeling that I would hate to be on this Alyssa chick's bad side. Mainly because I like living to tell my ridiculous stories.

"I'm sure she's going to turn up," I try to reassure Daisy, who grips me and Jones even tighter to her sides. My breasts are hanging down in front of us.

"No, she's not! I just know it," she cries.

"Okay," I say softly as I try to pat her somewhere to console her, but Daisy has me pinned across her lap. "How long has she been gone?"

"Five days!" She lets out another sob. Shit. Five days is kind of a long time to be missing. "We have to find her!"

"Okay," I agree again. "We'll find her."

"The hell you will!" Trent hollers from the foyer.

"Oh, shit," I bite out.

"And while we're at it," he shouts while gesticulating wildly. "What the actual fuck is going on here?"

"Daisy's friend Christina is missing," I explain. "She's upset, honey, and rightfully so."

"Jones, man, I like you a lot. You're a good man and a great cop, but none of that will stop me from shooting you where you are if you do not step away from my naked girlfriend right fucking now."

"Got it, boss!" Jones says as he jumps up from the sofa like his pants are on fire.

"And for fuck's sake, put on some fucking clothes on, Shelby!" he roars.

"You know," Daisy says as she slowly blinks at me. "I always wondered if the carpet matches the curtains. I guess they do . . ."

"I haven't had time to get a wax," I argue.

"Well, you should."

"Gee," I mumble, feeling more than a little irritated. "Thanks."

Later, while Trent was still fuming over Jones seeing me naked and Daisy wanting me involved in the search for her missing friend, I wrapped my arm around Trent's belly like I did every night and hitched my knee over his thigh, also like I did every night. But tonight, just before I drifted off to sleep, I said something I never have before.

"Love you."

And because I was practically asleep already, I missed Trent's arms getting tighter and his hoarsely whispered "I love you too."

FUNERALS AND FREAK SHOWS

Beep . . . beep . . . beep . . .

The alarm on the nightstand blares. It's one of those old-school ones that look like a big black box with giant red digital numbers on the front. It plugs into the wall and emits a noise that could make a person think they are under a nuclear attack when it goes off. This is Trent's trusty alarm clock. He has been in a committed relationship with it ever since college. Personally, I'm more of a T-Swift kind of a gal.

Speaking of the lady known as Taylor, my phone on the opposite nightstand blares *Reputation*. I reach an arm outside of my warm cocoon of down blankets. I know San Diego doesn't really get cold in comparison to other locales, but to me, it's freaking freezing at sixty-five degrees. Sue me.

I burrow back into my nest, waiting for Trent to turn off that annoying racket. Only, he doesn't.

"Baby, please turn it off," I mumble into my pillow, but I am greeted with nothing but silence and the blaring alarm.

Feeling more than a little worried, I worm my way across the mattress, underneath the big pile of blankets, toward Trent's side of the massive bed. *Beep . . . beep . . . beep . . .* the alarm continues to sound. I keep reaching and reaching for Trent even though I know he's not there.

I wiggle over inch by inch. I'm basically army-crawling across the bed as I slither on my belly; only, instead of moving gracefully under barbed wire, I'm flopping around while tangled up in a sheet under a ridiculous amount of blankets.

That is, until the mattress ends and there is nothing to keep me up in the bed. The carpeted floor rushes up to meet me, and it stings a little bit as it bites into my right hip and leg.

"Son of a bitch!" I cry out. That's going to leave a mark.

To add insult to injury, Trent's alarm clock bounces off of the nightstand and clocks me on top of my head. A small scrap of paper slowly floats to the floor, where it comes to rest in front of me. I must have hit the nightstand when I fell off the bed. I try to rub the stinging out of the top of my head and can feel the lump growing by the second.

I reach for the piece of paper, only to realize that Trent hadn't let go of his anger from last night after all. His jagged handwriting is scrawled across the page in a terse note.

Shell,

I HAD TO HEAD TO THE STATION EARLY. DON'T DO ANYTHING
FUCKING STUPID. WE'LL TALK WHEN I GET HOME. YOU
BETTER BE THERE.

-T

I'm fuming. Who the hell does he think he is to leave me such a rude note? That asshole! I am my own woman, hear me fucking roar, dickwad!

"'Don't do anything *fucking* stupid,'" I mumble.

No "I love yous" or sweet words.

I'm sure there is steam coming out of my ears. There is a red film covering my eyes, and I am feeling decidedly homicidal. I have half a mind to load up my cat and head for my own house, but that big idiot demanded I be here when he gets home tonight for what I'm sure will be a dressing-down.

Actually, big freaking chicken that I am, that's exactly what I'm going to do.

I don't even bother to shower and dress for the day. I throw on a pair of Trent's sweats—his favorite pair—the gray ones that say ARMY across the front of the sweatshirt and down the leg of the pants. That is step one in teaching him to give me ultimatums. Not to mention that if we're breaking up, I fully intend to take these with me as my consolation prize.

I toss my long red hair up on top of my head in a messy bun and slide my feet into the Converse sneakers I always keep in my bag before heading to go find Missy. Fortunately, I don't have to search long, as she is sitting on the nightstand where I left my phone. I open up her cat carrier and she jumps in. Most cats would hate a pet crate, but Missy and I are uptown women and always on the go. Plus, she knows that if we head to my granny's place, she'll get served a brunch of tuna.

I wad up the note and stuff it into the pocket of my permanently borrowed sweatpants, along with my cell phone, before ducking under the long shoulder strap of Missy's carrier. She meows softly while I carry her into the closet to grab the dry-cleaning bag that contains my clothes for today.

I grab my pocketbook from the table in the front hall and fish out my car keys. I lock the front door behind me and head down the walkway to where my cute little Jeep waits for us in the driveway. I hit the button on my key fob to unlock the doors and place Missy's carrier on the front seat. I tuck the rest of our bags into the trunk and slam the tailgate closed, letting a little of my frustration out.

I pull open the driver's door and climb in. I buckle my seat belt and crank my key in the ignition. The stereo comes to life, and I switch tracks to "Look What You Made Me Do." This isn't an "Our Song" moment. And I peel out of the neighborhood like Kanye just tried to steal my VMA.

The I-15 is packed with people most likely headed downtown for work, and the traffic, combined with my lack of coffee, has me fuming. My phone rings from the passenger seat. I pick it up and look at the screen. A picture of Trent and me smiling like happy, sadistic lunatics faces me, and I hit the button on the side to dismiss the call.

Before I can even place it back on the seat, it rings again. I don't let myself think twice about what I should and shouldn't be doing right now as my hand hovers over the seat with my phone buzzing away like a beehive in my hot little fingers. I bite down on my lip as I slide my thumb across the screen to answer.

"Hello?"

"Where the fuck are you?" Trent barks from across the line. "Because it sure as shit isn't at home where you should be."

"Was that meant to be as offensive as it sounded?" I snap.

"Probably not," he says with his voice low. "So are you going to answer me?"

"Driving," I answer.

"Meoooooowwww," Missy adds.

"Jesus Christ, you took my fucking cat?" he thunders.

"You . . . your cat?" I can barely get the words out. "Missy is my cat!"

"There stopped being a yours and a mine months ago, Shelby. And you know it!"

"That's not true at all," I say, pushing back.

"Oh yeah?" he asks. "How so?"

"You have a house up north and I have a condo in the city."

"So you want to move in with me permanently? Kane has a lot of time on his hands with Sophia being out of town at some skating thing. I could probably get him and a bunch of guys from the station to move you in in a day with the promise of pizza and beer."

"No!"

"No what? You know we have to give them something," he explains like it's the most rational thing ever in the whole entire world.

"No, I'm not moving in with you. Are you insane?" I yell before realizing that I need to shut this crazy train down ASAP. "Wait, don't answer that."

"So we settled that," Trent says. I can hear guys in the background. He must be in the bull pen. "Now put my cat back."

Hand to God, I have to bite down hard on my tongue to keep from screaming.

"One, Missy is my cat, and two, we are not available this evening," I tell him. We can both hear my voice shake with restrained anger.

"Excuse me?" Trent's voice is eerily quiet. The calm before the storm.

"I am not available to be ordered around at your whim," I say, my voice just as soft.

"Is this about the note I left you?" Trent asks me.

"That's certainly part of it," I explain as calmly as I can. "You do not get to yell at me in written or verbal form."

"Shell—" he starts, but I don't let him finish.

"Now, give me a call when you feel like talking like rational adults," I say before hitting the red button to hang up.

Traffic isn't letting up at all, and I decide to swing through a Starbucks drive-through around Carmel Mountain Ranch for some much-needed coffee. I figure the world is probably a lot safer if I put some carbs, sugar, and a truckload of caffeine on deck.

Missy is unusually quiet for a car ride.

The morning commuter traffic seems to have cleared a little, and I make my way southbound toward my grandmother's apartment in the Gaslamp Quarter. It was about two years ago when my grandfather passed away and Granny sold their home and moved into Peaceful Sunset Retirement Center, a high-rise of condos for the freewheeling octogenarian set. She likes to call it "Hell's Waiting Room," but really, it's home to her and her friends. A home we fiercely protected last year when a lunatic decided to play Russian roulette with the lives of the residents at Peaceful Sunset.

The exit for my own townhome development comes up, and I pass it by. I need my granny. Whenever life gets tough, she helps me get going, usually with a stiff upper lip and a belly full of tequila, but who am I to judge?

I take the exit for their less-than-sleepy corner of downtown, no longer driving like a mad woman when upset. The last time I did, Trent had a conniption and it almost ended our relationship. Although, a year later, I'm not sure we're much better off. We'll have to wait and see where we stand with each other once the dust settles. I pull into the circlar drive in front of the tall building to hand my keys over to the valet.

I put the strap of Missy's carrier across my body and grab my dry-cleaning bag from the trunk before thanking the kid working valet this morning and walking through the big glass doors. I sign in and head for the elevator.

"Meow." Missy lets out her little kitty battle cry of heartbreak as we ride the elevator to the tenth floor.

I press the button to ring the doorbell, and Granny pulls the wood panel open with more gusto than a woman of her slim frame should be able to. She has rollers in her hair and a shower bonnet over them. A zip-front gown covers her thin body, and she has hot-pink leopard-print slippers with marabou trim on her small feet. That's Granny in a nutshell.

"Well, hey there, Shelby," she greets me with a smile on her face. "What brings you by early? The funeral isn't until eleven, right?"

"That's right," I answer. "I was just thinking we could get ready together like old times, and then we could sit and visit for a bit."

"Well, that sounds great!" She smiles brightly at me. Something gleams in her knowing eyes, and I know that she notices more than she lets on. That's fine. We can all keep our secrets for a little while. "I just put a pot of coffee on. Have you had any yet?"

"Yes," I tell her. "Trent left early this morning, so I just hopped out of bed and headed here by way of the Starbucks on Carmel Mountain Road. But I could always use more."

"Well, come on in," Granny says as she gestures for me to follow her into the kitchen even though I could trace these same steps in my sleep.

"Thanks," I say as I pluck a mug from her cute little countertop tree.

"I've got that," she says as she swats my hand away. "You go on and sit down. I bet you haven't eaten anything either."

"Fine, but I can make the bagels," I say on a sigh as I move around her petite kitchen. I pop two sesame seed bagels into her four-slot toaster and push the little tabs down before grabbing a couple of plates down from the cupboard and a knife from the drawer.

"Here you go, Granddaughter mine," she says, handing me my mug.

"Thanks, Granny." I shoot her my smile. I will always be thankful for this time with her. As my last living grandparent, I know all too well how fleeting time may be. I don't want her to leave this world not knowing how much I love her.

"I love you, Shelby girl," she whispers, using the nickname my grandfather used to call me as she places a soft hand against my cheek. The arthritis in her knuckles causes her more trouble now than they used to. "Rest assured that I know you love me. And also know, Shell, I'm not leaving this world yet. I have got shit to do, Shelby girl!"

I can't help but laugh at her joy for just . . . life. "Okay, you caught me."

"Good, now drink your coffee," she orders when the bagels pop up. I move to reach for them, but she stops me in my tracks. "I got that. You go sit down and I'll bring this on over."

"I hate having you wait on me," I tell her. "I'm a grown woman and should do those things for you."

"To me, you will always be the little girl in pigtails standing at the kitchen door asking me for a ham sandwich. I will never see you as anything else. Even when you have babies of your own."

I pad around to the little bistro table in the corner and pull up a chair. I lift my mug to my lips and take a huge sip of the nectar of life. I'm really not sure how I even got here, let alone function without a cup or two, or twenty, filling my bloodstream. The cup that I had on the road barely counts as a drop in the bucket to get me going in the mornings.

"So now you can tell me what the hell has you looking so down in the dumps," she demands as she drops a plate with a bagel and cream cheese on the table in front of me before walking around to the other side of the table and taking a seat herself.

I choke on the coffee I was about to swallow.

"What?" I gasp between coughs. Shit, this is how I'm going to die. Although, if I die right now, Trent totally won't want these sweats back, so bright side! "Wh-what are you talking about?"

"You really are a terrible liar, Shelby," she says, shaking her head in disappointment. "You really should be ashamed of yourself for lying to your sweet, old granny like that."

"I'm not sure 'sweet' is the right word, dear," I mumble under my breath.

"I heard that!" she shouts. "Now tell Granny all about it."

"I'm so screwed!" I wail, breaking out into body-racking sobs.

"Now, what could be all that bad?" she asks me as she makes her way around the table to stand beside me and rub my back.

"Daisy's friend Christina is missing, and she wants us to help find her," I explain.

"Well, that doesn't sound bad at all," Granny says, and I can almost hear the wheels turning in her mind—all her devious plotting and planning. "Now that sounds like just the ticket to liven things up a bit around here."

"Trent forbade it!" I tell her.

"Trent knows we're never going to take his edicts seriously."

"Well, he's serious now!" I tell her. "H-h-he was so mad," I cry harder.

"And then what happened?" she asks me.

"He left for work early, and then he called me and yelled at me because I got mad and I left his house, and he told me to bring his damn cat back, but, Granny?"

"Yes, dear?"

"She's my damn cat, so I can't!" I wail, knowing full well that I'm not making any sense.

"That's true, dear." She pats my back again.

"I don't know what to do," I admit as I take deep breaths, my tears having all run dry for now.

"Of course you do," Granny tells me.

"Care to clue me in, oh wise one?"

"Of course," she says with a laugh. "We're going to eat our breakfasts, and then we're going to go get ready and make ourselves look just a shade too glamorous for a funeral. And then we are going to covertly help Daisy and not tell Trenton at all."

"Granny—" I start.

"What?" she chuckles. "Marla will love it. She needs a little excitement in her life."

"And what will happen when Trent dumps my ass for being an idiot and not respecting his wishes?" I ask, feeling a little put out still.

"He'll come around, honey. He always does. Besides, Trent will think we're doing nothing but our usual yoga and lunch dates. What he doesn't know won't hurt him." She winks at me.

I can't help but laugh. "Okay, you do know best."

"I always do," she says with a conspiratorial laugh. "Now tell me what's new with Miss Havisham . . ."

And I do. I tell her all about Missy's evil ways.

"Oh my gosh!" I exclaim. "You'll never believe what happened when Daisy showed up at dinner last night!"

"Baby girl." Granny laughs. "There is probably not a damn thing on this earth that our Daisy girl does that would surprise me anymore."

"Well," I begin to explain. "She did this thing with a meatball, and it looked a lot like . . ." I clear my throat to combat the massive wave of embarrassment that suddenly takes over my body. One would think that, at this particular juncture, I couldn't be embarrassed by anything anymore, but wonders never cease and all that. I press on, explaining about Daisy's magical meatball skills.

"Well." She clears her throat. "Maybe we should have our girl do a little demonstration . . . I mean, with meatballs. Not . . . you know, *meatballs*. Like a master class on fellatio or something."

"That's exactly what I thought!" I exclaim. "But then I was afraid that maybe it was just the wine talking." I shrug my shoulders, making Granny laugh.

"We should probably go and get ready before we miss that funeral," she tells me softly.

"Yeah."

"Come on. I'll curl your hair," she says, and the idea of my granny, who grew up in the South, with all of its gigantic hairdo awesomeness, has my butt puckering like Big Thunder is headed for it full speed ahead! But I love her, so I give her the only reply I can.

"That sounds great, Granny."

And then we head to her bathroom to get ready for a funeral of no one we knew.

Praise Jesus.

"Jesus, this is terrible," Granny stage-whispers from the seat next to me.

"Shh," I admonish her as quietly as I can.

"But it's *so* boring," she says to me as if that should justify her harsh critique of the service that is *still* happening.

"Granny—" I start, but she cuts in again.

"Christ, I might be dead by the time this crapfest wraps up. What the hell are they singing, anyway?" she asks me.

"Those are monks," I explain calmly, but I can already feel that vein in my temple throbbing. "They're chanting."

"Well, it sounds like someone is drowning a cat," she harrumphs.

"Shhh," the woman in the row in front of us, wearing too much rouge and Chanel No. 5, hisses as she turns around and shoots us a death glare. Shit. She's going to leave me a bad Yelp review; I can just feel it.

"Or more like ten cats," Granny continues as if no one had interrupted her. I just sit there stunned, my eyes peeled wide, and wondering how this became my life. Like, at what juncture did I take an off-ramp when

I should have continued on?

I just have no idea . . .

I stare at Mrs. Chanel No. 5 while the minister drones on and on about what an amazing woman Mrs. Carmichael was and how much she loved her cats—all sixteen of them. As I sit here, in the middle of this terrible service—Granny was right, but I'll never admit it out loud or sober because I'm a fucking professional—I make a resolution to myself that when I'm ninety years old, I'm going to wear as much rouge and Chanel No. 5 as I damn well please. And who is going to stop me, anyhow? No one, that's who.

Speaking of fragrance over use and advancing age, there's something niggling at the back of my mind that I just can't seem to put my finger on. There is something about this whole service, about Mrs. Carmichael, that is just out of reach. But before I can figure it out, Granny grabs my arm and pulls me toward her, and I forget what I was thinking about. She's surprisingly strong for such a tiny thing.

"You have to promise me," she implores.

"What do you need?" I ask her. We both know that I would promise her anything, that I would do anything for her.

"You have to promise me, Shelby."

"But you have to tell me what it is first so that I can promise." I all but laugh.

"Don't let my funeral be this dull," she says in all seriousness, and the smile I was wearing falls right off my face. This is something I can't think about without feeling a sharp pain sear across my chest. Losing Granny is not something I want to think about. I know it's part of life, it's natural, but I don't want to rush it.

"Granny—" I start, and my breath catches in my lungs and tears sting the backs of my eyes.

"Now, don't be sad, honey," she says softly. "One day it's going to happen."

"I know," I whimper softly.

"And when it does, you have to promise me that my funeral will be awesome!" she says just a little too loud, but not loud enough to stop the service.

"Okay," I whisper back. I have to swallow back the ball of tears that's lodged in my throat. "I'll make sure it's awesome."

"And nothing like this train wreck," Granny adds.

"Granny," I admonish gently. "That's not nice."

"Promise!" she whisper-shouts.

"Fine," I agree reluctantly. "I promise."

"Good. Now that that's settled, let's talk details."

"I'm kind of working here," I remind my grandmother.

"Bah! Who cares? You could literally make anything up, and it would sound better than what is currently occurring here," she tells me loudly enough to garner us a little bit of attention.

"Shh!" I whisper harshly. I'm beginning to panic. Somehow, by the grace of God and the skin of my teeth, I haven't been kicked out of a funeral yet. Barely. And that is no small miracle considering I usually have Granny with me.

"You better listen to your granny, or I will scream this funeral home down!" she challenges.

"Fine. You win."

"Good," she says triumphantly. "Now, no dying

monks."

"They're not dying, for Pete's sake."

"I don't care," she says. "They are terrible. I want rock 'n' roll."

"What?" I laugh.

"I'm thinking some heavy metal bands should keep the show rolling," she says seriously.

"I think you'll have the other old dead people rolling in their graves," I mumble.

"What was that?" Granny asks me. "You wouldn't be giving your old granny any shit, now would you?"

"No, Granny," I lie through my teeth that had to be straightened after I went over the handlebars of my first ten-speed bike. "I would never do such a thing."

"That's what I thought," she harrumphs before rallying back to her cause. "Now, I'm thinking AC/DC is the way to go here."

"A little 'Highway to Hell' action?" I snicker at my own joke.

"Yes!" Granny cheers. "That exactly!"

"Oh dear."

"I think it'll be hilarious," she says.

"Granny—" I start, but she doesn't let me finish.

"I just knew you would be the one to get me. It's like I always said: God made you just like your granny."

"I'm not sure Mom would find it so funny," I say.

"Oh, you don't give Mary enough credit. She really knows how to lighten up," Granny reassures me.

"I'm not so sure about that," I say, my voice low.

"She used to be a shit-ton of fun before you hit puberty and made all her hair turn gray," Granny explains.

"Well, thank you for that."

"You have to admit that if you had a daughter who developed a body like that and had my penchant for shenanigans, you'd be worried all the time too," she explains, and she's not wrong.

"You have me there." I raise an eyebrow.

"She'd probably calm down if you made an honest man out of Trent and gave her a mess of grandbabies," she says.

"I don't know about that."

"Besides, I was lucky," Granny says wistfully. "I had boys, so I didn't have to worry about all that. I just had to pray they didn't knock anyone up, but then your dad did and I got you and your mama out of it."

"I'm not so sure I'm enjoying this little stroll down memory lane, Granny."

"You're right. I'm getting off track here," she says.

"Good." I breathe a sigh of relief. I just wish I was smart enough to realize my confidence came too early.

"Now, when you put me in the ground, put me on top of Pop Pop," she says matter-of-factly.

"Granny—" I start, but she just keeps on keepin' on.

"He always liked it when I got on top," she says on a sigh. "You know, on account of his bad knees and all."

"I hear that," the elderly black man sitting on the other side of Granny says as he offers up his fist for a knuckle bump.

"Sweet Christ," I say, mostly to myself.

Granny doesn't seem to notice what I said, or she

isn't paying me any mind, because she is now lost in her debate over the best positions for sexual congress for the geriatric crowds with her new friend.

She doesn't seem to notice that I can't get any air into my lungs. I feel my face heat, and I try to force more air into my lungs. Despite my best efforts, I seem to be suffocating. Stars dance in front of my eyes and I try to shake my head to clear them, but it's no use.

I hear what sounds like Trent's voice saying, "Someone grab her." But that can't be right. Trent wouldn't be here. I'm here covering the service for the paper, and he's working the case he caught last night.

The stars twinkle just a little brighter, and then everything goes black . . .

chapter THREE

THE RONNIE MILSAP MISCOMMUNICATION AND CHILI TUESDAY

'm warm and cozy all snuggled up next to Trent in bed, and I don't want to wake up. This has been the best night's sleep of my life, and I am reluctant to let it go.

"Yes, I need an ambulance at Peaceful Oaks Funeral Home on Miramar Boulevard," I hear Trent say in the distance. Why would he be calling for an ambulance to a funeral home when we're snuggled in bed at home? Something isn't quite right here . . .

And then somebody slaps my face. And that somebody would appear to be my grandmother.

"Was that really necessary?" a disgruntled Trent asks.

"Yes, she needs to snap out of it," Granny answers him.

My eyes spring open.

"Welcome back, beautiful," Trent says, smiling in

my face.

"Who needs an ambulance?" I ask. Trent opens his mouth to answer, but Granny beats him to the punch line, which is apparently me.

"You do. You fainted just like a little bitch," she answers.

"Is that really how you'd answer right now?" Trent asks, incredulous.

"Yes," she answers without preamble.

I push myself up to a sitting position and clear my throat. "I don't need an ambulance."

"You do," Trent disagrees.

"I don't," I say again. "Tell them." I indicate the phone still pressed to his ear.

"Shelby—" he starts.

"I'm fine," I say again as I regain my bearings, and the events of last night and this morning come crashing back down on me. Seeing him makes me feel angry and . . . sad. I need to be away from here, away from Trent, just for a bit, so that I can get my balance back, and then I can take on the world and one six-foot-four, New Jersey–born homicide detective with a bossy nature and a penchant for spankings. "I just want to go home."

"She says she's good," he says into the phone. "Thanks, April."

"Come on, Granny," I say as I push myself up off the floor. "I just want to get out of here."

"Shelby—" Trent says again.

"Granny?" I ask as I bug my eyes out at her. She looks sad, maybe even a little disappointed, but nods her head.

"I'll look out for her, Trenton. You go catch the bad guys," she says as she links her arm in mine, and we head for the door.

"Now wait just a minute," he demands, and we turn to look at him. But just then his phone rings, and once again it's his work ringtone. "Fuck," he bites out, shoving his hand through his hair.

"It's all right," I say softly, seeing the look in Trent's eyes promising that it—*whatever that may be*—is anything but all right. Then I turn back and walk out the door.

We push through the heavy doors of the old-fashioned funeral home and head toward my car at the rear of the parking lot. I unlock the doors and we climb inside. I settle into the driver's seat, feeling loads older than when I woke up this morning. Life is hard, yo.

"You know, you're going to have to talk to him," Granny says softly as she turns to me.

"I will," I promise. "Just not right now. I've had enough for one day."

"And it's not even noon. There are so many hours left in the day. So much to accomplish!"

"Yay," I mock-cheer.

"And it's Yoga *and* Chili Tuesday," she says enthusiastically.

"Oh, shit," I mumble.

"Nah," she says, making a face. "No one's done that since Ruth stopped drinking all that Metamucil at breakfast."

"That really makes me feel a lot better," I tell her as I signal to turn out of the lot.

"Really?" She asks me with such a hopeful tone in

her voice that I can't help but want to accommodate.

"Loads."

"Good," she says as she settles back into her seat for the duration of the ride back to her apartment building downtown.

I reach over and turn the knob on the dash to fire up the radio. Before we know it, Miley Cyrus is at a party in the USA and Granny and I are both singing at the top of our lungs. I take in the looks on the valet guys' faces when we pull in bumping our choice cuts, and throw my head back and laugh. There is a lightness in my chest that wasn't there a few hours ago.

I link my granny's arm in mine, and we walk into the building. She smiles and waves in greeting to a few of her friends as we make our way through the lobby and to the elevator banks. I push the button, and it's not long before the loud ding sounds, signaling the elevator, and the big steel doors slide open. I have often thought these elevators ding louder than normal because the old people here are so hard of hearing that they can't hear a regular bell. I don't know this for sure or anything, but it's an educated guess.

The elevator stops on the tenth floor, and we make our way down the long hallway, with its muted beige walls, gold-framed mirrors, and fancy end tables scattered throughout. Our footsteps are silenced by the plush carpet. Altogether making this seem more like a posh hotel than a senior living community.

"What the hell?" Granny says sharply, pulling me from my woolgathering. This whole time I had been lost in my thoughts, wondering if Trent and I are really a good fit or if I am falling in love with a man who isn't capable of loving me for me.

And there I said it. I am falling in love with Trent. This is a lie I haven't said aloud to anyone else yet, and the harsh truth of it is, it's even a lie to myself because deep down I know I have already fallen.

But Granny's harsh words draw me back to the here and now, and I realize that you can hear the ball game coming from inside her apartment. She slides her ID card past the reader and pushes the heavy door open as soon as the lock clicks open.

"I said, 'What the hell?'" We stop in our tracks because sitting in the middle of the living room with a cup of coffee in one hand and the TV remote in the other is my dad.

"Well, if it isn't the two prettiest girls in all of California," my dad says, standing up to wrap both Granny and me in his still-strong-even-after-retirement arms.

"Jack, what are you doing here?" she asks with a huge smile on her face for her oldest son.

"I came to have lunch with you and found out pretty quick you were with Shelby when that demon of a cat of hers bit the shit out of me." Dad winces, holding up his ravaged thumb for inspection.

"Meow," Missy calls as she weaves between my legs, and Dad jumps back a step. He looks me straight in the eyes, challenging me to comment on the fact that he is scared of a little kitty cat.

I raise an eyebrow in comment as I bend down and scoop her up into my arms.

"Missy isn't a demon," I say softly as I scrunch my fingers in her fur. "She's just a sweet, misunderstood girl."

"Misunderstood?" Granny and Dad shout incredulously at the same time.

"Of course she is," I say, cuddling my pretty girl extra close. "And you probably scared her. You know how jumpy she is."

"Of course, darlin'," my dad says, his face gentling as he smiles at me the way only a father can smile at his only daughter. "My mistake."

"Apology accepted."

"Now, about lunch," Granny says, wading into the fray. "Y'all want to eat at the cafe here? It's Tuesday."

"Fuck no," my dad says a little harshly. "That chili gives me the worst heartburn. It's all those tomatoes, I swear."

"Dad, tomatoes can't give you heartburn." I roll my eyes.

"You just wait until you're my age and tomatoes give you heartburn. I am going to laugh right in your face. Of course, by the time you're my age, I might be dead . . ."

"Dad—" I roll my eyes again. He can be so dramatic sometimes.

"But I'll come back just to give you shit about the heartburn."

"Thank you," I say sarcastically.

"And don't even get me started on the farts," he continues. "Hand to God, baby girl, your mama was googling divorce attorneys after the last time I ate here. It was that bad."

"Gross."

"I just wanted her to shoot me. I was that miserable," he explains. "But she wouldn't. She kept mumbling something about looking bad in orange and wanting to be able to spend my pension."

"Dad—"

"I mean, should they really be feeding that shit to old people? Someone's going to die one day," he says and my eyes flash to Granny. It wasn't too long ago that people were dying at the hands of a crazy man my grandfather once knew. She shakes her head subtly, telling me Dad is better left in the dark on that one.

"How about I make some quick sandwiches if you don't feel like chili?" Granny changes the subject more successfully than I could.

"Sounds good, Mom," Dad says softly. I know it's been hard for him since my grandfather passed. These moments with my granny are as special for him as they are for me. "How about I help you?"

"That sounds great!" She smiles at him.

"I'll help too," I add.

"Excellent!" Granny cheers.

We all trek the five feet into the tiny kitchen, which is located directly off of the living room. I pull the chips and bread from the cupboards while Dad pulls down plates along with a knife from the silverware drawer. Granny roots through the refrigerator for an age before popping back out with her arms loaded for bear. She has packages of deli meats and cheeses, mayo and mustard, lettuce and tomato, and who knows what else. Dad and I both rush to her to help unload her haul.

"Everyone, pick what you want!" she cheers.

I pull a knife from the block and a small wooden cutting board out from behind it and lay them on the counter. I place one of the small tomatoes on top of the board and begin slicing it as my dad picks up the remote he carried in with him and turns up the volume. I will never understand why men cannot bear to be parted from their remotes.

"I love this show!" my dad says enthusiastically as one of those Time Life commercials for a CD set comes on. I can't help but smile.

My dad sings along with each snippet of song they play. He is clearly lost in his walk down memory lane with these songs of the past. I finish slicing my tomato and look up. There's a man wearing dark sunglasses in the middle of the day, before it was cool, and jamming while playing a piano.

"He must be one with the ko-kai-eene," I joke. My dad and Granny look up from fixing their sandwiches.

"What?" Dad asks me. "What are you talking about? I don't even know what that means."

"The ko-kai-eene?" I ask to clarify.

"Yeah, that. What is that?"

"You know, cocaine?" I answer. When I notice Dad's confused look still on his face, I point up to the TV. "You know, dark sunglasses . . ." Understanding dawns across my Dad's face, and he throws his head back and laughs.

"That's Ronnie Milsap," he corrects me. He's laughing so hard that he's crying, and I can't help but feel like he's laughing at me. "He's blind, you asshole."

And that would be why he's laughing at me.

"Whoops. My bad," I answer.

"Yeah, your bad." Dad laughs.

"Let's take lunch in the living room and find a scary movie on TV," Granny suggests.

"Okay."

"Sounds good to me," Dad answers.

We carry our plates and sodas into the living room and sprawl out on the sofas with our plates in our laps. Dad lifts the remote and flips through the channels until he finds an old-school Alfred Hitchcock movie that's just about to start.

"Does this satisfy your need for a scary movie, Mom?" Dad asks.

"Sure does," she answers. "I'm pretty sure your brother was conceived during this movie."

"Marvelous," Dad mumbles under his breath, but I hear him perfectly. All those years in artillery and tanks left him a little hard of hearing. It's not bad, but he can't really whisper anymore, and I think it's hilarious.

I smile as we sit back, eat our lunch together, and watch *North by Northwest*.

Dad points the remote at the television and clicks the set off when the movie is over.

"I love that movie," I sigh.

"Me too," Granny says, and Dad smiles.

"You two are just alike," he says with a laugh. "Jesus, help us."

"Not funny." I shoot him a wink and he smiles.

"Well," he says, "I should be getting back to your mom about now," before pushing to his feet.

"It's always good to see you, Jack," Granny says as

she wraps her arms around him.

"Love you, Mom."

"And I love you," she says softly.

"Always love my girl," Dad says as he hugs me next.

"Love you too, Dad."

"Try to keep out of trouble." He winks.

"Speaking of trouble," Granny says. "We should get a move on if we're going to make it to yoga class. Are you sure you don't want to join us?"

"Fuck no." Dad laughs before heading to the door. "But you ladies have fun."

"Thanks, Dad."

"And don't crap your pants," he advises.

"So funny," I say, rolling my eyes. Dad chuckles one more time before the door closes behind him.

"Well, let's shake a leg," Granny says, and we both take off for our battle stations.

I race into the spare bedroom, where I keep my yoga gear, pulling off my dress clothes from the funeral as I go. I get stuck on my pantyhose and narrowly miss falling on my ass. I really hate those little suckers.

Not today, Satan!

I shimmy my tight gray shorts up my legs and over my ass before pulling a jog bra down over my head. I drop a loose-fitting tank top over that and slide my feet into my flip-flops before turning on my heel and racing back to the living room to meet Granny.

"Perfect timing, Shelby girl," she says, smiling at me when she walks out of her room.

"Let's go!"

We walk out the front door and run right into Marla, Trent's grandmother and my granny's ride-or-die chick, and she's making out with a man. There seems to be a little heavy-petting action going on in this jumble of bodies and walkers.

"Ahem." Granny coughs. Nothing. She turns to me. "They're like a couple of teenagers."

"I'm not sure I was that . . . *voracious* as a teenager," I admit.

"Ah." She winks at me. "I bet Trent gives you a run for your money." And she's right. My entire body flushes with my embarrassment.

One year later and the heat—the chemistry—between us is just as crazy as it was in the beginning, with no sign of slowing down. At least, that was the truth until this morning.

"Ahem!" Granny shouts down the hallway, making me jump and the randy couple in front of us break apart like they just got busted necking in the driveway by her mom.

"Hello there!" Marla breezes by us. "We were just on our way to yoga class."

"Funny. Us too," Granny says with a twinkle in her eye.

"Harold and I will go down on you," Marla says, and I choke on the saliva in my mouth. I can't stop coughing. Marla's eyes go wide, hearing her Freudian slip. She backpedals, trying to correct it, but it's no use. "I meant we'll go down *with* you . . . you know? In the elevator. Not *on* you or in oral copulation."

"You know, Trent might not be so grumpy all the time if you orally copulated more often," Granny informs me. By now I am bent over clutching my hands to my knees, trying to catch my breath, but to no avail. One day I am going to stop letting these two wily old ladies catch me off guard so often. Come to think of it, I'm pretty sure they do it on purpose.

"She's right," Marla chimes in. "I find that a good blow job settles most ruffled feathers."

"Or anal sex," Harold weighs in.

"Not happening," I gasp.

"Well, that's too bad," Marla says. "Young people nowadays never want to hear the wisdom of the elderly." Not that most elderly people advise their granddaughters on blow jobs and anal sex.

"Maybe if you offered him a little something extra on the menu, Trent would finally propose," Granny says.

"I'm not looking to get married, Granny," I say softly.

"Well, then who is going to give me grandbabies?"

"Um . . . my parents?" I ask and then answer. "Because I'm your granddaughter."

"I want a great-grandbaby," she says petulantly.

"Well, the way they fornicate, I'd say we'll get one sooner rather than later," Marla says under her breath, but as always, it's loud enough for us all to hear. The problem is she's right. Trent and I aren't exactly careful. Maybe that's a subject that should be broached before it's too late. Although, we may not be a couple anymore, so the point may be moot. I kind of like that idea because I'm not real big on the idea of a confrontation with Trent about condoms.

"Um . . . ," I hedge, still kind of worried about a multitude of topics. "Maybe we should head on down to yoga class."

"Yeah," Granny agrees, eyeing me like a hawk. "That sounds like a good idea."

Once we are all loaded into the elevator, I turn to Harold. "So, Harold, when did you decide to take up yoga?" I ask, reaching for any change of subject I can get my hands on. Too bad it turns out to be the wrong one . . .

"U-u-um," he stutters as his face turns bright red.

"We got this book on the internet all about incorporating yoga skills into the *Kama Sutra* for better stamina and flexibility," Marla answers proudly with a little shimmy to her shoulders for emphasis.

"Ohhh . . . okay," I say, for lack of anything else. Granny just laughs, and as the bell chimes for the basement level, where the gym is located, I take a deep breath and make a mental note to talk to Trent about his grandmother's extracurricular activities if we're still an item. And if it turns out that we're not, then that sounds like a big old case of *not my circus, not my monkeys*.

"Bet you wish you didn't ask." Granny laughs.

"You got that right."

We exit the elevator and walk into the yoga room, where the class is almost at full capacity, and head to the back of the classroom where the last spots available are located . . . right behind Ruth and her cohorts. It would all be okay if Ruth was a decent human being, but she and her friends are really just a bunch of mean cows, so of course Granny can't let the opportunity to rub Ruth's nose in the pants-crapping memory pass her by.

"Whatever you do, Ruth, don't toot," Granny stage-whispers loud enough for the whole room to hear while we roll out our mats. The room fills with wicked snickers. Ruth is one of the mean girls of Peaceful Sunset. She's popular only because everyone is afraid of her and her flying monkeys.

"Shut up, you old goat," Ruth barks.

"Oh, hell no," Granny growls. "Hold my earrings, Shelby!"

"Oh, no, you don't," I say as I grab her out of the air mid-leap by the waist and pull her back. "There will be no barroom brawls at yoga. Remember when we got suspended last time?"

"That wasn't my fault," Granny grumbles.

"That was totally your fault," I correct.

"It was never proven," she pouts.

"Yes, it was. That's why we were suspended."

"What's going on back there?" Harmony, the yoga instructor, asks.

"Nothing," everyone seems to mumble all at once.

"Are we ready to begin?" A chorus of yeses goes up throughout the room. "Let's begin with a simple Tree Pose."

Harmony leads us through the breathing involved in a Tree Pose. "Deep breath in . . . and let it out. Push through to find your balance just like the mighty oak tree."

"I love this class, but I will never get used to her hippie-dippie bullshit," Granny says from beside me.

"I hear that," Marla agrees.

I just roll my eyes as we switch sides.

"And another deep breath in . . . and let it out . . .

be the strength grounded in the firm terra that Mother Nature has provided."

"Jesus, it's worse than usual today," Harold says.

Fwwwwwaaaaarrrppptt.

"Dammit, Ruth!" Granny snaps. "That one's gonna stink."

"That wasn't me!" Ruth denies. I shoot her a side-eyed glare because even I'm not sure that I believe her.

"It's like my granny always said: 'You crap your pants once, you'll crap them twice!'" Granny barks back.

"And let's move into Warrior One," Harmony says as we all shift our bodies in the practiced movements.

"That was one time!" Ruth growls under her breath.

"I bet that's what all the pants shitters say," Marla says in a rare show of aggression. We're all so surprised that we almost missed Harmony's transition into the next pose.

"Now, drop an arm into Triangle Pose," she says.

Brrrrruuuupppptttt.

It sounds like a car backfiring.

"Jesus Christ, it's like the Bay of Pigs in here," someone moans.

"Oh man, chili again?" Harmony asks, just as she does during every class.

"Oh yeah." Harold chuckles from the back.

"I sure wish they'd serve you guys ham sandwiches or something," she complains, but in her weird, upbeat way.

"For real," I say out loud, though I really meant to keep it in my head. Faces all around the room, including my own grandmother's, swivel to glare at me. "Uh

. . . whoops."

"Let's move into Downward Dog," Harmony says.

I bend my body forward, dropping my hands to the mat, when I hear a round of whistles go up throughout the room.

"Well, hello there," someone purrs. I have a feeling I know what—or I should say *who*—has caused the commotion, but I would rather hide and hope he doesn't see me back here.

"Let's move into Upward-Facing Dog," she says, and I push through the move and arch my back.

"Nice package," someone says, and I hear him yelp. One of the wily old ladies must have pawed his junk.

"And back into Downward Dog," Harmony says.

I walk my hands back so I can push my rear back. When I do, I collide with muscular thighs and a startling erection. I let out an "Eep!" and try to move away, but firm hands grab my hips, holding my core against him.

"So I take it this means you were going to hide back here from me?" Trent asks as he continues to hold me in a definite dog position, but it's one more likely to be discussed by rappers than by yoga professionals.

"We should try something like that," Harold says from over to the side. "I hear you can go deep in doggie."

"Fuck me," Trent mumbles before turning back to me. "Are you going to answer me?"

"Uh . . . what was the question, again?" I ask, licking my lips nervously.

"I'll answer your questions, Big Daddy," someone

calls from the front of the room.

"Dude, stop with the old-people hormones," Harmony complains.

"We can't help it," someone says. "Our bodies stop making them, so our doctors pump us full of more than we know what to do with in estrogen pills and Viagra."

"Sure looks like he knows what to do with that anaconda in his pants," someone says.

"You hush your mouth, hussy!" Granny shouts.

"I asked if you were just going to hide back here from me," he says and emphasizes his words with a little hip thrust that sends sparks through my body to all the right places.

"Stop that!" I snap, unwilling to orgasm in front of my grandmother. "And yes, I was going to hide back here and let you walk past me."

"You do realize you're right next to my grandmother, right?" he asks me.

"I do."

"And you didn't think I'd see you?" he asks, and I can hear the barely contained laughter in his voice.

"Well, I was hopeful," I snap.

"And you weren't going to bring my cat back?" he asks me with another rock of his hips. I bite my lip.

"She's my cat." I roll my eyes, preparing to argue further.

"And what about my girl?" he asks. "Were you just going to run from me and never look back?"

"Probably," I mumble while wondering where my life took a sharp left turn when it clearly shouldn't have.

"But you forgot one thing, baby," he says softly.

"What's that?" I ask.

"That I love the chase," he says, and then he scoops me up and throws me over his shoulder.

"Trent!" I shout. "Put me down."

"We'll be back for Missy later, Verna," he calls over his shoulder.

"You have fun, kids!" she calls out with a definite smile in her voice. Traitor. "Don't do anything I wouldn't do." Which is also frightening because I'm not sure there is anything she wouldn't do.

"And try out that anal stuff," Marla calls out, and Trent barks out a laugh.

"We will not being trying out the anal stuff," I grumble.

"We'll see about that." Trent laughs.

"Don't forget to do a little deforestation, Shelby!" Granny shouts through the room. "I haven't seen a bush like that since the seventies!"

"Dear Jesus, please open the earth up and swallow me whole," I pray out loud. "I'm serious. Now would be a great time."

Trent throws his head back and his laughter roars through the room.

"I hate you," I gripe.

"No, you don't."

Trent marches out of the yoga room and to the elevator, where he pushes the button and silently waits for the doors to open. What he does not do is tell me what the hell he is up to. I would ask, but I'm also a chicken-shit and I kind of don't want to know. He's going to tell me when he's good and ready anyway, so why rush it?

The bell dings and the doors open. Trent stalks into

the car and hits the button for the lobby. My head is starting to feel a little fuzzy after being held upside down for so long. The doors slide open one more time, and Trent walks out of the retirement center with me over his shoulder like he does it every day.

He walks right out the front door, and no one says one word about it. If they find the scene strange, I'd never know it. His SUV is idling at the curb, waiting for him to retrieve me. Trent pulls open the passenger door and drops me into the seat before reaching across me to buckle my seat belt.

"Don't. Move," he orders before slamming the passenger door closed.

Trent rounds the hood, then jumps in and buckles his belt all at once. I can't really read his mood very well. He's mad, sure. I totally get that. He was kind of a dick and I maybe reacted poorly, but still. What else was I supposed to do?

Trent doesn't give me any answers as he drives us north toward his home in the Escondido hills, the exact one that I left this morning. At least he didn't ask me for his sweatshirt back. Yet. That sucker is mine.

He pulls into the driveway and tosses the SUV into park. Trent shoots me a warning glare before he unbuckles his seat belt and climbs out. He rounds the hood again and pulls open the passenger door before leaning across me—again!—and unbuckling me. His normal woodsy scent is ratcheted up with all kinds of sexy man smells, sending my brain into a whirlwind.

Before I know it, Trent scoops me up again and tosses me over his shoulder. He stalks to the front door and then inserts his key into the lock and pushes the heavy wood door open. He slams the door shut behind us and throws the lock closed.

"Trent—" I start.

But he does not answer. Trent marches down the hall to his bedroom, where he stops next to the bed. I take a step back, but the mattress at the back of my knees stops me.

"Wh-what are you doing?" I ask.

"We're going to have a talk," he says as he sweeps my top up over my head. Trent's eyes darken as he takes me in, in my tiny shorts and jog bra.

"Naked?" I ask.

"Yes," he confirms, and he sweeps my bra up next and removes it.

"M-maybe we should talk with clothes on," I suggest.

"Unh-unh," he denies as he presses in close to me, and I fall back onto the bed. Before I know it, I hear the snick of handcuffs closing around my wrist.

"What the—" I ask, feeling confused and more than a little angry.

"I told you we were going to have a conversation," Trent says as I test the restraints on my wrist.

I watch him warily as he pushes his body up from the bed and toes off his boots and socks. Trent takes off his holster and badge and puts them up on top of a tall dresser way across the room, which is smart because, at this particular juncture, I might find myself inclined to shoot him.

My mouth goes a little dry as he pulls his T-shirt up over his head, exposing his muscular chest and its light dusting of dark hair. I love looking at him, and he knows it by that arrogant smirk playing on his lips right now. Half of me wants to slap his face, and the other half of me wants to sit on it. Jesus Fucking Christ, I need to get it together.

Trent unbuckles his worn leather belt and pulls it free from the loops of his jeans before letting it fall to the carpet with a muted clank. His eyes lock on mine as he pulls on the waistband of his jeans and all the buttons pop in succession like Fourth of July poppers, and I can't help but gasp.

"Like I said," he starts as he stalks over to the bed and climbs up at my feet. "We're going to talk about you leaving me this morning."

"I-I don't want to talk about that," I say after I clear my throat.

"I think we can both agree that that did not make me happy," he says as he slips his fingers into the waist of my shorts and pulls them and my panties down my legs and tosses them to the floor, leaving me a whole lot of naked, handcuffed to his bed, and more than a little turned on.

"Wh-what are you going to do about it?" I ask.

"Good question," Trent says, eyeing me like a lion would his next meal. "I'm going to convince you not to do that."

"And what if you can't convince me?" I ask, my voice husky.

"I'm not going to stop until I do." And then he pushes my legs wide and settles in between them.

The first swipe of his tongue has me arching my back off the bed. The second and third have me groaning as I squirm in his sheets. I'm not sure whether I want to get away from him or pull him closer. When he spears me with his tongue, the decision is taken out of my hands because my body has run away with all of my rational thinking, and I wrap my legs around his neck.

Trent chuckles against my center, clearly acknowledging his win, but at this point, I don't care. He sucks my clit into his mouth and I see stars, crying out my release in the process. Trent pries my legs from around his neck, kissing the inside of each thigh as he lets them drop down. I try to catch my breath, but it's a lost cause because clearly Trent isn't done with me yet.

He pushes his jeans down around his hips, and that cock I have come to love so much springs free. I pant as he pushes my legs wide and settles on his knees in between them, sliding the tip of his cock through my wetness and up and over my clit in an achingly slow circuit.

"Are you going to leave me again, baby?" he rumbles, his voice low, as he lines up the tip of his cock to my pussy and slides just the tip inside.

"I-I don't know," I say.

"Wrong answer, baby." And then he slams home.

"Trent," I pant as I pull on the cuff, trying to reach him.

My core pulses around him in a precursor of what's to come as he pulls out and drives back in.

"I need you, baby," Trent admits as he glides out again and thrusts back in deep. "I'm going to get angry and so are you, but we have to fight it out together. Preferably like this."

"Yes." He slides out and tips his hips when he

pushes in again so that he hits that magic spot when he pushes in again.

His thumb finds my clit, and I think I might die when he asks me again, "Are you going to leave?"

"No," I answer honestly.

"Good answer, baby," he says, and then he leans over me further, picking up his pace as he moves his thumb in time with his hips. And I'm a lost cause.

"Trent," I breathe as I spiral closer and closer to the edge.

"That's right, Shell," he rumbles as he pumps his hips faster and faster, hitting that spot again and again. "You're there."

My toes curl in the sheets and I come. Again. But Trent does not. Instead he pulls completely out and flips me over to my knees. I brace my handcuffed hand against the headboard to keep my balance as he drives deep inside me. I can't help but clench around him.

"Yeah, baby," he says as he pumps his hard length into me. "I love the way you grip my cock."

"Yes," I moan as I push back against the headboard, seating myself on him again and again.

"Yes," he growls. "Fuck yourself on my cock."

Trent's dirty talk heats my body up even more, making a rush of wetness coat him between us. I moan as I claw at the headboard. He grips my hips in his hands so tight I wouldn't be surprised if I see bruises tomorrow, but I couldn't care less right now. I love it. I revel in it as he pumps his cock into me repeatedly.

"That's it," he says as he drives in again and again. "Fuck, you feel so good."

"Yes, Trent," I agree as I arch so that he hits that

spot again.

"So fucking good."

"Yes." He slides his hand down my hip to where we come together.

"You should see how good you look taking my cock, baby." His finger circles my clit again, and even though I can feel another orgasm building already, I want to deny it. I don't think I can come again.

"Trent," I gasp as he circles my clit. "I can't."

"Oh, yes, you fucking can, baby, and you will," he growls. "Now, take my cock like a good girl and come all over it."

"Trent," I cry out. He pumps harder and harder.

"Come for me and show me that you're mine," he demands. My need for him hurts. He's built it so strong in me and he knows it. My nails scratch at the headboard, useless to stop the tidal wave that is no doubt about to take me under. "Come all over me."

Black spots burst before my eyes and I scream his name, helpless to stop it, but then again, where Trent is concerned, all I can do is hang on for the ride. And this is a great ride.

My third climax doesn't roll over me like a wave but explodes like napalm, blowing outward and burning across my skin.

"Yeah," he says as he drives deep again and again. "You're mine." And then he growls my name and follows me over the edge.

"Trent," I whisper, or maybe I mumble because my face is mashed into the pillows where I collapsed under the force of that climax.

"Yeah, honey," he says, and I can hear the smile in

his voice.

"I've decided to hear you out," I tell him.

"That's good of you, baby, because I'm fa—" But he doesn't get to finish that thought because his phone rings. "Hold that thought."

Trent pulls back, sliding free from my body, and stands up. He walks over to the dresser where he left his stuff, pulling up his jeans as he goes. He grabs his phone and answers.

"Foyle," he barks into the phone. "Are you fucking kidding me right now, Kane? Yeah, no, I'll be there . . . You could not have worse fucking timing . . . You better." And then he hangs up.

"Trent?" I ask hesitantly.

He lets his head hang back to his shoulders as he stares at the ceiling. "As much as I hate to say it, baby, I have to go."

"What?"

"They found Daisy's friend," he says quietly.

"She's okay, right?" I ask.

"No, honey," he answers softly. "She's dead."

"What? How?" I try to jump up and am stopped by my wrist in the cuff like a junkyard dog at the end of his rope.

Trent holds up his hand to stop me. "I can't answer that yet."

Trent buttons up his jeans and plucks his T-shirt off of the floor before turning it right side out and tugging it down over his head. He sits on the edge of the bed and pulls his socks and boots back on before standing to retrieve his holster and badge from the dresser top.

Trent smiles at me over his shoulder before heading to the doorway.

"Um . . . are you forgetting something?" I ask as I shake the hand in the cuff, making Trent smirk.

"No." And then he walks out of the bedroom door.

"Trent!" I scream. "Get back here, you miserable bastard!"

"I shouldn't be too long," he calls from the front door.

"I hate you!" I call out.

"No, you don't. Besides, I definitely don't hate you, baby."

And then I hear the door click shut. I sit there and fume until I get bored, and then I fall asleep. His bed *is* pretty comfy.

FOUR

INVESTIGATIONS AND PRETTY ASSES

I am pissed.

No, I'm not pissed; I'm furious. I am drive your car into the supermarket and mow down your good-for-nothing, piece-of-crap boyfriend in the parking lot eighty-seven times on the way in, soul-shaking enraged.

Why am I this mad? I'm this furious because that big, beautiful bastard left to work a case and did not unlock me. Sure, I had a great nap for a while, but then I woke up to a crick in my neck and a sore shoulder.

I look over at the digital alarm clock on Trent's side of the bed. The red numbers tell me he's been gone for four hours. That's four hours of me being cuffed to a hidden eyebolt in the lower part of the headboard where the box spring sits on a platform.

I let out a frustrated sigh and then plump the pillows with my free hand. Was the sex really worth this shit? Sadly, yes, it was and I will no doubt sign up to do it again. I'm such a sucker. I lie back against the pillows, and before I know it, my boredom takes over and I fall back asleep.

"I'm so sorry, baby," Trent whispers in my dream, but I can't for the life of me figure out what he has to be sorry for.

"Ung," I groan before trying to roll over and go back to my dream.

"No, Shelby," Trent says. "You've gotta wake up."

"I don't wanna," I grumble, and then something pinches my wrist, and my whole arm is engulfed with the freezing flame of the worst pins and needles imaginable. "Ahhhhhh!"

"I'm so sorry, honey," he says as he puts pressure on my arm.

"It hurts," I cry out. "Why does it hurt so much?"

"It's my fault, baby. I shouldn't have left you tied up for so long," he explains. My eyes flash open and I'm furious all over again.

"You!" I shout. "How dare you?"

"I know, honey," Trent says, trying to placate me. "I didn't think I would be gone so long."

"You shouldn't have left me like that. Period." My voice is quiet. I could scream and yell, but honestly, I am too mad.

"I know," he says. I jump up. "Where are you going?"

My face flushes what I'm assuming is an embarrassing shade of red. "I have to pee," I whisper. Trent's face goes soft, and that only serves to ratchet my embarrassment higher, so I race toward the bathroom. I only look back as I move to close the door. Trent is sitting on the side of the bed with his head in his hands. Watching him like this softens my resolve to be pissed.

With a heavy sigh, I slam the door closed and twist the lock. I take care of business and it takes a while. As I was my hands, I look in the mirror and wonder how long I was in that bed. My muscles are screaming, but on the flip side, I feel incredibly well rested. So how about that?

I reach over to turn the faucet off when I hear a muffled scream that sounds a lot like my good friend Daisy's from the other side of the bathroom door. But why would Daisy be in Trent's bedroom? I shut off the tap and move to the door. I unlock it and pull it open and realize that a pretty-good-sized crowd has amassed in Trent's master bedroom, and he looks less than impressed.

I turn to shut the door again. Taking the chicken's way out and hiding in the bathroom seems like a grand idea right about now. Unfortunately, Trent, who has always been pretty in tune to wherever I am in a room, catches my cowardly attempt and calls me out on it.

"Oh, no, you don't," he says. "You better get your pretty ass back here, Shelby."

"Dammit." I turn around and step out of the bathroom. "So what's going on, guys?"

"Oh dear," my granny says as she and Marla try to hold Daisy back. Daisy is shaking, and tear tracks stain her beautiful cheeks.

"What's going on," she shouts, "is that Christina is dead and Stacy is missing!"

"Oh, honey, no," I say, moving toward my friend.

"Not so fast," Trent says as he snags me around the waist and hauls me back to him. Before I can utter a protest, he drops one of his T-shirts over my head. I look down and realize I was still naked.

"Whoops," I whisper before he lets me go.

I rush over to Daisy and open my arms to her. She practically takes me to the ground as she hugs me tight. Her hot tears pour into my hair and down my shoulder. I turn to look at Trent.

"Is this true?" I ask him. "She's really dead?"

He sighs. "Yeah, that was the call that took me so long."

"How?" I ask.

"I can't tell you that," he says softly.

"What about Stacy?" Daisy shouts.

"Is that true too?" I ask, still holding Daisy in my arms. "Is another one of her friends missing too?"

"Yes," Trent says. The word echoes around the room like a gunshot.

"How long have you known?" I ask, breaking the silence.

"I didn't until just now when Kane showed up to this circus." He sighs again. I look over my shoulder and see that Kane is, in fact, standing at the back of the bedroom. Once again, he's seen me acting more than a little crazy with no clothes on. This is excessive.

"Hey, Kane," I say.

"Hey, Shelby." He smiles gently at me.

"We gotta stop meeting like this, Kane."

"No kidding," he says softly.

"How's Sophie?" I ask him.

"She says the tryout is going really well," he answers. "Says she might get to come home soon."

"Awesome. Do you know who the guys is?"

"No," he grumbles. "Some Frenchman namby-pamby."

Whoops. Looks like I touched a nerve. Time to redirect this conversation. Too bad I choose the wrong direction.

"So what are we going to do?" I ask. Trent narrows his eyes.

"You are going to do nothing," he growls.

"We can't just do nothing!" Daisy shrieks. "Tricks are going missing or dying!"

"Daisy—" I start.

"No!" she shouts as she pulls away from me. "We have to do something."

"Shelby isn't going to do anything," Trent orders.

"But she's my friend and I need her," she pleads.

"She's my girlfriend and I need her alive. You guys almost got her killed last time," he says softly, making my heart clench because it's true. Trent and I almost died last year when we tried our hands at amateur investigations.

"No, last time, Sophia almost died. I was in on the rescue," I correct him. Apparently, that was also a wrong turn to take the conversation in by the low growl coming from Kane in the back.

"That does not make it better," he says, his voice low and menacing.

"Sorry," I say quickly. "My bad."

"Everybody out!" Trent orders.

"Now, Trent—" I start.

"No," he growls. "You and I need to have another conversation." I'm not real wild about another conversation about me staying out of Trent's investigations, but the one this afternoon was pretty great, and thinking about that conversation causes a definite tingling sensation happening in some not-so-public places.

"Trent—" I start.

"Unh-unh," he denies me. "Baby, you got a pretty ass—a great fucking ass—that I love to look at and enjoy in a multitude of ways, but I will throw you and your great fucking ass in jail if I catch you anywhere near my investigation and not even fucking blink."

The room goes silent.

"Maybe we should all get some rest, and we will regroup in the morning," I suggest.

"I don't know," Daisy says.

"We'll figure out what to do," I promise.

"We have to find her," she pleads.

"We will do our best to find her," Trent says. "You will live your normal, everyday lives and leave the police work to the actual police."

"It's a novel idea," Granny says, breaking the tension. I have to bite my lip to keep from laughing.

"Are you sure we can trust them?" Marla asks.

"Nana!" Trent shouts. "I'm right here."

"Well, it is an important task," she explains. "We can't leave it to just anyone."

"We'll do our best," he sighs.

"All right, son," she says softly. "We'll leave it to you."

"But—" Daisy starts, but Granny interrupts her.

"Let's leave it to the professionals," Granny says. "We'll talk over brunch in a day or two."

"I love brunch," I mumble.

"Don't we all, dear," Marla says with a wink.

"Now, let's let these two have their conversation, or else I'm never going to live long enough to hold my great-grandbaby," Granny says as she herds everyone out of Trent's bedroom and then out of the house. "And don't forget to trim the hedges!"

"Would someone please just shoot me!" I shout with my arms held wide and my head dropped back to look at the ceiling of Trent's bedroom, only I'm not looking at anything because my eyes are closed.

"No!" both Kane and Trent shout at the same time.

"Well, thanks for nothing, guys." I sigh.

I look over to see Kane chuckling from the doorway.

"I need to talk to Kane for a minute, baby," Trent says softly to me before placing a kiss against my temple. "Don't. Move."

I sigh. "He's so bossy," I say to Kane.

"Gotta say, man," Kane says. "I like it better when you're the one in the hot seat." I'm not sure what they are talking about, but I am positive that it is not flattering, so I'm going to ignore them.

Trent walks Kane down the hall, and I hear their muffled voices, but I can't make out the words. I pull a celebrity gossip magazine from the nightstand and plop myself down into the chair in the corner to wait for Trent to come back so we can have our conversation. And that thought sends a shiver up my spine—the good kind.

A couple minutes later, I am deep in an article about the royal baby when I hear the front door click closed one more time, making my palms start to sweat like I'm on a first date with Channing Tatum. The sounds of Trent's footfalls moving down the hall have my lady parts raring to go. Down, girl!

"Hey, baby," he says from the doorway. Somewhere along the way, he discarded his shoes and locked up his duty belt.

"Hey," I whisper, suddenly feeling really shy.

"Come here," Trent says, and I don't have to be told twice. I drop my magazine to the floor and push up from the chair before heading straight to Trent's open arms. "You're so damn beautiful."

"Thanks," I say, ducking my head as a light heat hits my cheeks.

"You know why I need you to stay away from the investigation, right?" he asks me.

"Trent—"

"I mean it," Trent pleads before cupping my cheeks in his palms. "I can't let anything happen to you." And then he drops his mouth to mine, kissing me so deeply that I forget what I was going to say anyway.

He breaks the kiss to sweep his T-shirt up and over my head, dropping it to the floor. Trent kisses me again, and this time I squeal through it as he grabs me by the hips and lifts me up. I have to wrap my legs around his waist to keep from falling as he carries me back to the bed. Not that Trent would ever drop me.

Trent tosses me down onto the mattress, and I laugh as I bounce a little, but that laughter dies when he strips his own T-shirt over his head and removes his jeans, dropping both to the floor. The outline of his erection is hard to miss in his gray boxer briefs, and I lick my lips absentmindedly as he crawls over me on the bed.

"I can't be without you," he says softly as he traces a fingertip down my cheek and over my jaw. Trent trails that finger down between my breasts and over my belly, and down even farther still to the apex between my thighs.

"Trent—"

"I won't live without you," he says before lowering his mouth to my center.

As Trent licks and nips, my eyes roll back in my head, and it doesn't take me long to get to that knife-edge of oblivion as he eats me.

"Oh God," I moan.

"That's it, baby," Trent hums.

"Oh, yes," I pant as he swirls his tongue around my clit.

"Shell," he says to me in between licks and kisses. "Promise me you won't do anything crazy." He kisses me again and again.

"Yes," I ignore him as I rock against his mouth, moving closer and closer.

"Promise," he commands as I spiral toward the edge.

"Yes!" I cry.

"You promise?" he asks me again, but I'm too far gone.

"Sweet petunia, yes!"

"I'm so glad we agree. You have no idea how happy this makes me, Shelby." Trent smiles against my thigh and then slithers up my body before sliding in deep.

"Aah," I say as my climax drags on and on while Trent pumps in and out.

"I love how you squeeze my cock," he says between thrusts. "Only you, baby."

"Yes," I breathe. "Yes, yes."

"I need it," he says. "Give it to me."

"Trent—"

"I need the words, Shelby," he orders as he drives his cock deep.

"What?" I ask, lost in the moment, about to come again, and wondering what Trent is talking about.

"Tell me," he says again, his body moving faster and faster in mine. "Tell me you love me."

"Trent," I gasp as I fall over the edge.

"Tell me," he repeats as he pumps his hips harder and harder. "I know you do."

"I love you, Trent," I say when I wrap my arms tighter around his shoulders.

"Thank fuck," he says before following me over.

What Trent doesn't do is say it too.

THIS IS SOME BEAR GRYLLS SHIT

The morning sun shines brightly through the soft curtains in Trent's bedroom. I stretch like a cat in the warm glow, working out all of the muscle soreness in my body from yesterday as I go.

I toss the covers back and head into the bathroom. But my reflection in the mirror stops me in my tracks.

Holy shit! I have let things go too far.

I mentally tick down the weeks since my last waxing appointment, and I am totally alarmed when I realize that (a) I have run out of fingers on both hands, and (b) I have no idea when the last time this had been taken down.

I quickly scurry back into the bedroom, snatch my phone off of the nightstand, and call my favorite waxing salon in town. It rings twice before they answer.

"The Bee Keeper, how can we help you today?" the girl who is always a little rude answers the phone.

"Hi! I was wondering if you had any slots open for an emergency Brazilian?" I ask hopefully.

"Girl, we're booked solid for the next six months!"

"You're kidding," I say, hoping she's really just in a mood and not being an asshole.

"No!" She laughs. "Didn't you see the write-up on us in the Promenade Magazine? It was great for business." I did see it and thought, How trendy am I that I go to the best waxing salon in the county and that even some real housewives come down from farther up the coast to get their bushes tamed at the same place I do? Well, that was really fucking dumb because now I'm left in the lurch.

"I did see it," I admit.

"Well, then you should know that we can't help you last-minute!" she chastises me. "Shame on you. I swear . . ."

"Well, thanks," I say before hanging up.

I let out a sigh and place my phone back down on the nightstand. What am I going to do now? Think, think, think, Shelby! Ugh. And then I remember this one time when I was watching some show on the day-to-day life of Denise Richards and she was like, "Ain't nobody got time to go to a salon to get a wax," so she does it herself at home. I remember thinking, *Well, if Denise Richards can wax her va-gym-jam at home by herself, then so can I*!

So I downed a glass of pinot grigio like it was my job and hopped on the internet and ordered an at-home kit that guaranteed no pain and no icky strips. So I checked that "Buy Now" box, and when it showed up two days later in an envelope with a smile on the side, I promptly stuck it under the bathroom counter because I had a waxing appointment at The Bee Keeper the next day.

Goddammit, I was so lucky and I didn't even know it.

I wonder if I brought it over here when I grabbed a bunch of stuff from my condo to keep here. I normally wouldn't have, but Trent was in a hurry to come home and break in the bedroom because our new semi-cohabitational status, and that imagery had inspired me to just throw things in bags and run for the door like my pants were on fire. And they were on fire, a fire that only Trent could put out with his magical hose. And by that I mean penis. But I digress.

I pop open the cabinets below the sinks and start digging around. Trent apparently buys toothpaste and beard balm in bulk, which is more than a little weird, but whatever. To each his own and all that jazzy bullshit. And then—way in the back—I spot that little pink box. Victory is mine, motherfuckers!

I snatch up the box and rip it open, skimming the instructions. The wax is in a microwavable container with a cute, easy-to-hold handle. It says to pop it into the microwave for thirty seconds and then stir it with the popsicle stick that comes with the kit.

So I race down the hall to the kitchen with my newfound treasures in my clutches. I pop the lid off of the cup and toss it into the microwave, slamming the door shut, and hit the quick thirty seconds more button. When the timer dings, I pull the cup out and poke the stick into the cup, but the wax is still hard. What the fuck? I followed the directions. Well, I'm pretty sure I followed them. I skimmed them mostly, but how hard can it be to heat up a little mug of wax in the microwave?

I drop the stick onto the counter and put the mug back into the microwave for another thirty seconds. This time it will definitely be done. It probably just needed a teensy bit longer. When the timer dings, I pull the cup out of the microwave and go to mix it with the little popsicle stick, but, again, the wax isn't melted.

Now, I'm a little overeager to get this show on the road. It's still late morning, but I want to start my day in case the ladies call and want to get together for a planning session. I don't want to get caught with wax in unfortunate places, so I toss the cup back into the microwave for a full minute. Take that, stubborn wax! Surely this will do it.

When the microwave dings this time, steam pours out when I open the door. Bet it's done now. I poke the stick into the wax, and a seal that was covering the top flops to the side and hot wax splatters on the T-shirt I'm wearing. Oh, damn. I must have thought the seal was the wax. I hope I didn't burn the wax. I don't have time to order another kit on the internet even if it does come with free two-day shipping.

I stir the wax and it seems okay, so I head back down the hall to the bedroom, where I camp out in front of a full-length mirror with my legs spread like I'm getting ready to stretch for a marathon. Joke's on me because I have no idea how one would stretch for a marathon since I don't fucking jog.

I place the cup and the popsicle stick on a towel on the floor in front of me. I'm pretty sure the instructions said to use the popsicle stick to spread an even layer of wax over the area and, when it hardens, to peel back an edge and then let her rip.

Like I said, I'm pretty sure.

Mostly sure.

Well, we'll just see what happens.

I dip the stick into the mug of wax and scoop up a huge glob of wax and smear it down my bikini line. And Holy Mother of Christ, this sucker is hot! I should not have kept putting it in the microwave because now I have burned my pussy off and there will be nothing left. Shit, it hurts!

I try to wipe it off, but the pain must have delayed my brain functions, because the wax has hardened. Holy shit. It's cooling, and I no longer feel like my kitty cat has been set afire. Okay. This isn't so bad. I can do this. I take a deep breath and peel back the edge of the wax strip and let her fly.

And holy fucking shit that stings!

But then I look down, and my skin is as smooth as a baby's bottom. All right. I can do this! I scoop up another huge blob of wax and smear it on the other side. The wax in the mug has cooled down since the last side, and my skin no longer feels like molten lava. I peel back the edge and rip. And . . .

Holy fuckballs that stings!

I take a deep breath and wipe my brow. Now, on to the nether regions. I scoop out more wax and just glob it on real think because one look in the mirror tells me that things have gotten pretty out of hand down there. I scoop up another big blob, smush it onto the other side, and wait for it to cool and harden.

But here's where things go a little sideways on me. When I go to pull up the edge to take off the wax, it won't budge. Like, at all. I scratch and claw, and I'm not ashamed to admit that I cry a little, but it will not let up. The wax, which is now hardened, is tangled in hair and knotted all around while being stuck to my skin.

Shit! What am I going to do? I have to get this off of me! The longer it sits, the more worried I get. This can't be good at all.

Maybe a bath will help loosen it up so that it will come off. That's the ticket! I quickly hop up and run back into the bathroom. I turn on the taps and fill the big tub with warm water. I strip off the T-shirt and climb into the tub. I think that maybe if I let the wax soak while I wash my hair and the rest of me, it will soften up and I can pull it off without dying. So I take my time soaping up my hair and lying back in the water to rinse it. I do the same with my body, lathering it up all over with a bar of soap and then rinsing.

I pull the plug on the tub and stand up as the water drains down. I climb out of the tub and grab a towel to dry off before pulling the wax-stained T-shirt back over my head and down my body.

I walk back over to the mirror and sit down to see if the wax will come free. But now it's worse. Not only is the wax still knotted completely around the hair and stuck to my skin, but it also seems to have migrated over, and now my vagina is sealed shut. Ancient chastity belts have nothing on this shit.

I pull at it for a minute or two, and then I pull my knees to my chest and have a good cry until I fall over onto the towel and fall asleep.

"Shelby," I hear Trent call out, waking me from a deep sleep. "Shelby, are you home?"

"I'm back here," I reply, wiping the dried tears from my cheeks and pushing up to sit on the towel. The sun has gone down for the night, and the room is much darker than the midday light that shone when I fought my battle against the bush and lost.

"What are you doing back here, baby?" he asks, taking one look at me, and his whole body goes on red alert. "What's wrong?"

"S-something happened," I whimper as I sniffle.

"What is it?" Trent demands. I shake my head. There is no way I can tell him what happened. I will die of embarrassment. "I can't fix it if you don't tell me."

"I had an accident," I admit.

"What were you doing?"

"Trying to give myself a bikini wax," I admit.

"Well, it can't be that bad," he says, smiling down at me. "Let me see."

"No!" I shout. "You can't see it."

"Well, I'll have to see it sometime," he says with a laugh.

"No, you will never be seeing my vagina again. It's over. It's closed for business. I'm sorry for your loss." I nod my head solemnly.

"I highly doubt that," Trent says. "It's one of my most favorite things. Now let me see it."

Trent gently pushes me back to lie on the towel. I clench my thighs tight, but eventually, Trent eases them open. I throw my arm across my eyes, unable to see him look at the monster that my va-gym-jam has become. Trent is silent for a while, obviously studying the car crash that is now my pussy, before he finally finds his voice and speaks.

"So . . . wanna tell me what happened here?" he asks me.

"I accidentally glued my vagina closed!" I cry out.

"It'll be okay," Trent says, trying to reassure me. "We can handle this."

"I don't think so," I whimper. "I-I think I'm going to die like this."

"You're not going to die." I can practically hear Trent rolls his eyes. I hear a clear snick in the air, and my eyes snap open to see Trent popping open a fairly large folding knife that he keeps in his pocket.

"Wh-what the fuck is that?"

"My knife." He smirks obviously enjoying my discomfort.

"But what are you doing with that?" I ask.

"I'm saving your pussy, babe, because it's too good to be lost for all time. But I have to say, this is some Bear Grylls survival shit here that needs to go down."

And then he pinches the edge of the wax between the side of the blade and his thumb to pry up the seal it's created on my skin. Once he has a good purchase, Trent grabs the wax and rips upward quickly. And then he repeats the process on the other side.

Meanwhile, I'm trying to catch my breath because I feel like I might have just died.

"It's so pink and so smooth," he muses as he gently strokes my slit with the very tip of his finger. "Does it hurt?"

"Not too much anymore," I admit. "But I still might die now."

"No, don't do that," he says to me. "I'm thinking . . . I'm thinking that maybe I should kiss it better."

"What?" I ask, but he doesn't answer. Instead he places a tender, openmouthed kiss to my center.

I gasp when his tongue spears into me as he kisses me again and again before licking up to suck my clit into his mouth. Trent plunges a finger inside me and curls it to hit that magic spot as he circles his tongue around me, pushing me over the edge.

I hear his belt clank as he pushes his jeans down to mid-thigh before covering me with his body and driving his cock deep inside. I forgot how much more you feel after a fresh wax, and right now I feel everything. I feel the slip and slide of Trent's cock as he plunges through my wetness and the way he skates over my clit in the process. And it all heightens my arousal more than I thought it could.

"Trent," I gasp as I clench around his hard length.

"That's right," his deep voice rumbles. "Fuck, you feel so good."

"Yes," I pant as he drives in deeper and deeper.

Trent crushes his mouth to mine, and he swallows down my cries as I come for the second time. He pumps again once, twice, before breaking his connection to me at our mouths. Trent throws his head back and roars out his completion before dropping down to let me take more of his weight. Before he rolls to the side, taking me with him.

"It's never been as good as it is with you, baby," he

rumbles into my hair, and my heart is full to bursting because it's never been as good with anyone else as it is with Trent for me either.

I hug him tighter to me in hopes that he hears what my actions say when I can't find the words. Trent picks me up like a bride and carries me into the bathroom, where he takes great care to shower us both before dropping a clean T-shirt over my head and picking up his phone to order a pizza.

Talk about the man of my dreams.

chapter SIX

BRUNCH AND HOOKIN' 101

"Open this mother fluffer up," Daisy calls through the heavy wood and glass of Trent's front door. "We have got shit to do!"

"And pancakes," Marla calls out sweetly. "Don't forget the pancakes, dear."

"Hell no, I won't forget the pancakes!"

I take another sip of my coffee and let out a sigh before setting it down on the counter. I make my way to the entryway, knowing what I will find when I open the door.

"Hey, guys," I say, opening the door for them. "What are you guys doing here so early?"

"Brunch!" they all shout in unison.

"Isn't brunch usually at a more decent hour?" I ask, knowing it can't be any later than eight.

"Usually," Granny confirms.

"But we got important shit to do," Daisy finishes for her. I'm not gonna lie, the undefined shit to do has me concerned.

I take a deep breath and lead them back into the kitchen. I start pulling mugs down from the cabinet, knowing they will all most likely want a cup of coffee while I get ready for the day, and start pouring.

Earlier this morning, Trent woke me up with his head between my legs. By the third swipe of his tongue, my eyes opened, but by the fourth, they were rolling back in my head. After that he had crawled up my body and slid inside.

Trent had put his mouth to mine as he plunged deep inside me over and over. I'm still not sure if he triggered one orgasm on the heels of the first or if Trent and his magic penis managed to pull off the longest climax in the history of the world. By the time I was done, he pushed in once, twice more, before dropping his head to press his face into the side of my neck. His groan sent chills up my spine as he claimed his own release.

Trent pressed a sweet kiss to my lips as he pulled out, taking me with him while he rolled out of bed and headed for the shower. Apparently, we weren't done. Yippee!

He turned on the taps and then backed me into the counter while we waited for the water to heat up. I watched his face for any insight into his mood this morning. I could be upset that he forced me to share my feelings for him, but really, I'm not. It feels like a huge weight has been taken off my shoulders. And I was never very good with secrets anyway.

Part of me wonders if Trent doesn't feel the same way because he can't. I know how much it hurt him to lose his ex the way he did. And I'm okay with it if that's why. Maybe, just maybe, I can love Trent enough for the both of us. Or I'll get burned in the process. Only time will tell.

His face softened as he ran a fingertip from my temple, down over my cheekbone, and then to my jawline. I turned my face into his hand and kissed his palm. Trent framed my face with his hands and kissed me soundly. I opened my mouth underneath him and enjoyed making out with him until the steam billowed out from the shower and Trent dragged me inside.

Trent pulled us under the warm spray before filling his palms with shower gel. He soaped me up all over, pinching a nipple or two in the process, before helping me rinse the suds clean. He was very thorough. I rolled my eyes at him as I grabbed the shampoo and washed my hair. Trent did the same, only I couldn't help but watch the play of his muscles as he rinsed the soap from his dark hair.

He caught me watching him and winked. I decided then that turnabout was fair play and reached for the body wash bottle. I filled my hand with the soap before rubbing them together to create a heavy lather. I placed my hands on his chest, working the soap into his tight muscles. Trent tipped his head back and groaned, and I continued my massage down his body. When I reached his hard length, I took it into my fist and stroked him until he gripped my hips tight in his fingers and I knew he was close.

Then I let him go.

"Shelby," he growled as I pulled the detachable showerhead down, rinsing the soap from his body.

"Don't worry. We'll get you all clean." I winked and then dropped to my knees in front of him, placing my hands on his thighs and taking him deep into my mouth.

"Shelby," he rasped as he thrust a hand into my wet hair. The other he braced on the tiled shower wall behind me.

It didn't take long for Trent to find his second release of the morning, calling out my name as he did. Afterward, he shut off the water and held out a hand like a gentleman to help me up. Trent reached for a towel on the rack and wrapped me up in it before grabbing his own.

He pulled one of his T-shirts out of a drawer and dropped it over my head. I pushed my arms through the armholes and let it fall around my knees before turning to watch a naked Trent dress for the day, and I thought, I hope I never get used to this, that it never becomes something I take for granted, because if the dice had fallen differently, I would be married to James right now and hating every minute of it. Instead, I'm here with Trent, whom I love more than anything, and he cares for me in his own way.

"You going back to bed, baby?" he asked me once he was dressed and ready to head out for the day.

"Nah," I answered. "I think I'm going to go make some breakfast and relax before I have to meet the girls this afternoon."

"Remember," he warned. "We made a deal."

"I know, I know," I said, trying to placate him, but it fell on deaf ears. "No investigating."

"Promise me," he demanded.

"I promise," I said before placing my hands on his chest and pressing up onto my toes so that my mouth could reach his. My kiss started out soft, but before I knew it, Trent took over, deepening it, owning it, and I loved every second of it.

"I should go before I'm late for work," he whispered, leaning his forehead on mine.

"You should go before I give you a reason to be late for work." I smirked.

"You already do," he said softly, backing away.

"Have a good day," I told him. "Be safe."

"You too," he told me as he pulled open the front door.

"Really," I scoffed. "What could possibly happen to me?"

"Really?" Trent raised an eyebrow.

"Don't answer that."

"I'll see you later." He laughed before shutting the door behind him. I made my way to the kitchen and started a pot of coffee, barely having poured a cup when the doorbell rang. All in all, it was a decent way to start the day. But now here I am—my morning-sex buzz is wearing off, and as I look at Daisy, my sweet, incredibly kind and generous friend, asking me for help, I'm pretty sure I had just made a promise to Trent that I wouldn't be able to keep.

"Let me just go get dressed real fast," I say.

"You do that," Granny says, eyeing me like she knows all of my deep, dark secrets. Mainly because she does. But I don't think about that as I hustle down the hallway to throw on some clothes and brush my hair.

I hustle into Trent's bedroom and don't stop until I'm in the closet, where a collection of my clothes are squished into a spare drawer and my duffel bag sits in a corner. I root through it like my life depends on it, settling on a pair of black leggings and a couple of layered tank tops. I throw Trent's shirt into my duffel bag, because why stop now—in for a penny, in for a pound—with the amount of his shit I've managed to swipe since we've been dating?

I pull on an emerald-green lace bra and panty set that the lady in the store said set off the red in my hair. Personally, I think she just wanted to sell me over a hundred dollars in undies and collect the commission, but who am I to judge? I bought it. And then I slide my leggings up my legs with a quickness before pulling my tank tops down over my head.

I run into the bathroom and gather my hair up into a messy bun on top of my head and then brush my teeth as I do normally, because dental hygiene can't be rushed. I race back into the bedroom, grab my sneakers, and I step into them as I run back down the hall.

"Ready," I say, a little out of breath, as I reach the entrance to the the kitchen. Everyone stops what they're doing and turns to look at me with their mouths hanging open. I discreetly check my nose for a booger but can't feel anything. "What's wrong?" I ask.

"Honey," Granny starts. She's always the one to lay the truth on me. "Your shirt is on backwards and your boobies are hanging out."

I immediately drop my gaze to my ample chest.

"Oh, damn," I mumble.

It appears she's right. I did put my tanks on backwards, and the way they dip lower in the back is just enough for my boobs to hang out. Well, shit.

"Um . . . I'll be right back," I tell the crowd.

"Why bother? You're about to be naked in front of strangers," Daisy says offhandedly.

"Shh!" Granny and Marla turn to reprimand her.

"Excuse me?" I ask even though I am 100 percent sure that I do not, in fact, want to know what she's talking about.

"We'll talk about it at brunch," Daisy says, evading my question.

"Sure," I say as I pull my tank tops over my head and flip them around before tugging them back down.

"Everyone ready to go?" Marla cheers just a little too brightly as she claps her hands like a preschool teacher. "To the Caddy, ladies!"

Yep, I'm definitely fucked.

I pull on my cardigan and lock the front door behind us with my key. Trent and I hit the key-exchange phase of dating about three weeks ago, and I was enjoying it until recently.

We all pile into Harold's classic baby-blue Cadillac convertible, and I think, not for the first time today—or ever—that I blindly follow behind this group of women, whom I love more than life, while more than a little regretting my life choices to do so. But hey, no one's perfect.

Daisy and I stuff ourselves into the big back seat while Granny and Marla climb into the front.

"Sweet baby Jesus," I whisper to Daisy as Marla adjusts her rearview mirror. "What are we doing here?"

"We're going to find out what happened to Christina and Stacy," she whispers back. "We just have to be brave."

"Okay," I tell her, taking her hand in mine and feeling guilty for not having her friends be my top priority. I can be brave. All I have to do is sit back as we ride to the restaurant, and then we will figure out what to do together. We're all in this together.

We roll down the highway past a couple of exits with the wind in our hair like a few *Thelma and Louise* extras before Marla takes the next ramp. When she pulls into the parking lot of The Egg Yolk, I have to hold myself back from doing a happy dance. This is one of my most favorite breakfast places in all of San Diego County.

We climb out of the car, some of us faster than others, and walk arm in arm into the restaurant. It's not very busy with today being a weekday, but on weekends it's standing room only. It's that freaking good.

"Right this way, ladies," the hostess says as she leads us to a booth.

"Thank you," I tell her with a smile as we all take our seats. She hands me a menu before smiling at me and walking away back to her station.

I'm perusing the list of usual delicious breakfast suspects, wondering if I should get a side of French toast with scrambled eggs or if I should order eggs Benedict—both are sound options—when Daisy breaks into my thoughts with a bang.

"So let's cut the crapola," she says. I'm still weighing my options, but I've pretty much decided I'm getting the Benedict with orange juice and coffee, while she talks about her plans. And I'm sure they are important plans, but let's face it, I can't really focus without more caffeine in my bloodstream.

"She's not ready yet," my granny says. "You have to ease her into the idea."

Speaking of coffee, I wonder when our server will come and take our drink orders so I can get to it.

"Well, I say there's no time like the present to tell someone you're about to train them to be a hooker!" she practically shouts, drawing my attention, barely. Who's going to be a hooker? It must be another one of Daisy's friends. Maybe I should order pancakes. "Rip it off like a Band-Aid."

"I don't know about that," Marla chimes in. "Trent seemed awfully mad earlier. Maybe we should abort this mission." No, I'm going to get the Benedict. You don't go to a steak place and order chicken, so I'm not going to go to the best egg place in the county and order pancakes. That's just lunacy.

"We don't have time and you know it," Daisy says, pushing me towards their way of thinking.

"I need some coffee," I say over my menu. "Have you guys seen the waitress?"

"Shelby, we're sending you in to be a hooker and find a killer," Daisy says point-blank. I drop my menu down onto the table with a clink. That, I was not expecting.

"What?" I ask, sounding like an absolute idiot to my own ears and, I'm sure, to everyone else's as well. "I thought we were here for brunch."

"And to figure out what to do about Daisy's friends, honey," Granny says softly.

"But I've never heard anything about it. Last

night—"I start to explain my confusion.

"Last night, we left your place—" Daisy says.

"It's not my place. It's Trent's," I add.

"Two nights ago, we left Trent's house," Marla says with a look on her face that suggests the words tasted bad for her to say out loud. "And we went to grab a cup of coffee and hash out a plan."

"But that's what we're supposed to do now," I say, trying to rationalize, but really what I'm getting is a feeling of being left out.

"We're running out of time, Shell," Granny says as gently as she can.

"But—" I start.

"There is no time."

"Then what do we do?" I ask, not knowing at all that that one little sentence spoken in a breakfast joint in Rancho Bernardo would change the course of my life irrevocably.

"We have to find out who is doing this, honey," Granny says.

"But how?"

"We're going undercover."

"I don't understand," I tell them.

"We're going to George Washington's," Marla says brightly.

"To the strip club?" I ask, confused.

"Everyone knows there's always a trick working the back of the club," Daisy says like we're talking about what kind of jam we want on our toast. Incidentally, I am no longer vacillating between strawberry and orange marmalade.

"A trick?"

"A hooker," she says seriously, and I feel my eyes go wide. "A working girl."

"There's a hooker working George's place?" I whisper-shout.

"Of course not," Granny says, shooting me a *Don't be stupid* look. "But we need to trap a hooker killer."

"And Christina and Stacy were both working the back room at Girls! Girls! Girls!" Daisy adds when I looked confused. "It's the strip club off the 5, just past O'side."

"And what can I get you ladies this morning?" the waitress asks as she steps up to our table, interrupting my world exploding because there is no way I could have heard them correctly. And if I did, Trent is going to kill me. Guess I don't have to have that birth control talk after all.

We go around the table giving our orders before she leaves to put them in. I sit there sipping my coffee for a minute before I realize that I have to find out once and for all if my friends are really about to pimp me out.

"And I have to be this hooker?" I ask hesitantly while throwing up prayers to Jesus, Joseph, Mary, and the damn camel that I misheard them. They don't want me to be a hooker, a job that is against the law in most of the fifty US states.

"Yes," Daisy affirms.

"But . . . but . . . why me?" I ask.

"Well, most of the johns know me, seeing as how I used to be in the business," she explains. "And no offense to the grannies, but no one is going to pay to do them."

"None taken," Granny agrees.

"Of course, dear," Marla says like Daisy just asked for an extra chocolate chip cookie after dinner.

"So, as you can see," Daisy begins. "You're up."

"I'm up?" I ask.

"You're up," Daisy confirms with a nod. "We're going to make you into the best trick there ever was."

"But I can't be a trick," I shout, losing my tenuous grip on my control.

"Why not?" Daisy asks.

"Because, for one, it's illegal!"

"So what?" She shrugs.

"So what?" I repeat. "My boyfriend is a homicide detective!"

"Trent's cool," Daisy says.

"He's not that cool!"

"Maybe he doesn't have to know," Marla says quietly, and I know I'm so incredibly screwed.

"Yeah, I—" I start to reject the notion, but I'm interrupted by the server bringing a huge tray of food to the table.

"Here we go, ladies."

After that I dove into my eggs Benedict like it was my job and completely forgot to tell Daisy, Granny, and Marla that I was not going to be their prime hooker and I most definitely wasn't going to keep it from Trent either.

But like I said, I was already screwed.

WHEN IN DOUBT, CALL GEORGE WASHINGTON

"It's all about the tease," Granny says, and somehow, the idea of taking stripping advice from my octogenarian grandmother has brought a whole new dimension to my life.

"No, it's all about the blow jobs," Daisy says plainly.

"What?" I screech at the top of my lungs.

"Look," George Washington, my granny's friend from back in the day and strip club owner, says. "You just need to let go and dance."

"Dance," I repeat.

"That's it." He smiles at me like a sweet grandpa and not at all like a man who wants me to climb up onto his stage and take my panties off. "It's just dancing."

Marla snickers. "Sure, Georgie, it's just dancing with no knickers." She's not wrong. I'm going to be dead meat when Trent finds out.

"I'm a stripper," I say blankly.

"Yes," Marla and Granny say together.

Unfortunately, at the same time, Daisy says, "No, she's a hooker."

"A what?" George Washington shouts. "There are no tricks in my club."

"George—" Granny starts.

"No, Verna. Not now, not ever has there been a trick working my club."

"That's not true," Daisy says softly.

"Name one," he demands.

"Christina and Stacy."

"Motherfucker!" he roars. "You're lying."

"I wouldn't lie," Daisy promises, and by the tone of her voice, he can tell her veracity rings through.

"Why now?" he asks with a resigned air.

"Christina is dead and Stacy is nowhere to be found," Daisy explains.

"Shit," George bites out.

"I have to find out what happened," Daisy says and her full lower lip quivers.

"Shit," George repeats on a sigh.

"So, can we stay?" Granny asks.

"Fuck me, yeah," he says before giving me a good once-over. "Well, at least you got a great ass, so maybe you can bring in some decent money."

Dead. Meat.

Let's backtrack a little.

Sometime after I ate my feelings in a mountain of eggs, ham, and hollandaise sauce, we settled our check and climbed back into the Caddy. After that, Marla drove hell-bent for leather for George Washington's strip club, The Pink Pussycat.

The whole drive, my stomach twisted and turned, and I regretted not only taking down that entire breakfast platter, but also the choices I have made in my life that lead me to being hurtled down the I-5 to be taught to dance naked on a stage all while pretending to be a hooker in order to catch a hooker killer.

When we finally made it to the asphalt parking lot of our destination, I breathed a sigh of relief. And then I looked up into the pink neon lights and had to swallow back the bile that was rising up in my throat. As we walked inside the dimly lit club with its huge stage, the feeling didn't get any better.

"Like, I said," Daisy presses on. "It's all about the blow jobs."

"I can't do that!" I shout. "I have a boyfriend."

"I know." She shrugs. "That's why I got you this Taser."

"Great idea, dear." Marla beams at Daisy as if she just discovered the cure for cancer.

"What?" I shout.

"When things progress, as they naturally do," she begins to explain. "Then you just zap 'em with this

Taser."

"And then what do we do?" I have to bite my lip to keep from screaming. The panic I'm feeling is mounting in my body and I am at DEFCON *stroke* level.

"You just zing 'em, and we'll figure out what to do with them after," Daisy says. This is not a good plan but we don't have a better one. What the fuck are we supposed to do now? What am I going to do when Trent eventually figures out that we've gone off half-cocked on his investigation—again?

"Look," George Washington says as he wades into the conversation. "My club is your club; just don't get me shut down."

"I would never do that," I am quick to promise him.

"If you're anything like your granny, you would . . ." He lets that thought hang in the air and tosses me a wink as he leaves me in the overly capable hands of a retired hooker and two senior citizens. Jesus Fucking Christ.

"Well, let's see what we're working with here," Daisy says, giving me a look that I have decided I do not, under any circumstances, want to know what in the hell it means. I stand there and stare back at her. I fold my arms across my chest, determined to wait her out. "Shelby."

"Daisy," I volley back.

"Take off your clothes."

"No," I deny.

"How in the hell are you going to be any kind of a decent stripper if you don't get naked?" she snaps.

"I don't want to be any kind of a stripper," I tell her.

"I know that." She rolls her eyes. "But we don't

have any choice here."

"Fine!" I shout, throwing my arms up over my head. "Where is there a dressing room?"

"The real girls are back there, and they would eat you alive," Daisy tells me. "Just get naked here. It's not like you have anything we haven't seen before."

"How naked?" I ask.

"Bra and panties."

I sigh and begin unbuttoning my cardigan before letting it slide down my shoulders. I pull my tank tops over my head as one big blob and then get tangled in my leggings. How can something I love so much try to kill me every day?

"Lord love a duck, this is going to be a disaster," Marla says before making the sign of the cross.

"George is right," Granny says. "She's got a great figure. If she can shake what I gave her even just a little bit, she'll be fine."

"Hey, bitches," a brown-haired girl says as she walks in. "Who's the fresh meat?"

"Hey, girl!" Daisy greets the newcomer with a warm smile. "This is my girl Shelby, the one I was telling you about. And the old ladies are her granny and her man's granny."

"Nice," the brown-haired girl says.

"This is my girl Alyssa." Daisy introduces us, and I can't help but feel like life with this angel-faced hooker is going to be anything but normal going forward. Something tells me that behind her dimples is a rule breaker.

"Can she dance?" Alyssa asks.

"Probably not," Daisy says as if I'm not even here.

"I'll have you jerks know I took classical ballet for seventeen years!" I harrumph.

"All right!" Granny cheers. "That's my girl!"

"Now we're cooking with gas," Marla adds. I can't help but let out a sigh. It's easy to get caught up in the whirlwind that is Marla and Verna. I only hope that Trent understands. Who am I kidding? Trent is going to be furious.

"I have just the thing," Granny says, pulling off her teal cowboy boots. "Put these on and then put that boring librarian cardigan back on."

I follow her orders, slipping my feet into the boots. I bend over to scoop my sweater back up and hear whistles from over my shoulder as the early crowd starts to trickle in.

"Don't worry about the day drinkers," Alyssa says from beside me. "They'll be too drunk to remember whatever happens by supper time."

"Awesome?" I ask.

"Sure." She shrugs. "Just . . . uh . . . button these." She does up three buttons in the middle of my cardigan, but not enough to cover my navel or my cleavage. I'm sure I look ridiculous.

Daisy walks across the room to fiddle with a stereo. The opening strains of "Party in the U.S.A." sound, and a groan erupts from my chest.

"I love this song!" Marla and Granny call out at the same time before laughing uproariously. I sigh.

"We can work with this," Alyssa says to me.

"Yeah, we probably can," I unfortunately agree because I love this song too.

"All right," Daisy calls out as she claps her hands,

drawing everyone's attention. "Let's get down to business of the business and learn some moves."

We all climb up onto the stage, which, as it turns out, is easier for some of us than others. Poor Marla's false hip seems to be giving her some trouble. It takes both Alyssa and me to hoist her up as if she fell overboard from a ship, which reminds me never to leave dry land with this crowd.

Once we are all lined up on the stage, Daisy maneuvers me into the middle with a hooker on either side of me and an octogenarian on their other sides. What a floor show we must be for all the day drinkers, as Alyssa so accurately called them.

"Now roll your hips," Daisy instructs us. "Think of it like yoga class on Chili Tuesday, only sluttier and without the farts."

"It already is sluttier with that tart, Ruth, and all her cronies," Marla snipes.

"That's unlike you, Marla," Daisy says.

"Shh!" Granny tries to quiet the line of questioning before Marla can hear it. "Ruth locked her sights on old Harold, and now our sweet, fun-loving Marla is fit to be tied."

"Oh, shit," Daisy says. "My bad."

"It's okay, dear," Granny tries to reassure her, but it falls flat as Marla continues to grumble under her breath about coldhearted slut snakes who are old enough to know better.

"Suuuuuree," Daisy says. "Now bend over slowly, like a cross between you dropped your keys and Harmony's Triangle Pose but less baked."

I laugh and decide to put on a little bit of a show

for all these nonbelievers. I arch my back as I bend forward in my best *Legally Blonde* impression. Bend and Snap, anyone? I pull the band from my tresses and shake my hair free.

I get so lost in the Miley Cyrus lyrics I enjoy so much that I don't realize my fellow dancers have left the stage. I just dance and dance and dance. I shake it like I know what I'm doing. I shimmy my shoulders in time with my hips as I pop the buttons over my chest—*slowly*—one by one.

The day drinkers have moved closer and are eating it up.

I lean forward and shake my lace-encased breasts toward the mostly drunk men and watch them come a little undone as I slide my cardigan off my shoulders and down to the stage floor.

Suddenly, I feel sexy, I feel empowered, and, most importantly, I feel like I've got this stripper shit down. I know the song is coming to an end, so I head for a dramatic finish, dropping into a split and throwing my head back and shaking out my long, red hair.

The day drinkers cheer and high-five each other before throwing dollar bills onto the stage. Granny and Marla hug each other like proud mamas, which is both exhilarating and absurd.

"That's all yours," Alyssa says, nodding to the discarded money. "That was a good show, girl, so go on and collect your earnings."

"Really?" I ask, a little shocked. I was just enjoying myself, letting myself get sucked into my movements and the flow of my body forgetting my problems for just a moment. I had no idea that I might have been doing a decent job.

"Yeah, girl."

"Sweet." I smile for the first time in ages.

"Sophia would be so proud if she was here to see you," Marla says.

"Did she die too?" Alyssa asks.

"No, she's at some big figure-skating competition in Chicago this week," I answer.

"Cool," Alyssa says. "That's definitely better than being dead."

"True story," Granny agrees.

"We should probably get back before it gets too late," Marla says. "I don't see so well in the dark."

"What time is it?" I ask, suddenly panicking. I look everywhere for a clock and can't seem to find one.

"It's almost five o'clock," Daisy answers, looking at her phone.

"Shiiiiit!" I shout as I jump down from the stage and run around collecting my discarded clothing. "I have to go."

"I'm sure it'll be all right," Marla says in that strange tone of voice that normally wouldn't bother me so much, but when mixed with that funny look on her face, I know she's lying to try to make me feel better; however, we both know it falls short.

"I have to beat Trent back to the house," I tell her as I pull my leggings up my legs, only to get tangled in them and fall to the ground. Again.

"Curse these mistresses of death and torture!" I shout from the ground as I try to push myself back up.

"I'm not so sure that has as much to do with her britches as much as it has to do with her," Granny snarks.

"Hey!" I shout as I jump up.

"But I'm not wrong!" she says before sticking her tongue out at me.

"Ugh, fine," I admit. "Let's just get going."

"Sure thing, doll," Marla says before pointing her walker toward the door and leading the way out to the parking lot.

"I'll head out with Alyssa," Daisy says. "I'll catch up with you guys later."

"Sure thing, babe," Granny says as she hugs her farewell.

Outside, the parking lot is still. There is no movement and no sound, and it's really freaking creepy. The hair on the back of my neck stands up, and it feels like my spine has been zapped with electricity. It's that weird feeling that someone is watching me, and I can't shake it. But when I look over my shoulder, there's nothing there.

"What's wrong?" Granny asks me, always in tune with my emotions.

"Nothing," I say as I pull open the door of Harold's baby-blue Caddy. "Let's just get going."

Granny, Marla, and I all pile into the Caddy, and Marla fires her up before peeling out of the gravel parking lot of The Pink Pussycat.

Thankfully, the drive back to Peaceful Sunset is short, as Marla navigates all the one-way streets of the Gaslamp Quarter like a rabbit in his warren. When she pulls up out front, we dive out of the car.

"Are you going to head out from here, doll?" Granny asks me.

"No," I answer. "I have to run up and get Missy, or Trent will be upset. He wasn't a fan when he realized I took her with me this morning."

"Well then, let's hop to it," she says.

"Yeah," Marla chimes in, pushing her walker away with a quickness after she handed her car keys off to the valet guy. "Shake a leg! You can't keep my grandson waiting. How will Verna and I ever get a great-grandbaby if you don't go fornicate?"

"Sweet Christ," I mutter as I follow them through the big sliding glass doors in the front of the building and to the elevator.

We step into the elevator car, Marla and Granny still chattering about how beautiful Trent's and my children will be, and I am just about to roll my eyes at their ridiculousness when I realize that I don't have a car here.

"Shit!" I bark as the elevator opens onto the tenth floor.

"What's wrong, dear?" Marla asks me.

"You guys picked me up this morning," I explain to her. "I don't have a car here."

"Shit," she says.

"I know."

"Make like The Donald and grab your pussy," she says with all seriousness. "And then let's make for the elevator again."

"Marla, with that hip," Granny says as she opens the front door of her apartment, "you'll never make it in time."

I run in like my red hair is on fire and grab Missy's carrier, opening the door as I go.

"Go on without me," Marla says seriously before ducking into her own apartment.

"This isn't D-Day, guys!" I shout as I chase Missy around the living room. "Goddammit. Get back here, you little bitch. Now isn't the time to play."

"I'll head her off at the pass!" Granny shouts, and Missy hisses.

"Motherfucker," I bite out as she slithers out of my grasp one more time. "We're not going to the vet. We're going to Trent's house."

And it would seem my asshole of a cat knows exactly what I told her because, all of a sudden, she turns on her heels and trots her happy ass back to her carrier, where she hops in, and I quickly flip the little flap at the top over and zip it close it before she can change her fickle mind.

"Got her!" I cheer as I toss the carrying strap across my body.

"I'll come with you," Granny says. "We just have to borrow a car . . . and a driver's license."

"No time!" I cry out, looking at the clock that hangs over her mantle. "I'll take an Uber."

"Good plan!" she shouts, opening the front door and waving me through like a member of a NASCAR pit crew. "Go! Go! Go!"

I run to the elevator and push the button. Thankfully, it hasn't been called elsewhere yet so the doors open right up. I could have run down the stairs if it wasn't there, but not really, because this ass was built on tacos and not at the gym. I don't fucking run.

The elevator lets Missy and me out on the ground floor, where I make a break for it, barreling past the sliding glass doors, which take their sweet time opening.

By nothing short of an act of God, there is a yellow taxicab waiting on the curb. It's going to cost me a small fortune to get to Escondido in a cab, but I don't have time to find a better alternative.

The cabbie sees me coming and jumps out of the driver's seat to pull open the rear passenger door.

"Where to?" he asks me.

"Escondido," I answer him and see the dollar signs flash in his eyes before slamming the door and rounding the hood. He hops into the driver's seat and peels out hell-bent for leather. I instantly decide that I love this guy and we should be best friends.

He makes it to Trent's neighborhood in record time. I don't know whether to be horrified or impressed. I'm going to go with impressed.

He tells me my total, and I have to fight back the vomit that rises in my throat before sliding my credit card through the card reader on the back of the front seat.

"Call me anytime you need a ride," my new cabbie BFF tells me, handing me one of his business cards. "The name is Ned."

"Thanks. I'm Shelby and this is Missy."

"See you around, Shelby," he tells me as I make a break for the front door to the house, fumbling with my keys as I go.

I push open the front door and look at the clock on the mantle. Trent could be here at any time. Shit, shit, shit!

I set Missy's carrier down and open the zippered

door. She immediately jumps out and heads for greener pastures. I won't see her again for a while.

I run into the kitchen and rifle through the cabinets for something quick to fix for dinner that might distract Trent from realizing I was helping the girls look into Christina's death and Stacy's disappearance.

I spot a couple of steaks in the freezer and quickly pop them into the microwave for a quick defrost while I pull my favorite cast-iron pan out of the cabinet and heat it up with a shit-ton of butter. I season my steaks with my secret mix and drop them into the pan to sear while I preheat the oven. I grab some rolls and butter and season them for garlic bread before wrapping them up in tinfoil and popping them into the oven.

I flip my steaks and pull some salad fixings out of the fridge before turning off the range and placing the whole pan into the oven for a few minutes with the bread. I spread all of the salad vegetables on the cutting board, and then the blinking light on my phone catches my eye. I missed a phone call while I was buzzing around like a busy little bee and have a new voicemail message.

I pick up my phone and tap in my code before putting it to my ear, but what I hear shakes me to my core.

"You would do well to mind your own business and stop looking into things you don't have any business sticking your nose into," a computer-generated voice says into my ear.

I panic and hit the Delete button, which is stupid because when a deranged killer leaves you a message to threaten you, you give that message to your boyfriend, the hot homicide detective. Not delete it and pretend it never happened. But I never claimed to be smart.

I jump when strong arms wrap around me from behind, and let out a squeak before the scent that is inherently Trent invades my nose and I relax as he nuzzles his face into the side of my neck. The timer on the oven dings.

"You made dinner," he says like I just told him my vagina was gold plated. "Thanks, babe."

"It was no trouble," I tell him as I pull the steaks and the bread out of the oven. That's a lie. It was a lot of trouble. Especially the two-hundred-dollar cab fee to get here, but I'm not going to tell Trent any of that.

We plate our steaks, salad, and garlic bread before heading to the kitchen table. I run back to the counter and grab knives, forks, and napkins from the drawers.

"Wine?" Trent asks me when I was barely paying any attention.

"Yes, please."

I watch him as he gracefully moves around the kitchen pulling a bottle from the rack and opening it. He doesn't have to struggle with the bottle opener or muscle around it; he just opens it and pours two glasses as if he does it every second of every day, then saunters back to the table with a fat glass of red in each hand.

"This looks great," Trent says with a smile as he places a glass in front of me before dropping a napkin into his lap.

"Can I toss your salad?" I ask, making Trent choke on the sip of wine he has just taken.

"Uh . . ."

"That's not what I meant!" I shout, covering my

face with my hands. "I meant, can I serve you some salad after I toss it real quick."

"Sure you did," he says with laughter dancing in his vivid green eyes.

"I did too!" I snap.

Trent laughs out loud this time. "Shelby."

"Oh, just eat your damned salad," I growl as I drop the small bowl onto the table in front of him.

"Come here, baby."

"No," I say as I begin scooping salad into my own bowl.

"Don't be mad."

"I'm not mad," I deny as I pick up my knife and fork and begin to cut into my steak.

"Shelby," he says, plucking me from my chair at the table and pulling me into his lap. Trent nuzzles his face into my hair. "Don't be mad, baby."

"You do realize that I'm holding a really big knife, right?" I ask him and it's true. I never set down my silverware when he scooped me out of my seat, and Trent owns a set of ridiculously sized steak knives.

"I'm banking on the fact that you like me and my cock too much to want to kill us off or separate us from each other permanently because of a little embarrassment," he says. "So, forgive me for laughing?"

"Not yet," I tell him, still holding on to my anger for a bit longer. In truth, I don't really care. "Can I eat my steak now?"

"Yeah, honey," Trent says softly. But when I make a move to stand up from his lap, he tightens his arms around my waist.

"Trent?" I ask.

"I've decided that I like you right where you are," he tells me before sliding his plate over and pulling my plate to sit in front of me.

"How are we going to eat like this?"

"I don't know," Trent says. "But I just realized you're not wearing a shirt underneath that librarian sweater of yours, so I have a renewed determination to give it the old college try."

I look down and realize that I must have left my tanks at George Washington's club and that Trent has a bird's-eye view of my lace-encased nipples, and I let out a little "Eep!" while shifting uncomfortably on his lap.

"I'd advise against that if you want to get to eat, darlin'," Trent says as I feel a decidedly hard length pressing against my right ass cheek.

"Oh," I mumble.

"Yeah, 'Oh,'" he repeats, and I dive into my dinner with renewed interest.

Trent laughs when I shove a giant bite of steak into my mouth and have to chew on it for ages. He rests his chin on my shoulder and picks up his wineglass, bringing it to his lips to take a sip before offering it to me. I nod and Trent touches the rim of the glass to my lips before tipping the ruby-red wine into my mouth.

I cut a smaller bit of steak and hold the tines of my fork up to his mouth. I watch his lips close around the fork and slide the bit into his mouth from over my shoulder. Like all things Trent does, he even makes chewing sexy.

It's incredibly intimate to feed each other, and I love it. We slowly take turns feeding each other bites of dinner and sips of wine. We're in no hurry to finish even though Trent's erection never wanes; he doesn't press me to hurry our meal. Instead he lets the heat between us simmer the entire time. By the time the bottle of wine is empty and our plates are scraped clean, there is a low buzz in my belly of what's to come.

I stand and start to gather dishes to take them to the sink, and Trent stacks the rest and follows behind me. I turn on the faucet to let the water heat up, but he comes up behind me, wrapping himself around me and pulling me tight to him as he switches the faucet off.

"They can wait," Trent says, his voice rough with heat and sex. "But I can't."

I dry my hands on a dish towel before Trent scoops one of my small hands into one of his big, strong ones and leads me out of the kitchen and down the hall to his bedroom.

Trent drops my hand only to reach behind his head, grab his t-shirt at the neck, and pull it over his head in that sexy way that men do. I might be drooling as he reveals inch by freaking inch of those washboard abs. Trent clearly never let himself go once he left the Army. I, on the other hand, love a good donut.

He drops his T-shirt to the floor, then reaches for the buttons on my cardigan and slowly pops them open one by one before peeling the soft purple knit down my arms. He reaches behind me and unhooks my bra like a pro. Not for the first time since I have known Trent, I wonder just how much practice he's had taking undergarments off of women. Probably way more than I will ever care to know.

"Fuck, I could look at you forever," he tells me, his

eyes heating as they trail up and down my body.

I let out a little shriek, and Trent laughs when he rushes to scoop me up into his arms only to toss me down onto his bed. He reaches over me and slides his fingers into the waistband of my leggings and panties, dragging them both down my legs to toss them onto the floor.

I watch as Trent pops open the buttons on his jeans one by one. Slowly he pushes them and his black boxer briefs down his hips until his cock springs free. Trent lets his jeans fall to the floor before stepping out of them and then prowling over me as I lie on the bed. I let my legs fall open to cradle his hips.

When he touches his mouth to mine, I'm gone.

I moan into his mouth as Trent rocks against my hips, sliding his hard length against my center. I can't help but arch into him. My body heats for him, and Trent aligns the tip against my pussy and slowly pushes in just an inch before pulling back out again. He slides in just a little bit more, and I arch my hips against him, trying to force his cock deeper, but then he pulls out again. I whimper in protest, and Trent smiles against my mouth.

We dance this dance of Trent's teasing and my wanting for ages, which only seems to drive my need for him higher and higher, and the big bastard knows it. Finally, Trent thrusts all the way in and pulls back, only to dive back in again and again.

I pull my legs higher up against his sides and wrap my arms around his back in my shameless attempt to pull him deeper into me. All the while, Trent seems happy to go along at this leisurely pace.

Trent trails his lips down my cheek to behind my ear, where he nips at the lobe playfully while he slowly pumps his cock in and out. He kisses down my shoulder and to my breast to take my nipple into his mouth. I gasp as he rolls his tongue over my tight bud and arch into him.

"Trent," I cry out when he bites down. "Please," I beg.

He lets my breast go with a pop and grips the bed in his left hand while pinning my hip down with his other hand as he pumps faster and faster. I grab at his waist, needing to pull him closer.

"Yes," I pant.

"Touch yourself," Trent orders.

I can't do anything other than comply as I push my hand between us. I feel where his body meets mine as he plunges his cock into my center over and over again before circling my clit with my fingers. The feel of my hand on us where we come together makes him growl low in his throat.

"Fuck, you feel so good," he bites out as his fingers grip my thigh, pulling me down to meet him thrust for thrust.

"Yes, yes," I chant, and it doesn't take long for me to fall over the edge.

But Trent isn't done with me yet. He slows his movements back to what they were before, unhurried and steady as he teases my body. He kisses my mouth over and over as he makes love to me slow and sweet.

Trent kisses back down my breast and catches my nipple in his mouth again as he gently works my pussy. My breath catches in my lungs and my body begins to heat again, this time like a rising tide and less like a tsunami.

"Again," he growls against my breast.

"Yes," I pant.

I pull him flat against my body, loving the feel of his weight against me as he glides in and out, in and out. Trent picks up the pace and I love it. I love him. I went and fell in love with Trent Foyle.

"Shelby," he growls as he nears his own climax.

"Yes."

I arch my back as he rolls his hips again and again, and then I tighten my arms around him as my climax rolls over me. Trent buries his face in my neck and gently bites down as he follows me over the edge.

Trent pulls out and slowly rolls over to the side, taking me with him, before pulling the blankets up to cover us. He spoons me from behind, and I can't help but feel like everything is right in the world when I'm his little spoon.

Trent nuzzles my neck like he likes to do before he falls asleep, and I let his body heat and two orgasms take me to the brink of dreamland myself. In fact, I'm more than halfway there.

"Thank you for agreeing to stay out of my investigation," he says before relaxing into sleep.

I'm relaxed too. So much so that when he speaks, I can't respond. Instead I drift off the rest of the way, never admitting that I did not respect Trent's wishes or even remembering that there was a killer close by.

I will come to regret that later on. But now? Now, I sleep in the safety of Trent's strong arms. Here's hoping they can protect me . . .

ANOTHER DAY, ANOTHER FUNERAL AND GENITAL SMELLING

I'm flying through the forest, leaping tree by tree like a monkey as my glorious red hair shimmers and shines in soft, flowing waves behind me. My milky white skin sparkles just like all my vampire friends.

We're being chased by rogue vampires from the East and vampire hunters from the North. All I know is that we have to get away. I have to get to Trent before they find us.

The vampire hunters shoot arrows at us as we zig-zag and serpentine in order to evade them. I take a hit to the shoulder. Shit! I'm bleeding. Only, my blood doesn't smell like blood; it smells like the cherry-fla-vored body-oil-slash-lubricant that my granny and her friend Marla sell door-to-door. Come to think of it, the vampire hunters are launching not arrows but huge Big Thunder dildos from every bow. Those suckers re-ally hurt when you take one to the sternum. But I don't *have time to think about that . . .*

There is a wolf snapping at my heels, but when I look back, the wolf that has been chasing me isn't a wolf at all. It's Trent.

"Shelby!" he shouts as he grabs me.

"Shelby." Someone shakes me again. "Wake up."

"Wh-what?" I ask.

"Honey, you were having that dream again," Trent says with a soft, sweet smile, the one he saves just for me.

"A dream?" I ask again.

"Yeah, honey," Trent says softly, not at all looking like he wants to murder me. At least not yet. He doesn't know about the stripping and the fake hooking yet. "It was the one about the vampires again."

"Shit," I mumble.

"Yeah."

I have got to stop late-night snacking, which, let's be honest, was actually late-night stress eating while watching a *Twilight* marathon on TV. Those sparkly vampires get to me every damn time. And so did the old moo goo gai pan I found in the back of the fridge. I swallow back a burp that results in the world's worst heartburn. Fuck my life.

"I have to get going," he says.

"Okay."

"I won't be home until late tonight, so eat without me," Trent tells me.

"Okay."

"Now, kiss me goodbye," he orders softly.

"Okay." And then I do. I roll over to where he sits next to me on the bed already dressed for the day, with his holster on his hip, and press my lips to his. Trent smiles against my mouth before breaking the kiss.

"I'll see you tonight." And with that he saunters his sexy ass out the door and leaves me a little hot and bothered and more than a little worried about what's going to happen when he finds out about my new occupations.

But like the chickenshit I am, I shut all that guilt behind a heavy door and all the locks in my head and throw away the keys.

Well, I'd better get a start on my day. I throw back the covers and push up to sit on the bed, rubbing my temples with my fingertips. That *Twilight* dream gives me a headache every time. I love those movies though, so it's totally worth the dream hangover it gives me. I'm not even going to touch on Trent's appearance in it. My psyche clearly has a bone to pick with me, but I'm not in the mood for an ass-chewing—from myself or otherwise—at least not before I've had a cup of coffee or twenty.

I pad my way down the hall to the kitchen, where I question my love and loyalty to a man who left me not one fucking drop in the bottom of the pot. It's moments like this I think I would be better off as a lesbian.

I pick up the pot and carry it over to the sink, filling it up with water. I fill the tank on the coffee maker with it before breaking open the bag of grounds and inhaling deeply, as if I could absorb all the caffeine through every human sense, and adding them to the machine and turning it on.

I lean on the counter with my chin resting in my hands, like a little kid on Christmas morning waiting for the go-ahead to open their presents left by Santa, and watch the precious drops drip into the waiting pot.

Unable to wait myself, I pull a mug down from the cabinet and replace the carafe with my mug. When it's full, I swap the pot back and chug my mug of coffee like a beer at a frat party. It scalds my throat but I don't care. I can't taste the mana from Columbia, but that doesn't seem to matter either. My guilt over lying to Trent and my worry for Daisy and her sisters in arms—literally—have my subconscious doing cartwheels and backflips, and my stomach isn't exactly Willy Wonka's either.

I refill my cup, this time from the waiting pot, and add a little fancy creamer to my cup, which makes me giggle to myself and bust out the tune "Fancy" by Reba McEntire. That song is my jam, especially in the morning. It's an oldie but goodie, as my dad would say.

I take another sip, this time slower, and breathe a sigh of relief as my brain starts to function again. My phone chimes with a text alert from the kitchen island, and I turn to read it.

UNCLE SAL: Cover the funeral of the dead hooker today at 10 a.m. The regular guy is out with the flu.

Ugh. That sucks. I was kind of hoping to have the morning and afternoon to do some yoga and relax. I need to try to get into the right headspace for my first foray into fake hooking tonight. But maybe this will be a distraction. I quickly send Uncle Sal a text.

ME: I'm on it, boss! *Salutes*

UNCLE SAL: Smart-ass

ME: ;)

I wonder what a hooker's funeral will be like. I should probably invite Granny. If I don't, she'd never forgive me. I unlock my phone one more time and quickly shoot her a text.

ME: Hooker funeral at 10 a.m. Wanna go?

GRANNY: Hellz yeah!

ME: Dress to impress. I'm working.

GRANNY: Don't I always?!?!

ME: Of course you do. Do you need a ride?

GRANNY: No, Marla and I have the Caddy.

Oh boy. The thought of those two wild cards in a giant bathtub of a Cadillac on the streets of California is enough to strike fear into the hearts of many, but you know what they say: *not my circus, not my monkeys.* That battle is one my dad needs to take up, not me. Besides, I can't take on this mission on my own, and for that, they need wheels.

I carry my coffee cup back down the hall and into

the bedroom. I walk straight through the bedroom and into Trent's huge master bathroom, where I pull open the glass shower door and twist the knobs to let the water heat up before backing out of the shower. I lean my hip against the marble bathroom countertop and sip my coffee while I wait.

When my cup is empty—again—I strip out of the clothes I slept in, one of Trent's T-shirts I pulled on in the middle of the night when I got a little cold, and drop it in the hamper. I pull open the glass door to the shower and step in. I make quick work of my shower, not only not wanting to linger in the steam without Trent this morning, but also, I'm in a bit of a hurry.

I shut off the water and reach for the towel that's hanging on the rack before drying myself off. I look over my shoulder to the doorway. I could walk into the closet, get dressed, and then walk all the way back here to the bathroom to hang up this towel. I look toward the doorway again. I suppose I could just leave it in the closet like an uncivilized asshole, but I refuse to be that girl even though I'm lazy. I look one more time. I really am all alone in this house; Trent has been gone for hours, so . . .

My inherent laziness wins out. I mean it's one less thing I will have to carry back later.

There's really nothing to stop me, so I slip the towel from my body and hang it back on the rack before shaking what my mama gave me through Trent's master bedroom. I'm curvy and I own it. Sure, I probably have a little too much tits and ass, but I work it, so who cares?

I grab a matching pair of black lace panties and

bra from my coveted little drawer in the closet that has been assigned to me and my things. I slip them on before pulling up a pair of nude stockings. I wouldn't even bother with the little fuckers, but my granny has pretty strong feelings about ladies wearing stockings at a funeral, even if it is the funeral of a murdered hooker.

I pull my dress from the hanger. It looks like a simple black dress in the front, with cap sleeves, a neckline that skims my collarbone, and a hemline that touches the tops of my kneecaps. But the back is fabulous. The top of the back scoops down just a little, like a ballerina's dress, and then splits open as I move to reveal a hidden swath of lime-green silk. It is just a little bit sassy, and very chic, and I love everything about it.

I slip a simple but elegant pair of pearl earrings that were my mom's into my ears and put on a pair of basic, black patent leather pumps with a round toe before heading back into the bathroom to do a soft makeup look.

I love it—hair, makeup, clothes, all of it. Ever since I was a little girl, I have loved to play around and figure out what worked and what didn't. The good news is, it's made my morning routine pretty fast timewise.

I twist my heavy fall of hair into a ballerina bun on top of my head and secure it with some bobby pins before pulling a few soft tendrils down to frame my face. I look decent enough and it'll have to do.

I make my way back into the bedroom and look at the clock. Shit! I'm cutting it close, so I grab my Coach bag from the chair in the corner and toss my phone into it before racing down the hall toward the front of the house.

I pull open the front door and rush out, shutting it behind me before breaking into a run. I hate being late. I slip on the gravel that decorates the planter on the side of the driveway and barely recover my balance. Damn low-water-usage decor. I pull open my door and fling my body inside, starting the engine as I buckle my seat belt. The radio comes to life, and I throw my little SUV that could into reverse and peel out of the driveway.

I hit the highway and make good time going with the flow of traffic, so if Trent asks later, I didn't drive like the ghost of Dale Earnhardt had inhabited my body. I just rule the road like California driving standards dictates, which, to be honest, isn't all that great. And that's coming from a native Californian.

I pull into the parking lot of the funeral home and find a spot. I look around and don't see Harold's blue Caddy, so I sit in the car for a minute. I pull out my phone to text Granny to see where they are, when I hear tires screech and I look up just in time to see Marla take the turn into the lot on two wheels. Jesus. They squeeze into a spot a few cars down from mine—thank God—and I jump out of my car and rush over to help them.

"Woo-hoo!" my granny cheers when she pushes open the passenger door. "What a ride."

"I know!" Miss Marla says as she swings the driver's door open. "Harold doesn't know what he has in this old gal."

"But we do. Don't we, Marla?" Granny says as she smiles fondly at her friend. I can't help but hope that Daisy, Sophia, and I look at each other the same way in another fifty years.

"Hello, my darling girl," Miss Marla says, turning to me as she closes the big blue door.

"Hey," I reply as I bend over to place a kiss on her soft cheek. She's so tiny. Marla is barely five feet tall, if that, and I'm not tall by any stretch, but I tower over her. She looks me over, clearly deciding she's not thrilled with what she sees, and I decide to change the subject, like the big chicken that I am, before she has a chance to ask me any questions. That way, I won't have to tell her any lies.

"Let's head inside before we miss the service," I suggest. Marla looks like she wants to say something but has decided to hold her tongue. For now.

"Great idea!" Granny hops on board. This time she's oblivious to my plans and evasive maneuvers. Usually she's the one to see right through me and call me out on my shit.

We make our way into the funeral home, and surprisingly, it's a packed house. I'm not sure we're going to find seating because the room is a crush of people. Granny, Marla, and I shoulder our way through, and it's not looking so good until I hear Daisy's voice ring out in the building, full of authority. And I have never been gladder to hear my bestie yell at a room full of strangers.

"Can't you see there are old ladies here?" she shouts as she shoves a whole row of people to their feet. "What kind of animals don't give up their seats for some feeble old ladies?"

"They don't look so feeble," one of them says after looking over our motley crew.

"Look feeble," Daisy stage-whispers over her shoulder, and instantly Miss Marla and my granny break into their wailing about broken hips and the Great Depression. Their shoulders are stooped, where they stood proud before, and one of them is dragging a leg. I have to bite my lip to keep from laughing at this ridiculous display. *Feeble old ladies, my ass.*

"My apologies, ladies," one of them says as they clear the row for us.

"Don't worry, dear," Marla says. "It's all water under the bridge."

"Yeah, an old and feeble bridge," I mumble.

"Hush your mouth," Granny whispers harshly as she kicks my shin.

"Ouch."

"I'm sorry," she says to me. "I must have tripped. It's this trick leg of mine that's acting up again."

"Oh, no one's watching anymore," Marla says as she wades into the conversation. "You can let it go."

"Thank God," Granny sighs. "I hate pretending to be weak. It really chafes."

"Tell me about it," Marla agrees.

"You two are something else," I say with a smile.

"Don't deflect," Granny says. "Something is off with you."

"I don't know what you're talking about," I deny as I sit back in my stolen seat and cross my legs. "There's nothing wrong with me."

"If I didn't know any better, I would say it has to do with that grandson of mine," Marla says dryly.

"Are you kids on the rocks?" Granny asks.

"No," I whisper. "We're fine."

"Then why is he moving hell-bent for leather this way?" Marla asks.

"What?" My spine stiffens. Shit. I can't keep up the pretenses in front of Trent, and we all know that our grandmothers are shit liars. I am so fucked.

"You know? I always wondered what that saying meant," Granny adds.

"I think it means 'in a hurry,'" Marla explains. "Just like how Trent is knocking people over left and right to get here to her."

"Quick, scoot down a seat so we can eavesdrop on their conversation," Granny says, shooing Miss Marla over a chair.

"Granny!" I admonish quietly, but she just shrugs her shoulder in a *So what?* motion. She is incorrigible and so is Marla.

"I've been trying to get ahold of you all day," Trent says as he slides into the seat next to me. "Where's your phone?"

"Nice to see you too," I snark. It may be a little petty, but he could at least say hello to me before launching into *Where is your phone?* interrogations. I don't know how long we're going to be together or when he's going to find out about our extracurricular activities, so I need all the happy-couple stuff while I can get it. Of course, Trent has no idea, so I can't tell him that.

"Hi, Shelby," he says to me in that gravelly voice of his.

"Hi." I smile back before reaching into my pocketbook to pull out my phone. "It's right here . . . oh. It's dead."

"Shelby." Trent smiles as he shakes his head.

"What did you need?" I ask.

"To say hi, but when I couldn't get ahold of you, I began to worry," he says. A scowl pulls at his brows.

"I'm sorry," I say honestly and really I am. I am sorry for so many things. I'm sorry for Daisy and the loss of her friend. I'm sorry I'm lying to Trent. I'm sorry he has to worry about me because we both know that I am going to keep putting myself in sticky situations, and I hate that too. But I am not sorry for helping my friend. I want to find Stacy like nobody's business, and I wish we had found Christina before it was too late.

"It's okay," he tells me even though we both know that's not true. "What are you doing here?"

"Covering the funeral for the paper," I explain.

"Of course," he says quietly. "I should have known you were working."

"No worries." I shrug my shoulder. "You too?"

"Yeah." The room around us feels a little stilted. I feel awkward and uncomfortable, and I don't know what to do to resolve the issue.

"What the fuck is wrong with you two?" Granny snaps, drawing attention from all around us. I would ask her to lower her voice, but one look at her tells me she's a pot that's about to boil over and there is no stopping it.

"We're fine," Trent says. "Right, Shelby?"

"Yeah," I answer halfheartedly. "We're fine."

"Well, you don't sound fine," Granny claps back.

"Yeah," Trent agrees with her softly. "You don't sound fine."

"Things just feel a little . . . strained," I answer.

"Strained?" Trent asks.

"Yeah." I sigh. "I don't know. I'm worried about Daisy. I'm tired. And everything just feels so . . . hard right now."

"What can I do to help?" Trent asks, and part of me melts, but the other part of me feels guilty for lying all over again.

"I don't know," I answer him honestly.

"You two are acting like everything is so unsure," Marla says. "Like everything is undecided."

"Isn't it?" I ask. "Life just feels so undecided."

"Well, what about your genitals?" Granny asks, and all rational thought flies right out of my head. Fortunately, so do all the heavy thoughts that were weighing down my mind.

"What?" I choke out. I know I shouldn't ask, and yet, here I am with the words falling out of my mouth before I can stop them.

"You know? Your genitals," Granny says as if I should know exactly what she is talking about and that it makes perfect sense.

"No," I respond. "I don't know what you're talking about."

Granny sighs as if I have put her out somehow. "I read in *Cosmo* ages ago that if your genitals match, it's a soul match."

"What now?" I ask.

"What she means, dear," Marla says, trying to help, "is that if your genitals smell compatible, there is a chemical match to your bodies."

"Huh?" Trent says eloquently.

"That you physically were meant to be together," she says softly.

"I kind of like the sound of that," Trent says hopefully, and I swing my head around to face him with what I'm sure is a *You can't possibly be serious humoring these two nut jobs right now* look on my face. "What?"

"This is insanity," I answer.

"Is it insane if I want to be with you?" he asks me.

"No."

"And is it insanity that I like the idea that you were made for me and I was made for you?" he presses on.

"No."

"And is it insanity if I like whatever will give me the answer I want? You."

"Yes!" I respond. "I draw the line at ball sniffing." Unfortunately, the minister had just walked into the room and bent down to speak quietly with Christina's mother, so everyone heard me tell Trent that I wasn't going to smell his balls. I look to him for guidance, but based on the out-and-out grin playing about on his handsome freaking face, it's clear he is going to be no help whatsoever.

"I mean, a little decorum would be nice," Granny harrumphs.

"Really?" I growl. "You want a little decorum now? Not, say, when you were asking if our genitals smell compatible?"

"Yes," she answers. "That is correct."

"Ugh, fine." I fold my arms across my chest and sit back in my seat, silently waiting for the service to start.

"It's true," Marla says, obviously trying her damnedest to be helpful for her friend. "Just go ahead and google it."

"I'm not really sure that's a good idea," I hedge, eyeing Trent as he comes to the same conclusion I do, just a bit slower.

"It is," she says, her smile growing wider by the second. "I google things all the time."

"I'm not so certain that we need to know about your google habits . . ." I try helpfully to defuse the situation, but it's no use. This is a runaway train on the tracks and there is no stopping it.

"Like just the other day," she says, gaining steam. "I was reading in the paper the other morning about some kids trying to make a movie called *SMILF,* and I thought the article was fascinating and wanted to know more about this film."

Oh boy.

"I think we get the idea . . . ," I start. I look to Trent and his face is bright red. I'm not quite sure he's even breathing right now.

"And I thought to myself, I don't even know what a SMILF is," Marla continues, and I'm at a loss for what to do. "Do you know what it is?"

"Uhh . . ." is all I can say.

"Well, I do!" she calls out. "It's a single mom I'd like to f—"

"I think we get the idea!" I cut her off, not that I'm opposed to dropping an f-bomb from time to time, but I'm not sure I could handle my boyfriend's sweet old grandmother saying it right now in the funeral of a murdered prostitute. And I definitely know that Trent couldn't handle it.

"And do you know why I know what it means?" she asks us like a school teacher who has led her class to the one correct answer. "Because I googled it."

"I think we get the idea," I repeat, biting my lip to keep from laughing.

"So you should google it, because Verna is right," Marla finishes triumphantly with a haughty shimmy to her shoulders that makes me smile. I love that lady so much.

"Are you all right?" I ask Trent. I place my palm on his back to give him a little comfort.

"I-I'm not quite sure how to answer that question," he says after a moment.

"Well, you think on it," I tell him before leaning back in my chair. "I'm sure something will come to you."

"I don't know about that," he says.

"Well, at least she's not watching porn on the internet," I say helpfully. "Or is she?"

"That is not helpful," Trent tells me.

"My bad." I shrug my shoulders.

My shoulders tense as I hear the buzz that his phone makes as it vibrates in his pocket. Trent drops his head back and closes his eyes. I wish I could take his stress away, but I also know I am inadvertently a big part of his life's stresses. Trent pulls his phone out of his pocket and reads a text message.

"That was Kane," he explains to me. "I gotta go."

"That can't be good," I mumble.

"It's not," he answers for my ears only. "We've got another body."

"Oh no." Poor Daisy.

"Yeah," he sighs. "I don't know when I'll be home."

"Okay," I say, for lack of anything better.

"Eat without me. I'll see you later."

"Later," I tell him. "Be safe."

"Always." And then he was gone.

 chapter NINE

STRIP IT, STRIP IT REAL GOOD . . . DO DO DO DO DO

"I see someone did a little deforestation project since the last time I saw you naked," Daisy shouts across the dressing room as I drop trou backstage at George Washington's establishment.

"Uh . . . yeah," I blush furiously while I agree. "I cleaned up a bit."

"Nice work," she nods, making my face burn even hotter.

Sometime after the funeral services for Christina were over, Granny, Marla, and I stood up and went over to Daisy, who was sitting with Christina's mother. The two women were crying together into dainty little hankies.

"Oh, I guess we need to be getting you to the club," Daisy said when she looked up and saw me standing there.

"No," I said on a soft smile. "I'm sorry to have interrupted."

"Come here, girl," the older woman gently commanded.

"Yes, ma'am." I moved closer so that I could bend down into her space. I had the feeling that she wanted a private moment with me—or as private as one could get in a crowded funeral home.

"Are you the girl from the paper that Daisy has been talking about?" she asked me.

"Yes, ma'am, I am."

"You're going to find who did this to my Christina," she said, not asked. It was not a question to her.

"I'm sure the police are going to do everything they possibly can," I told her.

"I know that," she said. "I mean you."

And I knew deep down that I would not deny this woman any help, just as I could not say no to my dear friend Daisy when she had asked me for help. No, Daisy hadn't ask me either; she'd demanded that I help her, and I had readily agreed because it was the right thing to do. So I was going to help this woman too. I mean, I already kind of was, but with the decision made, I knew there was no going back. The die had been cast and the chips were going to fall wherever they may. Trent might not understand why I was doing what I was, but it was my decision—it was always my decision—and this was the only choice I could live with.

So I answered her the only way I could. "I'm going to do my best."

After my awkward yet life-altering conversation with the mother of Daisy's murdered friend, I decided I needed tacos.

"I need tacos," I told the group at large after we pushed through the glass front doors of the funeral home. "Today was tougher than I thought it was going to be." And yet, at the same time, it felt like a huge weight had been lifted off of my shoulders.

"And it's not even over yet," Granny said from beside me.

"True dat," Marla answered her as she raised her fist up to be bumped by Granny.

"And you still gotta get naked for a bunch of strangers," Daisy added helpfully while being not at all helpful.

"Yay," I fake-cheered. "Tacos. Now."

"I know just the spot," Granny said.

"To the Caddy, ladies!" Marla cheered, raising her cane like a claymore to lead us on a charge. The thought made me laugh.

We all climbed into the Caddy, Daisy and I squeezing into the back seat with Marla and Granny in the front. As Marla turned the key in the ignition to fire up the old gal and then peeled out of the parking lot, I gripped the seat to keep my balance in case my antique seat belt failed. I looked over beside me and saw that Daisy was mirroring my pose.

I really should offer to drive more often.

To my surprise, Marla drove us to a hole-in-the-wall taco stand I had never been to before. And suddenly, my life seemed just a little brighter. Funny how tacos could change my whole outlook on life.

We sat at a little picnic table beside the taco stand and enjoyed our lunch in contemplative silence before we all piled back into Harold's baby-blue Caddy and headed toward George Washington's strip club.

"Strip!" Granny commands as the door to the backstage dressing room closes behind us.

"What?" I ask.

"Hurry, girl!" Marla harshly whispers to me. "We don't have much time."

"Huh?" I ask again.

"Take your clothes off!"

"Oh," I realize. I guess that's what I need to be doing.

I step out of my black pumps and lose about four inches of my height. I reach under my arm and slide the zipper on my dress down, feeling the fabric loosen as I go. I reach down and gather the hem in my hands and scrunch it up as I raise it up and over my head. It's one of my favorite dresses, so I fold it gently, to be put back on later, and place it in the locker we've been given to hide our shit in while we try to glean some information out of a bunch of dudes with boners.

"Those stockings are nice, but you'll slide around in them too much while you dance," Daisy informs me honestly. She doesn't pull any punches. "Those are advanced maneuvers."

"Okay." I gently roll the silk and lace down my legs and pile them on top of my dress.

"What did you bring to dance in?" Granny asks me.

"Oh!" I jump up and run to my large Coach tote bag that I carry everything in. "I almost forgot."

"You almost forgot?" Daisy shakes her head. "Why am I not surprised?"

"Will this do?" I ask as I pull a black string bikini I had bought for a vacation with my douche of an ex, James, to the Bahamas. He ended up taking his mistress instead of me, and I had already taken the tags off of the swimsuit, so it was mine and has lived in the back of my closet ever since.

"That's perfect," Daisy tells me, and the grannies agree. Well, at least I could get something right.

I reach behind me and unhook my black lace bra and fold it to put it on top of my dress. I hook my fingers in the sides of my matching panties and slide them down my legs before depositing them on top of the pile.

"I see someone did a little deforestation project since the last time I saw you naked," Daisy shouts across the dressing room.

"Uh . . . yeah," I blush furiously while I agree. "I cleaned up a bit."

"Nice work," she nods, making my face burn even hotter.

I step into the bikini bottoms and stand up, checking the ties for security purposes. It's all fun and games until you accidentally hit someone with a beaver shot. I am just reaching for the matching top when Daisy's voice stops me in my tracks.

"Wait, where are your pasties?" she asks me. I freeze where I am, bent halfway over and reaching for my skimpy bikini top, while the girls swing free in the breeze. A skinny girl, I am not. Truth be told, I'm not heavy either; I just really like tacos and Starbucks and hate jogging.

"Uh . . . what pasties?" I ask her.

"The ones that cover your nips, girl," she admonishes me.

"Uh . . ."

"What's going to cover your goodies when your top comes off?" Granny asks me.

"You can't just give the cow away for free, dear," Marla shares.

"Christ on a cracker, this is why Trent hasn't married you yet!" Granny shouts.

"I'm not married because I'm not ready!" I shout back. Unfortunately, I don't keep my trap shut and quit while I'm ahead. "And at the rate I'm going, I probably never will be either!"

The room goes silent.

"Shell?" Granny asks me, breaking the silence. I don't answer. "Why would you think you're never going to get married?"

I sigh. "Really?" I ask.

"Yeah, hon. Why would you say that?"

"I mean, look at me. James cheated with my best friend—" I start.

"Excuse me," Daisy cuts in. "You know I would never do that, and besides, I have my hands full with Jonesy. And Sophia would die before betraying either you or Kane of the Fine Asses. So really, that ho wasn't your bestie. She was just a placeholder for us."

I smile at her. She's right. Daisy and Sophie and far better besties than Bella ever was. A real friend doesn't do that.

"You're right," I tell her.

"I know," she says, brushing nonexistent dirt from her shoulders.

"What else is there?" Marla asks, steering us back on the emotional-journey track.

I look her straight in the eyes. "You have to know?" I whisper. I can't bear to say it any louder. It hurts as it is to whisper those words.

"Know what, honey?"

"That Trent is going to dump me after this," I answer. "And that's all right. I deserve it. I promised him I wouldn't get involved, but I had to. I couldn't not help Daisy find her friends. And then after meeting Christina's mom today, I couldn't walk away and still be able to look myself in the mirror. And that means losing Trent in the end."

"He'll understand—" Granny starts.

"Will he?" I ask.

"Probably not," Marla answers softly. "I'm so sorry."

"It's okay," I try my best to reassure her.

"It's not and I'm sorry, honey," she says softly.

"Now what about her pasties?" Daisy shouts, breaking the sad moment.

"What pasties?" I shout back.

"The fact that you have none and every good stripper has some pasties," she answers.

"Well, I'm not a stripper!" I volley back.

"You're right," she agrees, but she's still shouting, so it doesn't exactly sound like she's agreeing with me. "You're a trick."

"I am not a trick!"

"Are you dancing in a private room?" she asks me.

"Yes."

"Are you taking your clothes off?" she asks.

"Yes."

"Are men expecting a little somethin' somethin' extra when they go back there?" she asks with a smug grin on her face.

"Maybe . . ."

"Then you're a trick!" she shouts.

I throw my hands up in the air. "Fine! I'm a trick. Happy now?"

"Yeah," she says and shrugs her shoulder, "a little bit, but you still need some damn pasties!"

"Well, I don't have any," I snap back.

"We're running out of time, ladies," Marla says.

"What are we going to do?" Granny asks.

"I got this," Daisy answers.

"You do?" I eye her warily.

"Of course I do!" She smiles brightly as she reaches into her oversized, bright purple pocketbook and starts to dig around. "I was at Wal-mart with my nephew this morning picking up some necessities, and they gave him this here string of happy-face stickers."

Sure enough, Daisy holds up a strip of smiley-face stickers like that monkey in the beginning of *The Lion King*. I always loved that movie, but even I'm not sure where she's going with this.

"Uh . . . what?" I ask as she peels a couple of happy

faces off of the wax paper strip.

"*Pow*! *Pow*!" she shouts as she slaps a bright yellow smiley face over each of my nipples. "There. Now you're covered."

"Ouch! You asshole, that stings!" I cry out.

"But now your goodies are covered." She shrugs. "See? Now, that's a good friend right there."

"Yeah . . . I guess," I say grudgingly.

"Good. Now, suit up, soldier," Granny says, slapping me on the back so hard that it knocks me forward a bit.

I reach for my bikini top, tying it first under my breasts and then around my neck. I slide my hand in and scoop up my right breast first and then my left to situate them in the teeny black triangles. I roll my shoulders back and take a deep breath before sliding my feet back into my black patent leather pumps. They may not be sky-high or clear acrylic, but it's what I have. I'm a classy trick, I guess.

"Let's do this!" I say as I clap my hands together.

"All right!" Granny cheers.

"Now, that's what I'm talking about," Daisy says.

"Go get 'em, tiger," Marla says, and I can hear the pride and love she has for me ring out through her voice.

"Okay," I say, mostly to myself. "I got this."

"Wait!" Granny shouts just as I'm about to pull open the dressing room door. "One more thing."

"What's tha—" I start to ask, but she splashes a small bottle of baby oil that I didn't see her open, let alone even holding, all over my chest and belly. "What the fuck?"

"You needed oil and glitter," she explains.

"There's no glitter in this oil," I say, looking down my body, so I don't notice that my lunatic grandmother is still armed and dangerous.

"I know," she says sweetly. "It's right here." And then she tosses the contents of a vial of gold craft glitter all over me.

"You should probably rub that in," Daisy says absently beside me.

"Thanks," I droll, letting the *s* hiss like a snake. I'm sure the expression on my face is just magical right now.

I look down one more time at the disaster that is now my mostly naked body and decide there really is only one thing to do now—rub in all the glitter. I let out another sigh.

"You look just like a real stripper now," Marla says proudly.

"Thank you, Miss Marla." I smile at her.

"Now we can go," Granny says.

"Thank you." I roll my eyes.

"I saw that!" she snaps.

"I meant for you to," I admit, smiling my sweetest smile.

She gives me her best grandmother glare.

"She's just like you," Marla says with a chuckle.

"Let's just get on with it," Granny growls, and I can't help but laugh.

"I love you, Granny."

"And I you, my darling girl." And just like that, all is right between us.

Marla is not wrong. Granny and I are exactly alike,

which is as amazing as it is terrifying. I wouldn't blame poor Trent if he saw the writing on the wall and got out while he still could. It would smash my heart to bits, but at this point, I wouldn't blame him.

We walk down the hallway in a single-file line with me bringing up the rear, just like a prizefighter and his entourage. We spill out into the room and shut the door behind us. Daisy reaches for a light switch next to the door and flips on the light outside, letting the patrons in the main room know that a private dancer is ready and waiting.

That knowledge makes my palms sweat and my knees quake. I'm freaking out.

"Shit!" I whisper. "What do I do now?" The panic is spreading throughout my limbs, and darkness swirls at the edges of my vision.

"Take a deep breath," Granny orders.

"It'll all be okay," Marla says as she pats me on the back. "This is what you've prepared for. You're ready."

"But I'm not!" I wail. "I'm not a real hooker!"

"We know that, dear," Marla reassures me.

"But what do I do once they're in here?" I ask.

"You dance," Daisy says seriously.

"And then what?" I grasp at anything.

"You ask them vague questions while you give them lap dances," she answers.

"But they're expecting a hooker!" I whisper-shout. "I am not a hooker. What do I do then?"

"Then you tase the shit out of them," she says blandly.

"What now?" I ask, a little shocked.

"When you get what you need to out of them and

you know that they are expecting you to finish your services for them," Daisy explains.

"Yeah?" I ask.

"You tase the motherfucking shit out of them," she finishes triumphantly. And I like this plan. But then I realize I'm still screwed.

"But I don't have a Taser on me!" I begin to panic again. Jesus Fucking Christ I thought they were kidding about the taser shit.

"Sure you do," Granny says, pulling a Taser out of her tan leather granny purse. It's a lot like Mary Poppins's magic carpetbag, but smaller and full of shit like Tasers and Valium. "We got you this."

"What? I thought you were kidding!""We never kid about tasers," Daisy says helpfully.

"I don't know about this," I hedge.

"Sure you do," Daisy says gently. "You have to do this in order to be safe. It sucks but it's what you have to do." And suddenly, I realize that she's right.

"Fantastic!" I breathe, feeling like a weight has been lifted off of my chest.

"I think you should hide it in the sofa cushions so that when you're down to business, you can hit them with the zap zap when you need to," Daisy says.

"I like it." I nod. "But what are we going to do with him when we zap him?"

"You just let us handle that," she tells me. I thank Baby Jesus and all the little angels that I have this group of women to lean on. I don't know what I would do without them.

A knock sounds at the door.

"Hide!" I furiously whisper.

Daisy and the grannies scurry around the room, hiding where they can. When I can no longer see them, I slowly open the door and get a good look at the man standing on the other side. He's wearing tan Dockers and a wrinkled blue-and-white-checked shirt without a tie. His five o'clock shadow grazes his cheeks, and there's a thin gold band circling his left ring finger. Gross. But it's the obvious tent in his pants that has me swallowing back against the bile that's rising up in my throat.

"Hey there, sugar," I greet him with a sultry smile. Well, at least I hope it's a sultry smile. It's the very best I can muster under these circumstances.

"Hey," he says as he breezes past me and into the room.

I send up a silent prayer that he won't discover one of my octogenarians hidden in a corner somewhere, and I shut the door, clicking the lock firmly in place. I walk over to the stereo system as he takes his place on the sofa, and I do my best to hide the shudder that racks my body when I think about all the jizz that's probably hit that sofa. With my back to him, I press Play and wait for the music to cue up.

When "Classic" by MKTO fills the room, I shimmy and shake just like we practiced yesterday. I make my way back toward him like a big cat stalking its prey.

"So," I purr. "Do you come here often?"

"Uh . . . no?" he asks, unsure of what the game is. He probably thinks I want to hear that I'm his first. What I really want to hear is who killed Daisy's friends. But I can play this game.

"So . . . I'm your first?" I ask as I trail a fingertip

down the front of his shirt.

I turn around and bend forward while I snap the strings of my bikini bottoms against my hip with my thumb. I glance at him from over my shoulder and see him watching me, so I bite my lip before arching my back and pulling to stand straight again.

"Y-yeah," he stutters. The man shifts in his seat, and his erection presses further against his trousers.

"So," I say as I turn around and brace my hands on the back of the sofa to lean over him, letting my breasts dangle close to his face. I watch him work his throat as he swallows. "Tell me what you want."

"I-I-I want you." He swallows again. He's nervous. He may come here often to drink and watch the ladies dance, but he doesn't buy a hooker often.

"How so?" I ask.

"I-I think I would like a blow job," he whispers, and I almost feel bad for what's about to happen.

"Sure thing, honey," I say, and then I place the prongs to the side of his neck and zap him. When the current hits his body, he comes in his pants.

"Well, that's . . . unfortunate," Granny says as she pops out from her corner to kill the music.

"So, what's the plan?" I ask them.

"We . . . uh . . . we don't really know," Daisy admits to me.

"What?" I ask them as the man twitches in his stained clothes.

"Well, we didn't really work that part out yet," Granny hedges.

"What do you mean, you didn't work that part out?" I ask, feeling my panic mount again.

"Well . . . things progressed at a more rapid rate than we were prepared for," she tells me.

"Shit, shit, shit!" I whisper-shout. I'm afraid, more than ever now, that we will draw unwanted attention while this guy is still incapacitated.

"I think he may be coming around," Daisy says absentmindedly as if she's a spectator at a horse race at Del Mar.

"What?" I screech.

"Don't worry. I got this," Marla says as she pulls Big Thunder out of her pocketbook and clubs the poor schmuck over the head. "And it's lights out, motherfucker."

"Jesus," I mutter.

"Look!" Granny practically shouts. "There's a back door. Let's see where it goes."

"Lord, give me strength and deliver me from evil," I close my eyes and mumble.

"I think you're mixing up your scriptures, dear," Marla says as she winks at me.

"Hey, it goes to an alleyway," Granny says over her shoulder. "This is perfect! Shelby, you and Daisy haul his ass outside here, but make sure not to come in contact with any bodily fluids."

"Gee, thanks." I roll my eyes as I help Daisy lift him up.

"Don't worry, girls," Marla says with a bright smile. "I brought wet-naps!"

"Awesome . . ." I say blandly.

"There," Granny says as she brushes her hands together as if she just did all the work. Daisy and I, on the other hand, are sweating like pigs. "No muss, no fuss."

"Easy for you to say," I complain. "Daisy and I are sweating like hookers in confession."

"Speak for yourself, chica. My conscience is clear." Daisy winks at me to show me there are no hard feelings.

"Sorry, doll. Bad choice of words," I say softly as we shut the door on the guy in the alley.

"No big deal," Daisy tells me just as there's another knock at the door.

"Christ on a cracker!" Granny jumps. "Who knew you were such a hot commodity as a lady of the night?"

"Granny."

"Not me!" she whispers.

"Just hide already and save the commentary," I say with an eye-roll.

"I saw that!"

"Shhh!"

Once they are all back in their places, I walk over to the door and pull it open. A couple stands at the door wrapped up in each other's arms. She's practically climbing him like a tree.

"Can I help you?" I ask them.

"Yeah, baby," the woman says. "We like to watch."

"O-okay," I say. I did not plan for this eventuality, but I have to admit that it's kind of hot. I wonder if Trent would want to catch a show with me sometime. "Well, come on in."

The woman leads the man over to the sofa by the hand, and they sit down. I shut and lock the door before walking over to the stereo. She said they like to watch, so I might as well give them a show. I cue up "Pony" by Ginuwine. If "Pony" doesn't get your freak flag flying, nothing will.

Something tells me this couple is just out for a good time and are not serial killers. Although, recently I watched a *48 Hours* on a crazy-ass chick, and she looked like an everyday suburban mom, so it just goes to show that you never really know a person.

"So," I say as I begin to dance. "Do you guys come here often?"

"Nah," the man says as they begin to paw at each other again. "Only every couple of months or so. We just like to watch a pretty girl dance and then go fuck like rabbits in the back seat of the car."

"Yeah, we only have the babysitter until midnight," the woman says.

"Awesome," I say as I dance closer.

I hate that I'm about to have to take them out, but also, I'm not sure how to get them out of here. I'm also not sure my new Taser has enough juice to zap two people back-to-back. I'm starting to really get worried when I see Marla rise up from behind the sofa faster than a woman with a false hip should be able to. And she's wielding Big Thunder like a battle-ax. I barely have time to dive out of the way before she knocks them both unconscious.

"Damn," Daisy says, popping out of her corner to turn off the music. "That's one hell of a club."

"It's the true vehicle anti-theft device." She snickers as she tucks it back into her purse.

"Thanks," I say, grabbing the man by the ankles while Daisy grabs his arms to haul him out into the alley. "I wasn't sure what I was going to do there."

"Me either," Granny agrees. "That Taser is good,

but not multiple-people good."

"Good to know." I nod.

Daisy and I make quick work of the woman, and then we close and lock the door behind them.

"I kind of feel bad about leaving all those people out there," I admit.

"Don't worry, dear," Marla reassures me. "We'll check on them before we leave."

"I'm not sure that makes me feel better, but okay." I shrug. There's not much I can do about it now.

"We're about to have a big old pile of unconscious dudes with boners, and that one chick who just wanted a sexy night away from her kids, in this slightly seedy establishment if you don't slow down, chick," Daisy says. "We need to start getting some evidence and shaking down these people for some information."

"You're right," I sigh. "None of these people felt right for the killings, though."

"I agree," she says. "I just feel so helpless, you know?"

"I know, honey," I say. "We're doing what we can. We just have to stay the course."

"Even if it costs you everything?"

"Even if it costs me everything," I reply.

"You know how I said that chick was a bad friend?" she asks me.

"Yeah."

"Well, you're a great one too. I'm glad you're mine, Shelby. Even if you are a pretty shitty hooker," Daisy tells me.

"Thanks, girl. I'm glad you're mine too," I say as I wrap my arms around her shoulders.

A knock sounds at the door. This time Daisy and the grannies pop back into their places like seasoned pros. I walk to the door and open it.

But this time is different.

Standing at the door is a tall man in a dark, three-piece suit that speaks volumes of its cost. He has a tie neatly knotted around his neck and tucked into his vest. I spy a gold Rolex on his wrist and large diamond studs in each ear. This man has as much money as he does muscles on his body—and that's a shit-ton.

But even more than that is the foreboding feeling that he ushers into the room.

"Can I come in?" he asks as he shoots me a sparkling smile.

"Y-yes, of course." I wave my arm to usher him in before shutting the door and locking it. Sweet Moses, I hope Marla is ready with her Big Thunder bat because this guy screams t-r-o-u-b-l-e—trouble.

I head over to the stereo and cue up my original song selection of the night, "Classic." The man raises his eyebrow at my choice, but whatever, this is still my show, for now. All bets are off if he decides to murder me.

"So." I begin to dance around him like the last one even though my belly is full of big, flopping-about bald eagles. "Do you come here often?"

"No." Nothing else, just a one-word answer.

"What changed your mind tonight?" I ask and I kind of want to throw up. I have a bad feeling about this guy. He's probably the hooker killer. He has that look about him. This man is probably going to kill me right now.

"You."

I audibly gulp as I swallow back the fear that is rising up from my belly. I stutter-step for a hot second but then continue my dance.

"Oh yeah?" I ask as I turn my back to him again and slowly pull the strings of my bikini top from behind my neck loose. I look over my shoulder and watch him watch me as I let the strings fall.

"Yeah," he agrees, but again, that's all I get.

I pull the strings under my breasts loose. I let the scrap of black fabric fall to the floor and try not to imagine which of the Four Horsemen are touching it. I lift the heavy fall of my hair from my back and neck as I swing my hips and undulate to the music.

"Turn around," he commands softly, but there is a sharp edge to his gentle tone. There is more here than meets the eye. "Let me see you."

"As you wish," I respond, making my voice low and husky as I turn around and let him get a good look at my happy-face stickers.

His dangerous mouth quirks at one corner. "I think I like you."

"Good," I say to him, but I don't have any good feelings about him at all. My stomach is clenched in knots, and for the first time in my life, I'm afraid I may have a Ruth situation right here in the back room at a strip club owned by my grandmother's friends. And by that, I mean crap my pants. I'm that nervous.

"Come here."

I do as he says and swing my hips as I saunter toward my impending doom. I can't help but wonder if I should add a little kick ball change to my steps if these are my last moments on Earth. I would rather go out with a little razzle-dazzle.

He spreads his thighs wide and I step in between them. My Taser is within reach and I feel an eerie calm settle over me. Too bad it would prove to be a little premature, just like my high school sweetheart's ejaculation.

"Closer." He crooks his finger at me, and I lean in so there is only an inch or two of space between our noses and I look him in the eye. A change rolls over him and it scares me down to my bones. "Now that I have your attention, tell your cop boyfriend to stay out of my business. I'd hate for a pretty little thing such as yourself to get hurt."

The more he talks, the wider I can feel my eyes getting. As he finishes voicing his threat, he reaches for a lock of my hair, letting it slip through his fingertips. Sometime during his diatribe, I had stopped breathing; he scared me and he knew it. But it's his stupid knowing smirk on his scary fucking face that does me in, so I reach for my Taser and put the prongs against his neck and press the button to zap the shit out of him.

When his body goes slack, I jump back, and when I do, Marla jumps out from behind the sofa and smashes Big Thunder over his head for all she's worth. I would stop her, but I'm too stunned by what he had said to me to be of any help.

Fortunately, Daisy jumps out from the corner she was hiding in and wraps her arms around Marla to pull her back. She forces her hand open to drop the massive dildo she carries around with her everywhere she goes, and Daisy hands it off to Granny, who tucks it into her modest granny purse.

"It's okay, Miss Marla," Daisy says softly. "It's all going to be okay."

But I don't feel like anything is going to be okay ever again.

I don't realize that I'm shaking until Granny wraps her deceptively strong arms around me. She holds me tight while the tremors subside. Unfortunately, my work isn't done here.

"We're going to have to move him soon," Daisy says.

"I hate to leave him in the alleyway with all of those nice people," Marla says. I'm not so sure *nice* is the word I would use to describe them, but okay, we'll go with that for now. They are definitely a step up from Mr. Career Criminal.

"I'm okay," I whisper to Granny.

"Yes, you are," she reassures me, speaking low for my ears only.

I grab his feet, wanting to be as far away from him as possible, and we drag him out through the alleyway. Marla wallops our previous patrons one more time for good measure as Daisy and I carry Mr. Mobster out to the parking lot. A quick look around reveals no good hiding places.

"We could toss him in the dumpster," I suggest.

"You think a man dressed like that will be happy when he wakes up with the trash?" she asks.

"Uh . . . no," I answer.

"Right." She sighs. "Let's put him in a trunk."

"We can't just put him in a trunk!" I begin to freak out again. "Can you imagine Ma and Pa Moses driving down the 5 on their way home from church services when Mr. Al Capone Junior jumps out of their trunk? He'll kill them!"

"Do you really think good, church-going people currently have their cars parked in a strip club parking lot late at night?" she asks me.

"Uh . . . no again," I mumble. "But he will still kill them when he gets out!"

"Good point," Daisy agrees.

"Thank you." I let out a sigh.

"So we'll put him in his own trunk," she decides.

"How are we ever going to find out which car is his?" I ask her. This is too hard. We're never going to puzzle this out before he wakes up. And now we're all going to die, and I can't be responsible for my grandmother's death.

"Please hold," she says as she places her end of the guy on the ground before rooting around in his pockets. She pulls out a set of keys and remotely unlocks a flashy Mercedes that's parked just two rows over before picking up her half of the bad-guy load.

Maybe that wasn't so hard after all . . .

When we reach the car, she fiddles with the key fob again and presses another button that pops the trunk.

"In he goes," she says.

"Should we leave the keys with him?" I ask as we both stand there staring down at his unconscious body in the dark well of the trunk.

"Probably not," she says with obvious thought. "We don't want to make it too easy for him to find and kill you. It's bad enough he already knows who you are."

"Good point, well made," I say as I slam the lid of the trunk down just a little too hard.

"Thank you," she says as she places the keys on the front seat and hits the lock button on the open door before closing it. "Like I said, we can't make it too easy for him now."

We walk back to the rear door of the club, and Granny and Marla are wringing their hands. They want to come up with a plan of action. They want to know what we're doing now, but all I know is that I'm just done. I need to put clothes back on because I feel too exposed, too naked. I need alcohol, and a lot of it. And most importantly, I need to get these bikini bottoms off because they are starting to ride up, and it's all fun and games until you have a wedgie on one side and a camel toe on the other. That shit hurts.

"What do you need, Shell?" Granny asks. They all wait for my answer, and I give the only one that really matters anyhow.

"Tequila," I say seriously. "I need a lot of tequila."

"I know just the place," Marla says.

TEN

TEQUILA AND SNORING

"**H**it me again, Mack." I slam my shot glass down onto the bar just a little too hard and cringe. "Whoops."

Sometime after Daisy and I locked the mobster, who seemed to have detailed knowledge about who I really am and my life, in the trunk of his Merc, I decided I needed hard liquor. So, like a pack of wild lionesses, my posse and I stalked back to the dressing room like we had a mean fight in front of us and weren't about to back down.

Granny pulled a pair of leggings with tacos all over them out of her bag and a bunch of tank tops for me to layer.

"Thanks, Granny." I choked back the tears that were clogging my throat. This woman always knew exactly what I needed and was ready. "This is exactly what I need right now."

"No, what you need is tequila," she said softly.

"That'll do it," I agreed.

I changed into my new outfit as quickly as possible, pulling on my panties and bra and dropping my bikini into my oversized Coach tote. I tossed my heels and dress in there too. The dry cleaner could take care of everything else. The leggings felt like butter as I slid them up my legs, and I wondered where these had been all my life before pulling my tank tops down over my head and slipping my feet into the pair of Chucks that I kept in the bottom of my bag for emergencies.

After that Trent's grandmother and mine, not to mention Daisy, my hooker mentor and BFF, whisked me down the hall and out of George Washington's strip club. They bundled me into the back seat of Harold's baby-blue Caddy, and off we went to some hole-in-the-wall dive bar, where I promptly ordered all the tequila.

I'm not even sure how many shots I've had. All I know is that it was probably too many, which is where we're at now.

"The name's not Mack," the bartender says as he tips the bottle to fill my glass again.

"That's okay," I tell him as if he is the one who offended me. Unfortunately, I get like this when I drink the tough stuff. "Just 'play it again, Sam.'"

"The name's not Sam either."

"I'm okay with that too. Just keep 'em coming." I nod.

"Should we cut her off?" I hear Daisy ask, and I slide my glass close to me and lean over it protectively while I send out my best murderous glare like I'm a hobbit protecting a ring.

"Nah." Granny laughs. "She's fun like this. Just

wait and see."

I relax a little, sitting back on my barstool, and sip my drink. Not Mack comes over and tops me off.

"I like you." I wink at him and he smiles back.

"Don't smile at her," Daisy snaps at him. "She has a boyfriend and he is one scary mofo. He's a badass cop in the city and a former Army Ranger to boot."

"He's also my grandson," Marla says with a haughty air.

"Is that true?" the bartender asks me.

"It is," I say dreamily as I lean my elbow on the bar and rest my chin on my hand. "He has a magical penis."

"And that's the ball game, folks," Daisy says.

"I guess we'll be needing the check," Granny says.

"Coming right up, ladies," he says before turning to the cash register behind the bar.

I pull my wallet from my tote and smile as I up-end it on top of the counter. All the change and bills flop around on the bar top, along with a shit-ton of receipts—apparently I shop a lot—and Daisy and the grannies scramble to scoop it all back up.

"Slow your roll, girl," Daisy says.

"Was that too much?" I blink a couple of times.

"Uh . . . yes," she says hesitantly.

"My bad."

Not Mack the Bartender drops the tab in front of us. "Whenever you're ready, ladies."

Granny peels a couple of bills out of the stack she collected from the mess I made and lays them on top of the bill before stuffing everything else back into my bag and slinging it over her shoulder.

"Let's get the wild child home," she says to the group.

"Okay." I smile.

They fold me back into the Caddy and hit the 15 northbound for Escondido.

"We're here, doll," Granny says as she gently shakes me awake.

"I don't know what happened," I tell them.

"Tequila!" They all say, laughing at the same time.

"Oh, okay," I say before meandering my way up the front walk.

Before I can even think about where my house keys are, the front door swings open to reveal Trent standing in nothing but a pair of worn jeans, and I have to admit that the look is good on him.

"I'd ask where you were, but you reek of cheap alcohol and I just saw Daisy and our grandmothers peel out of the drive in Harold's Caddy, so I guess I already know the answer to that," he says after he gives me the once-over.

"Yeah."

"You drunk?" Trent asks me.

"Yeah." I let myself fall forward and brace myself against his muscular chest. My hands seem to have a mind of their own as they wander all over.

"You want something?"

"Yeah."

"If you want my cock, you have to ask for it," he tells me.

"I want your cock," I mumble, feeling my cheeks heat.

"That's good, baby," Trent says softly. "Because I

want your mouth on my cock, and then I want to fuck you while you're still drunk."

"Okay," I mumble.

"Does that work for you?"

"Yeah."

"Good," he rumbles. "Now come inside."

"Okay." Trent takes my hand in his and leads me into the house, then he shuts the door behind me and locks it.

"Tonight, we're not going to be interrupted by anyone, right?"

"I don't think so," I answer him honestly.

"Good," Trent says as he slides the strap of my giant pocketbook down my shoulder and drops it on the table by the door.

"Meowww," Missy chirps from the floor, and I bend down to pet her.

"There's my sweet girl," I coo.

Missy weaves her way through my legs and then moves on to find either some form of cat entertainment or a good place to nap. I stand back up and smile at Trent. He's so pretty, with his muscles and tattoos and dark stubble. Not to mention an ass that I just want to bite.

This may be the tequila talking, but I think I'd really like the opportunity to bite his ass.

I toe off my sneakers and sexy-walk my way over to Trent, who smirks at me. I have a funny feeling that my sexy sashay is more of a drunken stumble, but that's all right. I'm like Tyra Banks, boo. I can work it like Missy Elliott.

I turn my back to Trent and let my jacket slide

down my arms and hit the floor while looking at him from over my shoulder. "Catch me if you can."

And then I take off down the hall. Trent, not being one to willingly lose a challenge, is hot on my heels as I cross the threshold of the bedroom. He grabs me by the waist from behind and swings me around. Trent crushes his lips to mine and I get lost in his kiss.

When he breaks away from me, I gasp to catch my breath before wrapping my arms around my waist to pull my tank tops over my head and toss them to the floor. In my inebriated state, I'm feeling pretty damn confident, so I assume a Superman pose with my hands on my hips and my head held high, but my confidence flags a bit when Trent doesn't say anything or make a move to touch me again.

"Wow," he says, sounding a little taken aback. "That's a lot of glitter."

Oh, fuck. I totally forgot about the jar of fucking craft glitter that Granny had dumped all over me before my fledgling foray into fake hooking. Shit, shit, shit! I scramble to come up with a plausible excuse, but when I open my mouth, only stupid bullshit falls out.

"It's a new trend," I explain. "Do you like it?"

Trent seems to slow-blink, realizing that he has unknowingly wandered into dangerous does-my-butt-look-big-in-these-jeans territory. "It's great, honey," he backpedals. "Very . . . um . . . shiny."

"Thank you," I fake-preen, shimmying my shoulders as I go. Time to get this train back on the sexy-times tracks. "Maybe you should take off your clothes too."

Not one to be told twice that he needs to get naked in order to get laid, Trent opens the button fly on his jeans in one swift move, and it sounds like a string of muffled firecrackers as one pops right after another. I roll my lip into my mouth between my teeth as he pushes his jeans down to the floor and steps out of them as he goes, revealing that Trent is wearing nothing at all underneath.

"Well," I purr. "What are you waiting for?"

And then Trent pounces, racing toward me like a linebacker. I brace for the sack as he tosses me back onto the bed. He flops on top of me, but because of all the baby oil and glitter, Trent slides right off of me and shoots onto the floor, but then he pops right back up.

"Jesus, you're as slippery as an eel."

I pop up to my knees in bed, only I'm drunk and covered in oil, so I flop around a bit too until I can get a purchase on my knees.

"Come here." I crook my finger at him. "Come lie down and let me lick you all over."

Trent must like the idea because he practically jumps from halfway across the bedroom and flops down onto the bed with his hard length pointing straight up.

"Impressive," I mumble, mostly to myself.

"It's all for you, baby." He smirks. "So, what's with the smiley-face stickers?"

I panic and say the first thing that pops into my head. "Uh . . . just trying something new, I guess."

"I like it."

Where was I? Oh, right, I need to get this naked party back in action.

I kiss my way down Trent's muscular chest and feel a little adventurous, so I flick my tongue over one of his flat nipples. He adjusts to lie propped up against the pillows with his legs spread, and as I slide down his body—finally getting a handle on all this freaking baby oil and glitter—I settle in between his legs and grip his hard cock in my hand.

"Shelby—" Trent groans as I pump my fist over him a couple of times before leaning forward and taking his tip into my mouth.

He pumps his hips gently, encouraging me to take him deeper into my mouth, but I'm in no hurry. I rest my head against his firm thigh as I slowly slip him in and out of my mouth while holding his base tight in my hand. I love this. I love driving Trent wild, giving him something no one else does. I could do this all night . . .

"Shelby," Trent says softly.

"Huh?" I ask when I let him slip free from my mouth with a pop.

"Honey, you fell asleep," Trent's voice seems to rumble as if he was laughing, but that can't be, because I was in the middle of giving him a fantastic blow job.

"I did?" I ask softly, still not opening my eyes.

"You did," he confirms. "A lesser man would get a complex from a pretty woman falling asleep on his dick. Fortunately for you, I'm not one."

"Okay," I mumble.

"Sleep, honey," he gently commands me.

"Okay," I repeat as I feel him grab me under my arms and place me on the pillows beside him. Trent pulls the covers up over me, and then I do as he says and fall asleep.

chapter ELEVEN

STINGS AND SEMI-CHUBS

I'm having the best dream.

I am spread out on the bed in the middle of Trent's bedroom. The dove-gray curtains blow in the breeze as a late-morning glow glimmers in the air. I bask in the warm sunshine, and Trent has his head between my legs.

This is the best kind of dream—the one where a real orgasm is coming. The mind is a beautiful thing. I could be embarrassed about it, but why? I am a healthy, red-blooded woman in my prime. And for the time being, I am involved with a superhuman hunk of a man, so I'm going to enjoy that both in my dreams and in real life.

I arch my back as he takes another slow swipe of his tongue—tasting me, teasing—and Trent rumbles out a little growl. He slowly brings me to the edge of bliss. But it's when he slides a finger deep inside me to ghost over that spot that I gasp out a breath and my eyes snap open.

This isn't a dream at all.

The room is dark, and just outside the window, the hazy light of dawn is beginning to creep up the hillside. Somewhere in the shadows, my man plotted a sneak attack of the very best kind.

"Trent—" I gasp.

He rumbles his pleasure against my pussy just before he rolls his tongue over my clit, and I am lost. I thrust my fingers into his dark hair and pull him closer to where I need him most. I squeeze my eyes tight as I shatter into a million pieces.

I just start to catch my breath as Trent slides up my body. He positions the tip of his cock at my entrance and, with one firm thrust, impales me to the hilt. Tingles spread all over my body, and a fire that should have already been put out ignites.

"Fuck yes," he growls before he begins to really move.

Trent plunges into me over and over. This is a hard and fast coupling that won't last long, and I wouldn't want it any other way. I grip his hips between my legs and rake my nails down his back as he pushes my body harder and harder toward the completion he seeks.

It does something to me when Trent is this wild, and I love knowing that I'm the one to push him there. When this investigation is over and done with, or, at the very least, when he becomes aware of my involvement, I'm going to lose him forever, so why wouldn't I take as many memories like this as possible with me when he inevitably tosses me out on my ear?

"Trent," I pant.

"You're there, baby." He pumps harder and harder. "Fuck yes, you're there."

"Yes!" I shout as I come again.

"Shelby!" Trent shouts my name as he follows me over the edge.

We lie together for I don't know how long. Trent's heavy weight is crushing me into the mattress, and I love it. I bask in the feel of him here with me as our bodies lie still connected in the most intimate way, and I can feel the steady beat of his heart in his chest against mine.

"Good morning," I mumble shyly. A blush steals across my cheeks.

"It's always a good morning when I wake up with you, honey," he tells me softly as he brushes my hair back from my face.

"Trent—"

"I have to get in the shower," he sighs. "I wish I didn't have to but I do."

"It's okay," I tell him honestly. "I understand."

"I know you do, but I don't want to leave you this morning." Trent runs a frustrated hand through his hair. "I wish I could stay here in bed with you all day." He punctuates his words by squeezing my ass cheek in his large hand.

"Me too," I say truthfully.

"So," he starts as he pushes up from the bed to saunter, naked as you please, over to the bathroom. "What do you have on tap for today?"

The question is innocent enough, but it's as good as a bucket of cold water being thrown over my post-orgasm chill. I feel my spine go straight with the knowledge that I have to lie to Trent. Bile rises up in my throat. I pride myself on being an honest, straightforward, doesn't-pull-any-punches kind of a gal, and here I am lying to the man I love more than anything. And I do. Trent puts the color in my world.

"Oh, nothing exciting," I say with a quick quirk of a smile on my mouth. It's there, and then it's gone, hoping he doesn't see it for the forgery that it is. "I have to get some work done, and then I'll have lunch with the girls."

"What are you working on?" he asks me. It's probably best to stay as close to the truth as possible and limit my actual out-and-out lying whenever I can. Then maybe I can keep up the pretenses as long as possible. Not that it will matter in the end, because when Trent finds out what we've been doing, he will dump me for sure.

"Oh, just a follow-up after Christina's funeral." Which, I suppose, is true enough. We are following up and it started after her funeral. It's just not the write-up for the *San Diego Metro News* that Trent thinks it is. Ugh. I feel sick again.

Trent narrows his eyes. "Are you sure that's all you have going on?"

"Yeah," I say, smiling brighter than I feel. Trent does not look convinced.

"Okay," he says hesitantly before turning on his heels to head into the bathroom.

My phone buzzes on the nightstand next to me, and I reach for it on autopilot. I slide my thumb across the screen to unlock it. I have a new text message from an unknown number, but when I open it, I feel all the air whoosh out of my lungs. It's picture after picture of dead cats, and the message with it is just as cruel.

UNKNOWN NUMBER: Dead pretty puss-
ies. Will you be smart or will you
be next?

I scroll through all of the pictures, glad that I haven't had anything to eat yet, while praying I won't find a picture of my Missy in the bunch. When I get to the end, I quickly hit the Delete Message button and toss my phone back onto the nightstand, where it bounces with a clatter.

"Everything all right?" Trent asks from the doorway with a towel slung low around his hips. Shit. I didn't notice him there, and I can't help but wonder how much he saw.

"Yeah." I smile brightly. "Why wouldn't I be?"

"I don't know," he says cautiously. "You looked pretty upset for a minute there."

"Oh, it's nothing," I say quickly. "Granny is mad at Ruth for something else ridiculous. She's hatching her next diabolical plan as we speak."

"You sure that's all it was?"

"Yes, of course," I rush to answer. "Why do you ask?"

"You know you can tell me anything, right?" Trent asks. "I will always help you, even if I'm angry. I promise that I will always be there for you, Shelby." I wish that were true. I blink quickly to stop the shimmer of tears in my eyes.

"I know," I whisper.

Trent opens his mouth but stops and closes it again.

He looks like he wants to say something to me but quickly shuts it off. He's leaving the ball in my court, and I have no choice but to withhold vital information from him.

"Okay," he says. "I gotta get ready to go."

"Okay."

"Are you sure there isn't anything else you want to tell me?" he asks.

"I'm sure," I tell him and pray that he lets it go.

Thankfully, and heartbreakingly at the same time, Trent seems to let the issue go and walks into the closet to get dressed for the day. When he reemerges fully dressed—boots, gun, and all—he presses his lips to mine quickly before heading out the door without another word.

Missy hops up onto the bed silently, so very unlike her, but also in tune with the severity of the situation. I scoop her up and hug her to my chest. And, miracle of miracles, she lets me.

We're going to need to be more careful moving forward.

And I can't help but feel like everything is about to change, so when I hear the front door click quietly closed, I finally give in and let the tears that I had held at bay fall like rain.

"I'm going to need more of those happy-face stickers if you have them," I tell Daisy. I know they can all hear the dejected tone in my voice.

"Sure thing, honey," she says softly as she reaches into her big leopard-print bag. "I've got some more right here."

"Thanks." I take the stickers and apply them my-self this time while I quietly suit up for another day of pretend hooking.

Today feels different. Last night, after Christina's funeral, I was settled in my role in this game, but today I'm not so sure. That's not quite right. I am not waf-fling on whether or not to continue my own investi-gation. I will do whatever I can to find Christina and Stacy's killer, all while hoping against hope that Trent finds them first.

But I would be crazy not to be terrified after yes-terday. And I am a lot of things, but I'm mostly sure that crazy isn't one of them. Mostly. I'm almost posi-tive. Oh, just chuck it in the fuck it bucket. Who am I kidding? This group is crazier than a dog in a cat factory. Me included. That notwithstanding, my run-in with Mr. Mobster yesterday scared the pants off of me, and that's pretty impressive, seeing as how they were already off! It's not every day that a mobster knows who you are while you are operating under an alias.

I let out a heavy sigh as Granny flips the light switch in the private room announcing that I'm open for business. I stash my bag with my clothes in a cup-board at the back of the room and wait. The alleyway was free of tasered people when we got here, so I'm assuming they all found their way home sometime between last night and this morning. A certain black Mercedes was also missing from the parking lot, so hopefully he will be missing from my life for a while. Or forever. I would really like to not see him again. He was handsome and all, death threats and threats against my person aside, and I'm sure he's a great guy —well, not really, seeing as how he is a mobster—but I would probably be okay if I never saw him or heard his name spoke again.

Actually, I don't even know what his name is. That is particularly frightening because I won't know he's coming until he's right there, probably plunging the knife in.

There is a knock at the door.

Daisy, Miss Marla, and Granny all jump into their hiding places. I take my time walking toward the stereo system on the far wall. It feels like my heels are full of cement. I can barely make my body go through the motions that I know I have to do.

"Come in," I call out with my back to the door.

I brace myself against the shelf when I hear the soft snick of the door latch as the door opens and then closes. I hear light footfalls on the carpet behind me and the sounds of his clothing as it shuffles against the old, faux-leather sofa.

I take a deep breath to shore up my courage before switching on the music. I go back to my first night here in George Washington's club and select "Party in the U.S.A." again. It's light and fun and always makes me smile. Sometimes I play it on my phone and dance to it while I cook in Trent's kitchen. He has a great kitchen for dancing in. One time he even told me that he thinks it's his favorite song after watching me dance to it in one of his dress shirts while searching for ice cream in the freezer.

I turn around and begin dancing. His large frame is situated to peek out from the shadows. Even though I cannot see his face, there is something familiar about him. I shake off my thoughts of the mobster who knew my real name and had a hidden agenda of his own. But as I move closer, I can see that it's not him. So how do I know this guy?

"Do you come here often?" I lead in with my standard opener.

"Not particularly, but if you're going to be a regular around here, then I guess I should be too," Kane says and leans forward out of the hazy shadows.

I stop in my tracks.

"Oh, shit."

"'Oh, shit' is right, darlin'," Kane says softly.

"Well, fuck a damn duck," Miss Marla adds. The outburst from her would usually make me laugh, but this situation is too precarious. I have to get Kane to agree not to tell Trent about this.

"That'll do too," he agrees, and I swallow audibly.

"W-w-we . . . uh . . . ," I stammer. "We don't have to tell Trent about this, do we?"

"Shelby—" he starts.

"I mean . . . don't lie . . . that's not right." I swallow back against the panic that's climbing up my throat. "Just . . . uh . . . don't volunteer the information."

"Honey, he knows," Kane whispers softly.

"What?" Granny, Marla, Daisy, and I all shout at once.

"We got an anonymous tip this morning that someone was turning tricks out of a private room in George's club. This is a sting operation," Kane says cautiously.

"But I'm not really a hooker!" I practically shout.

"I know that," Kane says. "I still need to bring you

in for questioning."

"I was just trying to find out who took Christina and Stacy," I explain.

"I'm getting that impression," he says as he evades my reasoning. "I would even ask how you were planning on protecting yourself against a killer, but I can see you came prepared."

I look over my shoulder and see Granny, Marla, and Daisy all closing in, in a semicircle around me from behind. These women, whom I love so much, have all armed themselves against the police. For me.

"See? I couldn't possibly be guilty of what you are implying," I hedge.

"But still . . ."

"So I'll just be going before Trent finds out what happened here, and then we shall never speak of this again."

"Shelby, this room is wired," Kane explains, but I don't really understand what he's saying. I tilt my head to the side as if that will offer me some clarity on the situation.

"Fuck me running," Granny says from behind me.

"I don't understand," I say.

"The room is bugged, Shelby," Granny explains to me.

"Huh?" I ask.

"Trent is sitting in a surveillance van outside," Kane says.

"Fuck me running," I repeat Granny's earlier words. "I gotta get out of here before Trent can get in here. If I'm fast enough, I can probably beat him. Granny, fake a heart attack and buy me some time to empty out my bank account and head to Mexico."

"I don't think there's going to be enough time for that, darling girl," Granny says solemnly.

"Why is that?" I ask.

"Because Trent is walking through the door right now," Kane says with a broad smile, splitting his too-handsome-for-his-own-good face. "This is going to be fun."

"I don't know if 'handsome' is how I would describe it," I mumble to myself as Trent takes a couple of steps toward me. "Well, this has been real, but I gotta go."

"And she don't mean 'real fun,'" Daisy says with an eye-roll.

"I need a moment alone with my girlfriend," Trent growls.

"No can do, Big Chief," I say, shaking my head. "I am late for a . . . a . . . uh . . . dentist appointment. Yeah, that's it. I have a dentist appointment right now, so I have to run." I shuffle to the right and pivot, trying to guess his next move.

"I don't think you are going to make that cleaning," Trent says as he pivots to follow me. "Come here, Shelby."

"Nope." I shake my head quickly and then bolt like a bank robber with a sack of money.

Unfortunately, my former Army Ranger boyfriend hasn't let his level of physical fitness slack since he left the service and he catches up to me rather quickly. It's embarrassing, really. Damn you, tacos! But I love you so much. I'm going to need to insist on double bacon cheeseburgers more often to fatten him up.

"Serpentine! Serpentine!" Granny shouts, and I do my best to avoid him but he's gaining on me.

"Shit!" he grumbles as I make a great evasive maneuver.

"That's my girl!" Miss Marla cheers.

"Nana!" Trent says.

"What?" She shrugs. "Chicks before dicks."

"Ungh," he growls as he pushes harder and catches up to me.

Trent reaches out for me, wrapping his arms around my oiled-up waist as he pushes off from the ground with his feet like a cheetah and takes me to the ground. It was a sack that would rival any professional football player's.

"Damn it, Shelby," Granny growls. "I am disappointed."

"I'm sorry, Granny," I mumble. Unfortunately, my face is smushed into the syphilis carpet, so it sounds a lot like "Mheerrrmm shreermy, Geermy."

"I had a ten-spot on you lasting another five minutes."

"Mheerrrmm shreermy, Geermy."

"Again," Trent says as he pushes up from the floor. "I was a Ranger." Poor Trent. He has this really put-upon sound of frustration that he makes sometimes. Okay, it's all the time. Poor Trent almost always has cause to be frustrated where I am concerned. Wow, put it like that and I really feel bad. Kind of. Mostly. Well, sort of.

"We know, dear," Marla says with a bright smile.

I start crab-walking backward toward the door while his back is turned. But when Trent turns around, he spears me with a glare.

"And where do you think you're going?" he practically roars.

"Uh . . . the dentist?" I answer.

"I don't think so." He turns back to the room at large. "Do you all have a ride home?"

"Of course, dear," Marla smiles sweetly. "Don't you worry about us."

"Benedict Arnold," I gripe to the room at large.

"You'll thank me when I'm holding your baby," she says softly.

"Baby?" Trent roars. "You're pregnant too? How could you, Shelby?"

"I'm not pregnant!" I volley back.

"Are you sure?" Trent shoots me the side-eye.

"Very." Mostly. Sure, we'll go with *mostly*. I'm terrible about taking the pill, but I have been on it for so long my ovaries are probably all shriveled up anyway. Plus I should have my period in a few days, which is probably why I have been acting crazier than usual.

"Okay," he says after watching me for a moment.

"Thank you."

"Now, we gotta go," he says with finality.

"What? No." I panic. I panic so hard. Now that Trent knows what our investigative plans are, I'm doomed. This is it. He's going to end it. I just know it. And the worst part is, I'm not even close to ready. But I won't beg or plead. I am just going to apologize, and then I'm going to let him go.

Granny hands me my bag with all of my clothes in it from the cupboard.

"Thanks," I whisper to her.

"It'll be all right, honey," she says. "You just gotta have a little faith."

"Okay," I agree because, really, what else would I say in front of all of these people anyhow, and then I follow Trent out of the room.

We walk through the club and out into the parking lot. As we reach his SUV, I realize that I should have snuck out the back door to the alleyway. Somehow, I must have forgotten about it in the moment.

We climb into his car and he heads toward the I-15. I guess I should be glad he didn't break out the cuffs, and neither did Kane. Kane, who said he needed to bring me in for questioning. I wonder if this means that Trent is driving me to jail . . .

"So . . . ," I hedge. "You wouldn't be driving me to jail now, would you?"

"I should," he mumbles under his breath, but I can still hear him. I see his knuckles whiten as he grips the steering wheel tighter in his hand. I'm surprised the heavy plastic doesn't crack under the pressure.

I know that I'm about to myself. Crack, that is.

Before I know it—or am even remotely emotionally prepared to deal with the fallout—Trent pulls into the driveway and cuts the engine. Without saying a word, he climbs down from his SUV and starts up the walk. I follow him like a death row inmate headed to the electric chair.

When I get to the front of the house, he's standing there holding the door open for me, but his head is tipped down and he won't meet my eyes. Shit. This is worse than I thought. He's not just going to dump me; he's going to tear out my heart on the way out.

I walk past him into the living room and sit down on the couch, which is weird because I'm wearing a string bikini and covered in baby oil and glitter. It makes sitting on the worn leather couch harder than you would think, and I slip around all over the place. I hear the door close and the lock slide into place as I finally get my purchase on the sofa and settle in.

I open my mouth to say something—what, I don't know yet, but I'll figure something out.

Trent holds up a hand to stop me. "Not yet."

"Okay," I whisper. I worry my hands in my lap. Shit, this is bad. But worse, he's holding it off instead of ripping the Band-Aid off for a clean break.

"What do you have to say for yourself?" he asks me after a while.

"I-I-I don't know."

"You don't know what?" he asks quietly, and it's the quietness that has all the air rushing out of my lungs.

"I don't know," I whisper. "I just wanted to help."

"You wanted to help?" he asks incredulously. "Were you helping when you were hooking out of the back of a strip club? That's illegal, by the way."

"I wasn't really hooking."

"You could have fooled me," he says. "Were you helping when you maimed a bunch of people last night?"

"That wasn't me. That was your grandmother," I explain.

"Jesus Christ."

"It's not so bad. I swear."

"How about when you were giving half my unit

semi-chubs and the rest full hard-ons?" he roars.

"Well, yes, that," I huff. "That knowledge is going to make next year's Christmas party really awkward."

"If there even is a next year!" he shouts.

"You really mean that, don't you?" I ask quietly.

"Let's just go to bed," he says with a predatory gleam in his eye. "I'll let you know when I figure it all out."

chapter TWELVE

ANGRY F*CKS AND FIRE FLAPS

"I-I-I don't know if that's such a good idea."

I slowly start backing away from Trent. I know he would never hurt me, but when he's this mad, I can never really be sure if I have finally pushed him so far that he's finally going to snap and strangle me once and for all.

"I think it's a great idea," Trent growls with the confidence of a lion. Only the true king of the jungle can prowl with the knowledge that he is about to get his next meal served up for him on a silver platter.

And by the look in his eyes, that meal is me.

What I didn't realize was that as I was slowly edging away from Trent, he was herding me like a lost baby sheep toward the bedroom. Only, if I were a lost little lamb, Trent wasn't a sheepdog; he was a wolf just waiting for the kill shot.

Unfortunately for me, the hallway in Trent's Spanish-style home—while gorgeous in its Southern California-style—is a straight shot from the living room to his master bedroom. He had backed me through the door and shut it behind me before I realized what had happened. The sound of the lock clicking over makes me jump on the balls of my feet. I know that I'm not trapped, that I could leave at any time, but Trent like this is unpredictable. I'm no longer afraid that he will break up with me right now, but I'm not really sure what else is going on either.

Trent prowls forward and all the air is sucked out of my lungs.

He unbuckles the duty belt from around his hips and places it on the tall dresser next to him. Maybe he thinks I'll shoot him if he leaves it on. That, or maybe he'll be tempted to shoot me.

Trent toes off his boots and reaches down to pull off his white socks. The sight of his bare feet does something to me. He balances effortlessly before straightening back up. If I tried such a move, I would fall on my ass.

He takes a step toward me as he reaches behind his head and grabs the neckline of his T-shirt, pulling up, up, up and over his head, revealing inch by tantalizing inch of his washboard abs.

"Wh-what are you doing?" I can barely choke out the words because my mouth is so dry.

Trent just smirks and keeps on moving toward me. The room seems to be shrinking in on me, but really, I know that it's Trent. His confidence and swagger seem to take up the entire room. Usually I love it—it's a heady feeling—but today it just makes me a little . . . nervous.

"Just getting a little more comfortable."

Trent pops the buttons on his jeans one after another before pushing both his jeans and boxer briefs down around his ankles. His hard cock springs free and I lick my lips. I can't help it!

"See something you like?" he asks me as he steps free of his jeans.

"Maybe," I rasp, my voice low and needy.

"Good," he rumbles as he steps forward and moves into my space. "I may just let you have it."

And then he lowers oh-so-slowly down to press his lips to mine. I know the kiss is coming, and still it blows me away. I sink into him, letting my hands slide up his firm chest as he licks into my mouth. He pulls the ties on my bikini top, and I feel the small triangles and strings tugged free from my body.

And then I'm flying through the air.

Trent has tossed me onto the mattress. I bounce once, twice, before Trent follows me down, covering my body with his. He kisses me again but, this time, grazes his mouth down the side of my neck, nipping every so often.

"I get the glitter and the happy faces now," he tells me.

Trent sucks the spot behind my right ear that drives me crazy as he slowly peels the sticker from my nipple. It stings, but not nearly as bad as it would if he had just ripped it off. He takes my wounded nipple into his mouth and works to soothe the hurt. I can't help but squirm underneath him as he continues to lick and suck and nip at my tender flesh. I close my eyes and let out a moan. I'm so lost in the feel of him.

That is, until Trent rips the other sticker off fast.

I gasp as the sharp sting rips through my nipple, and tears gather in the corners of my eyes. Trent moves his mouth to the new injury and begins the same treatment he administered to the previous side, but it's not enough.

He reaches over and pinches my other nipple, causing me to gasp again, but for a totally different reason. Trent continues to lick and suck on the fresh injury, which doesn't hurt at all anymore. Instead it heats me up from the inside out.

Trent pulls back, letting my breast go in order to focus his efforts on the strings of my slightly scandalous bikini bottoms. He pulls them free from around my hips and tosses them to the bedroom floor without a care in the world.

He slides his fingertip through my slit.

"Fuck, you're so wet for me."

I don't say anything at all because, well, it's true. I arch my back as he skates his fingers around my center, never touching me where I want him the most, yet, at the same time, only stoking the fire higher.

Trent aligns the tip of his cock at my opening. "Do you know how it made me feel to find you in that club today?"

"No." I gasp as he plunges forward, filling me completely. "Yes."

"Which is it?" he asks as he slides his cock out, only to trust it back in again. "Yes or no?"

"No." I raise my knees up around Trent's hips as he towers over me. "I don't know how it made you feel."

"And what was the yes?" He pulls back partway

and circles his hips. I have to roll my bottom lip into my mouth and bite down hard to keep from crying out.

"You feel good," I whisper.

"Fuck, you feel good too," he says with an accented thrust. Trent grips my thigh tight in his palm as he pumps harder.

"Yes."

"I need to know that you won't put yourself in danger anymore." He plunges in again and again, and I'm lost to the sensation.

If he keeps it up, I'm going to come soon. I guess I don't answer fast enough—I mean, what was he talking about, anyway?—because Trent slows his stride. I groan as he backs off.

"Maybe it's best if I don't make promises I can't keep," I pant, and Trent pumps hard again, but only once before pulling back out and circling his hips again.

"I need you, Shelby," he says as plunges in again and again, harder and harder. "I can't let anything happen to you."

"I need you." I rake my nails down his back.

"I can't lose you." He pumps in and out, faster now.

"You won't," I promise, and I hope to God that I can keep it.

"Come for me," he orders as he grips my thigh so tight that I know I'll see bruises tomorrow.

"Trent—"

"Do it." He pumps harder. I'm so very close to the edge of bliss. "Give it to me."

And I do. Trent plunges deep once more before planting himself deep inside me and following me over the edge.

He buries his face in my neck, and we lie there in the silence, our heavy breathing the only sounds. And I can't help but feel like everything is going to change.

Trent's phone trills on the nightstand.

"Who the fuck is texting me on a Saturday morning?"

Last night, after Trent dragged me home from George Washington's strip club, he screwed me into some kind of resolution. Only, I have no idea what it is. Afterward, we snuggled in the dark before drifting into sleep.

Now, his phone is bouncing around on the nightstand. We both should have been able to sleep in, but here we are—awake. He picks up the phone and slides his fingertip across the screen to bring it to life. He's silent as he reads over the message, and I think of the threats I have been receiving. Guilt pings in my stomach, and I realize that I should have told Trent about them, only now it's likely too late.

"Well?" I ask, feeling nervous. "What is it?"

"We've been summoned."

"By whom?" I ask.

"My grandmother," he answers. "And likely yours too."

"Ah." I should have guessed as much. "How much time do we have?"

"About an hour." He sighs.

"I guess I should go hop in the shower and wash

off all this glitter," I say, looking around. There's glitter everywhere. It's going to take me forever to clean all of this up.

"Probably." He sighs again. "I would join you, but I was told being late is not an option."

"I'll be quick," I promise as I hop up and run into the adjoining bathroom.

I wash off and dress in leggings and a V-neck T-shirt in record time. I see Trent saunter into the bathroom with his perfect ass exposed in the bathroom mirror as I comb out my hair. I need out of this room before he reemerges with water droplets dripping down his magnificent chest and his large cock on display—but I digress—so I twist my long hair into a bun on top of my head before leaving the bedroom like my panties are on fire.

I need to be busy with something when he comes out of the bathroom, and I also need my brain to function at least a little bit. So I head for the kitchen and start a pot of coffee. I walk to the entryway and grab my Chucks from their spot by the door and slide them onto my feet while my magical brew percolates.

When I head back into the kitchen, I pour myself a cup and chug it while I stand in front of the coffeepot. I let out an undignified squeal when Trent surprises me. I hadn't heard him walk in.

"Easy there, tiger," he says with a laugh. "Maybe leave some for the rest of us."

Trent comes to stand behind me at the counter. His arms cage me into the small space, and his body heat burns all down my back as he reaches around me for the carafe and tops off my mug.

"The early bird catches the worm," I tell him. Who the hell made my voice all breathy? It's like a red-headed Marilyn Monroe up in here. Can someone say, "Happy birthday, Mr. President"?

"But, baby, you forgot one thing," he says, his lips tickling my ear because he's so close to me.

"What's that?"

"You forgot about the cat that gets the bird." And then that fucker plucks my coffee mug from my hand and drinks it like he owns it. Which he does, because it's his house, but still! And I just stand there stunned as he does it.

"Need any more before we hit the road?" he asks, breaking me free from my stolen-coffee trance.

"No," I answer softly.

"Then we better go. We don't want to be late," he says as he turns my head to look at him. Trent gently presses his lips to mine. His kiss is short and sweet but definitely promises more to come. And suddenly I can't help but wonder if we really have to be on time.

Fortunately, Trent has no such distractions as he places my now empty mug in the sink and takes my hand, leading me out to the car in the driveway.

"We're here, honey." Trent wakes me from the first real sleep I've had since this whole thing began a few days ago.

I must have fallen asleep on the drive down to the senior living center where both of our grandmothers and their friends are living their best life. YOLO!

I blink my eyes and see that we're just pulling into the roundabout in the front of the building. Trent opts to park in the front lot instead of with the valet. They all know him here and that he drives a department vehicle, so they just smile and wave at us as we make our way to the large sliding glass doors.

We sign in at the front desk before heading to the elevator banks. Trent does not take my hand or lead me along with his own hand at the small of my back. In fact, he stands with at least a foot of dead air between us. The distance makes me question last night and this morning all over again. I hate feeling insecure. I try to live my life confident in who I am and where I stand, so walking this knife-edge with Trent has my stomach turning throughout the whole ride to the tenth floor, where our grandmothers live next door to one another.

"I thought you'd never get here," my granny shouts as she flings open the front door to Miss Marla's apartment.

"We're right on time, Granny."

"I told her you're young and in love and maybe found a moment that moved you," Marla explains while shooting Trent and me a nervous side-eye.

"Hi, Nana." Trent kisses her cheek. She's so tiny compared to his large frame, and he treats her like a porcelain doll. It's sweet to see.

"Hello, dear." She smiles at him. "Now, who would like some coffee?"

"Me!" I raise my hand like I'm in school, and Trent raises his eyebrow at me. "I'll just go start a pot or twelve."

I know my way around Marla's apartment like I do my Granny's home not only because the two are usually together but also because the apartments in this building are mirror images of each other. I make quick work of putting together a coffee tray of filled mugs, cream, and sugar.

I carry the tray back into the room, and all the current conversations stop dead in their tracks. By the looks on everyone's faces, they were talking about me. And by the look on Trent's face, he's not happy at all. I cringe and my steps falter for a split second before I rally and paste an overly bright smile on my face as I place the service tray on the coffee table.

"Granny? Coffee?" I ask, breaking the awkward silence. She eyes me like a hawk before answering.

"Yes, Shell. Please." I fix her a cup the way she likes it, which is just the way I like it—with more cream and sugar than needed to give an African elephant diabetes. "Thank you, my darling girl."

"Anytime." I smile.

"Miss Marla?" I ask.

"Yes, please, Shelby. Cream and sugar, but less than the truckload you Whitmore girls put in yours." She winks at me.

"Trent?" I ask him hesitantly. "Coffee?"

"I got it," he says quietly before fixing his own cup. The move only puts more distance between us.

"Okay," I say, sitting back before fixing my own mug when he's done.

The room goes back to being silent again, and I can't stand it. Thank God Trent clearly can't either, because he disrupts the quiet.

"So what did you bring us down here for?" he asks.

"Other than our charming company and sparkling conversation?" Marla asks dryly.

Trent chuckles. "Touché."

"We really needed Shelby, but I like to see you too." Marla winks at him. "We have a pleasure party this afternoon."

"And you need me?" I ask, tilting my head to the side, a little confused.

"Marla's arthritis is acting up again," Granny is quick to explain. "She can't move as fast as she needs to, so we agreed that you should help her. If you can."

"She can," Trent says on a sigh. I can't help but feel like he's a little glad to be rid of me for the day.

"Excellent!" Marla claps her hands together.

"You didn't have plans today?" I turn and ask Trent.

"I should work on the case," he says with a pointed look in my direction. A silent order to butt out. His response makes tears sting the backs of my eyes. He has me all topsy-turvy with his hot and cold routine.

"We have new creams," she says excitedly.

"Creams?" I ask.

"It's all right, dear." Marla pats my hand. I can't help but bite my lip to keep the tears that are welling up in my eyes from falling. "Even the best relationships run a little dry from time to time." I just nod my head. "You know, Trent," my granny says as she wades in. Shit, shit, double-shit, crap. "It's okay if you can't get her motor going. We've got a great nipple cream I can give you for a good price—"

Marla slaps the back of her head. "And by that, she means free.""Uh . . . Thank you." Trent grasps for an appropriate response and clearly comes up empty-fucking-handed. "Just remember, Shell," she says, pulling me back into the worst possible conversation ever. "Nipples only. Not your clit. Not your pussy.""Granny!" I yell, my face turning beet red. "What? You want your flaps afire, then don't mind me!" she huffs.I lean forward and drop my face into my hands, hoping once again that the earth will open up and swallow me whole, when that crazy old lady I call my grandmother fake-coughs into her hand and shouts, "FIRE FLAPS!"

"So . . ." Trent coughs. "I should probably go."

"Don't you dare," I growl-whisper.

"I'm leaving you in the capable hands of our grandmothers," he says, standing up.

"Capable?" I scoff.

"Don't do anything I wouldn't do." He strides to the door. Well, good thing for him that he would investigate the missing women, because that's exactly what I plan on doing too.

chapter THIRTEEN

BACK IN THE TRENCH COATS

"**A**re we really working a pleasure party this afternoon?" I ask the now female-only population.

"Hell no," Granny says.

"We're going back to George Washington's," Marla finishes.

"Are we sure that's a good idea?" I ask. "I mean, Trent was pretty pissed, and we did get rolled by the cops last night."

"Yeah, but they won't be back today because they know it was just a bunch of meddling old ladies," Granny adds.

"True enough," I agree.

"Now, who wants a cookie?" Marla asks, producing a tin of fancy cookies in little paper cups. And I'm not gonna lie, I could really use a cookie right now.

"I do!" I raise my hand again, and she passes me the tin.

"Thank you." I smile brightly at her. I love her like my own granny.

"I thought you could use some." She winks at me. "Now, let's review our case notes."

"What case notes?" I ask.

"These," Granny says as she pulls a ridiculously thick manila folder from her granny purse on the floor, "are our case notes. You didn't think we weren't paying attention, now did you?"

"Of course I knew you were paying attention," I say, shooting her the side-eye. The last thing I want is to make my granny feel undervalued. For one, she's amazing, and two, she'd probably whoop my ass. "I just didn't know you were taking notes."

"Not by hand, dear," Marla adds. "Arthritis is hell on my dictation skills, but those voice-recording apps are amazing."

"Really?" I ask incredulously.

I know I'm sitting here stunned with my mouth hanging open, but I can't help it. A month ago, Granny was accidentally downloading free porn from all over the internet and unable to get her DVR to record *Masterpiece Theatre* and old reruns of *The Lawrence Welk Show,* and now she's using voice-recorder apps to crack a homicide case wide open. I just can't believe it.

"You better believe it," Granny replies to my thoughts.

"I don't know whether to be impressed or horrified," I admit.

"In this case," Marla says sweetly, "go with impressed."

"Yeah, definitely be impressed," Granny says with

a laugh. "We're a couple of octogenarian badasses. No one ever expects it to be the old people."

"Trust me, after Ernie," I say softly, "I never underestimate the elderly."

"That's true," Granny agrees. "He was a real wolf in old man's clothing."

"So, back to your notes," I say, circling us back. "You can't possibly have gotten all of that from our brief moments in the back room."

"No. I AirDropped a bunch of it from Trent's home computer when he wasn't looking," Marla says with not even a teensy bit of remorse in her voice.

"Marla!" I shout.

"What? He's my grandson." She shrugs her shoulder.

"That doesn't mean you can hack his files."

"I'm pretty sure it does," she answers.

I'm not really sure how to combat those arguments, and really, is it my place, anyway? I'm not her actual grandchild; Trent is, so actually, he should be responsible for her shit, even if it is hacking police department files. I've got my hands full enough with my own hell-raising grandmother.

"So, show me what you've got," I concede.

"Well, from what we can tell, none of the people who darkened your door the other night were killers," Marla says.

"I agree."

"But where things get interesting is at the appearance of the mob boss," Granny says.

"He certainly seemed to know who you are," Marla adds. "Had you ever met him before?"

"No, never." I shake my head.

"He must have been watching you," Granny says, and I can't help but agree.

"No," Marla says as she wades in. "He had to have been watching Trent."

My stomach drops straight through the floor. I know without a doubt that she's right. He had to have been following Trent or having Trent followed for a while. I can't help but wonder what a man like that would want with Trent. Whatever it is, it can't be good.

"But I also don't think he's the killer," Marla says hesitantly. "But that can't be right, right?"

"I agree." I smile at her. "I don't think he's kidnapping and killing prostitutes, because that would mean less money for him if he dabbles in various criminal pursuits like I believe he does."

"That makes sense," Granny agrees. "Why kill some hookers if you're pedaling flesh just like it?"

"They could be competition," I suggest.

"No, he seems more like the kind to actually earn the spot as top dog, not cheat to achieve it, as ludicrous as it is to suggest he's an honest criminal."

"No," Granny says, championing Marla's theory. "If he wanted Trent and Shelby out of the way, he would have just killed them long ago."

"I agree," I say. "It's a disturbing thought to think about a mob boss wanting you dead, but I agree."

"So where does that leave us?" Marla asks.

"As much as I know I shouldn't ask, what was in Trent's files?"

"Just bits and pieces about Christina and Stacy," Marla informs us.

"Was there anything connecting them?" I ask. "Maybe a common enemy or john?"

"No." Marla shakes her head. "We even double-checked with Daisy's friend Alyssa. They never booked the same guy."

"Damn. Now what do we do?" I ask.

"We go back to George's, of course." Marla pats my cheek.

Of fucking course.

We're going back to the club.

To fake-hook.

Yay!

That was my fake cheer.

"Uh . . . what's that?" I ask as I stare at a couple of tiny scraps of electric-blue fabric and what has to be dental floss. "Have you gone to the dentist recently?"

"No," Granny says with a laugh. "Why?"

"I was just wondering where the dental floss came from." I still stare at the blue fabric in my hand like a car crash on the freeway. You just can't help but look at it as you drive by.

"No." She laughs. "I bought that for you on one of those Facebook stores. I'm surprised it got here so fast since it came from China."

"That explains why it's so small," I mumble as I glare at the bathing suit.

"It does look a bit small," Marla says.

"She'll be fine," Granny says with a confidence I

do not feel. "She's just going to take it off anyway."

"Maybe."

"Um . . ." I'm clearly incapable of thought right now.

"Anyway," she says. "Suit up, soldier!"

"Okay." I comply because, really, what else am I supposed to do here? I'm at a total loss. A catastrophic loss.

"Daisy's not here." Marla frets while I begin to remove my clothes. "Do you have any pasties?"

"Uh . . . no. I don't." Well, shit. Not that seeing my nipples is going to be a big deal after seeing all of me in this bikini, if we can even call it that.

"That's all right," she reassures me. "I picked up some Forever stamps at the grocery store this morning, and they're still in my pocketbook. What luck, right?"

"Yeah," I lie. "What luck."

I pull the G-string bottoms up my legs, and the string just slips into my crack as if I never had a choice in the matter. I'm not really sure how I feel about this. I adjust it so my downtown is covered as much as humanly possible while Marla peels off two of the tiniest little stamps ever, with waving American flags on them. It seems a little unpatriotic to put them on my nipples, but at this point, I'm in too deep.

I place them over my pink nips and then tie the top around my body and behind my neck. I try my best to adjust the girls, but every time I get one holstered, the other one pops out. It's at this moment that I realize I'm humming "Pop! Goes the Weasel." Fuck my life.

I—*finally*—manage to get the girls wrangled, and they look like they may stay put for the time being. I'm a little sweaty because that was kind of a workout and I don't fucking jog, ever, so I'm a little out of shape, but in a lovable way. When I turn around, I see Granny happily engrossed in her task of decorating the room with Tasers and a plethora of giant dildos just like Big Thunder, but glittery and in every color.

"Jesus Christ, are they multiplying like rabbits now?" I ask. I didn't mean to, really, but I was so surprised that the words just kind of fell out of my mouth.

"Don't you take the Lord's name in vain, young lady!" Granny snaps at me. "And besides, we didn't want you to be caught unawares again."

She's so earnest in her wanting to protect me, to help me, even a little, that I can't be mad at her. "Thank you."

She hugs me fiercely. "Anything for my girl," she whispers in my ear.

There's a knock at the door.

Granny and Marla jump into their hiding spaces as quickly as two eighty-year-olds, one with a trick hip, can. At first, they both hurried to the same spot and silently waged a war before deciding they would both find new hiding spots. I have to bite my lip to keep from laughing.

"Come in," I call out once they're both hidden. I'm just reaching for the stereo, the cool black plastic and metal barely within reach of my fingertips, when the door opens and the sound of a voice stops me in my tracks.

"You've got to be fucking kidding me."

chapter FOURTEEN

HANDCUFFS AND HARD-ONS

"Yes!" I cry out. My voice is muffled by the cushions of the sofa as I'm bent over and handcuffed behind my back. "Harder."

You would think that after the night before and then the way Trent stormed in on me in the private back room at George's, we wouldn't be here in this position—which is bent over the arm of the couch with my legs spread wide while Trent fucks me from behind. But truthfully, this was our only option.

Let me explain . . .

I was just about to turn on the stereo in the private room, and Granny and Marla were in their hiding spots, when the door to the room banged open and the jig was up.

"You've got to be fucking kidding me," Trent groaned in more of a how-is-this-my-life kind of way and less of a I-am-going-to-throttle-you kind of way. But then again, he had to have known there were witnesses in the room.

"You can come out, ladies," I sighed, and our grandmothers pushed out from wherever they were hiding.

"Jesus Christ!" he roared. "Are there more dildos or Tasers in here?"

"Um . . ." I worried he was going to blow a fuse. I took another look around the room and tried to see it through his eyes. There really was a lot of . . . um . . . *paraphernalia* scattered around the room. They didn't even try to hide most of it. "Well . . ."

"It's a toss-up." Granny shrugged her slim shoulders unrepentantly. "I bought the Tasers and Marla bought the dildos."

"No!" Marla jumped in, obviously not willing to let her best friend fall on her sword for her. "I think I bought the Tasers and you bought the dildos."

Trent rolled his eyes. "Are they even legal?"

"Who's really to decide what is and isn't legal?" Marla asked cautiously.

"Oh, I don't know," Trent roared. "How about the fucking law?"

"Don't you snap at me, mister," Marla clapped back, and my eyes went wide.

"You're right," he sighed. "I'm sorry."

"Apology accepted."

"Now you two collect your . . . *weapons* . . . and go home," he commanded softly.

Granny looked at me with deep concern in her eyes for all to see. She was asking me an honest question, and I answered her with the same honesty.

"I'll be fine," I told her.

They made their way around the room—well, as quickly as three out of four functioning hips could go—collecting their various items from their hiding spots and stuffing them into their oversized granny bags. Marla stopped on her way out to kiss Trent on the cheek, and he quickly folded his tall frame over so she could reach him. This was one of the things that made me love him so much. Before walking out the door, Granny stopped and turned back to look at me one more time. I smiled and nodded to her, and then she turned around and followed in Marla's footsteps.

"Are you out of your goddamn mind?" Trent roared. I opened my mouth to answer him, but he stopped me before I could. "No, don't answer that."

"Trent?"

"I have half a mind to cuff you and perp-walk you out of here," Trent said when the door snicked closed behind our grandmothers.

"Ha ha ha," I laughed nervously. "You wouldn't . . ."

"Don't tempt me."

I edged my way toward the door. I thought that if I could juke left and distract him, I could make it to the door. I should have kicked off these ridiculous heels first because Trent caught up with me faster than I was willing to admit, and one of my boobs popped out of the tiny bikini top and was now swinging in the breeze while Trent closed the cuffs over my wrists behind my back.

"Is this all your stuff?" Trent asked as he held up my oversized Coach tote with the pink and purple flowers painted on the side.

"Yes."

And then he tossed my very girlie bag over his shoulder and adjusted my boob. I questioned him with a raised eyebrow.

"I would hate to have to shoot anyone who looks at your breasts, babe." He just shrugged when I rolled my eyes.

Trent walked me out of the building and carefully loaded me into the front seat of his SUV and buckled my belt for me before tossing my stuff into the back seat. And then he drove straight home.

"I need some help here, Shell," he said when the front door clicked closed behind us.

"How so?" I asked hesitantly.

"I'm not real sure whether I should wring your neck for being so reckless or fuck the shit out of you and just be glad that you're still alive."

"I definitely think you should go with door number two," I said before my brain had a chance to catch up with the words that fell out. Maybe Trent didn't hear me? But one look at the sexy smolder he was unleashing on me had the room temperatures rising and my panties incinerating.

I stood there with my hands cuffed behind my back, wearing nothing but a ridiculous bikini my grandmother bought off of Facebook, and I was incredibly aroused. Trent took deliberate steps toward me. I rolled my bottom lip between my teeth as I watched him prowl closer with his intent clear and his eyes hungry.

When he reached for me, I went willingly, letting myself fall into his arms knowing he would catch me. And he did. Trent lifted my hair from my neck and nipped at the juncture of my neck and my shoulder, making me moan. He pulled at the strings on the electric-blue bikini top and tossed the itsy-bitsy pieces to the side. He looked at me standing there in nothing but the G-string bottoms, my red hair flowing like a wild halo all around me, and smirked. I was sure I looked like I should be sliding across the hood of a car in a classic-rock music video.

"Nice flags," he said with a chuckle. "It's very patriotic of you, and as a Ranger, I am the ultimate patriot."

"You're a regular Mel Gibson," I drolled.

"That I am, baby," his voice, deepened with his arousal, rumbled. "Now turn around."

I did as instructed and turned around facing away from him. Trent slowly guided me forward to lean over the arm of the couch, and because my hands were still cuffed behind my back, I had to trust him not to let me fall, and that only turned me on more.

Once I was balanced over the arm of the sofa, Trent kicked my feet farther apart, widening my stance so he could easily slip between my legs. I heard the zipper of his jeans being pulled down, our breathing the only other sounds in the room. When Trent hooked a finger in the string of my bottoms, if you could call them that, and pulled the fabric to the side, I realized how wet I really was.

He positioned his hard length at my opening and plunged in. Trent gripped my hips tight in his hands as he slid out and thrust back in, again and again.

And now here I am, after a pretty shitty day, about two seconds from coming like I never have before.

"Yes!" I cry out. My voice is muffled by the cushions of the sofa as I'm bent over and handcuffed behind my back. "Harder."

"I think you're forgetting who is in charge here, sweetheart," he says as he pounds unrelentingly into my body, effectively giving me what I asked for.

I couldn't hold back the tidal wave that is about to roll over me and swoop me under its crashing waves even if I tried. I press my cheek into the soft material of the sofa, letting that ground me as the orgasm of a lifetime erupts and I cry out.

Trent plunges into my depths again and again before planting himself deep and calling out my name and collapsing over me on the arm of the sofa. I feel the soft cotton of his T-shirt across my back, and the image of him fully clothed while I'm not heats me up all over again.

This Trent was a little rough and wild, and I liked it more than I ever thought I could.

He pulls out as he stands back up, and I miss the connection. I feel him reach into his front pocket for something. I realize it's the handcuff key when I feel the metal bracelets give way one by one. I suck in a breath as I become aware of the soreness in my muscles. Trent rubs one arm first and then the other before placing my palms flat on the sofa cushion over my head.

"Don't move," he commands softly.

I do as he says and I hear him leave the room. I let my eyes fall closed, and my breathing slowly returns to normal. I am beyond relaxed, my bones are basically pudding, so I don't hear his light footfalls as he reenters the room. But my eyes flash open when the rough terry cloth of a warm washcloth skates over my tender flesh.

"Relax," Trent orders as he gently cleans me up. "I need to do this."

"You need to give me a sponge bath?" I quip.

"No, I need to take care of you after I was so rough with you." His answer speaks volumes as to how he feels about me and our relationship and the complicated situation we've found ourselves in.

"Okay," I tell him softly.

When Trent is done, he pads back to the hall bath, where he tosses the washcloth through the door. I hear it land in the sink before he turns around and walks back to where I am still slumped over the arm of the couch.

He scoops me up in his arms and carries me down the hall to his bedroom as if I am the most important thing in his world. And I'm just starting to believe that I may be.

Trent places me on the bed before making quick work of removing his clothes. This time isn't for show but to join me skin to skin in this bed. He peels the G-string from my body and tosses it over his shoulder. Trent kneels between my thighs and looks down at me.

"You know I'm never going to be able to walk into a post office now without a stiffy, right?" he asks me as he eyes my makeshift pasties. I start to peel one off but he stops me. "No, allow me."

I let my hands drop back to the bed as he peels the stamps off of my nipples and places them on the night-stand. Trent kisses me deeply, and I let myself sink into that, into him, and I feel nothing but us. He swipes his finger through my slit before sliding it in deep. I wiggle against him, trying for more.

"Christ, you're wet for me."

Trent stretches out over me, slowly sliding his cock through my wetness and driving my reviving arousal higher. He pushes in gently. This time couldn't be more different than before. This is tender and sweet, and sexy but also loving. Trent is loving me quietly into the night, and then, like a sailboat in the bay, we ride over the wave and come together.

Trent pulls out and rolls over, pulling me into him as he holds me tightly to his chest. He presses his face into my hair and breathes in deeply.

"Is it too much to ask that you stop doing stupid shit?" he asks me, but by the tone of his voice, he has already come to the conclusion that it's a lost cause.

"Well, you can ask, but it's highly unlikely."

"No, shit," he drolls.

"Just . . . try a little harder . . . for me," he says softly. "I'd miss you if you were dead."

That's possibly the closest I will ever get to a true admission of love from Trent, and I respond to it the only way I can. I will try a little harder not to get killed. "Okay."

"Okay?" he asks, sounding as if he's unsure of what he heard.

"Yes," I confirm. "Okay, I will try very hard not to get killed."

Trent breathes out a sigh of obvious relief. "I'll take it."

And then he pulls me tighter to him and his breathing slows. Trent found sleep. I listen to his heartbeat next to my ear and wonder how I'm ever going to keep all the promises I have made to all the people I love.

And, most of all, not get killed.

Famous last words, right?

chapter FIFTEEN

DEAD MEAT

I blink my eyes open as the late-morning sun filters through the curtains. Trent is curled around my body. Sometime in the middle of the night last night, we found our way back to each other through the fog of this investigation.

We may not have all the answers, but at least now I am confident that together we might find them. Trent knows I have to help Daisy whether he wants me to or not. Just like I know he will worry about me until this is over.

My phone buzzes on the nightstand. Trent is still asleep, so I carefully wiggle my way out of his hold so that I can roll over and grab my phone. The message is from my granny, so I slide my finger across the cool glass to unlock the phone.

GRANNY: Coffee at 11.

ME: Where?

GRANNY: The regular place, and lose the tail.

I roll my eyes. She must be watching those old gangster movies on the old movie channel again. We really should really do a better job of monitoring what she's watching. Dad says she's fine, but I know she's watching soft porn on my streaming accounts. I can't prove it because she covers her tracks so well, but I know she's doing it.

And she knows that I know.

ME: We worked it out.

GRANNY: With his penis.

I laugh and cough and choke all at the same time. Only Granny would see right through everything and cut the bullshit. Trent rolls over and opens his eyes.

"Everything okay, babe?" he asks me.

"Yeah." I smile. "Granny is just being herself, like always."

ME: I'm not acknowledging that comment.

GRANNY: See you at coffee.

ME: See you.

Trent pauses before acknowledging my comment,

and as the air in the room thickens, I can't help but wonder if maybe we didn't resolve things as much as I thought we did. Well, shit.

"So you're meeting the old girls today?"

"Yeah," I answer.

"Be safe," Trent says as he rolls me onto my back before covering my body.

"I will," I breathe, but honestly, when I feel his cock slide against my center, all thoughts of safety fly right out of my brain.

"Stick together and don't separate," he says as he slides deep inside me.

"Okay," I whisper.

"And any situation that feels wrong, get out of it as fast as you can and call me." He slowly glides in and out over my center, managing to hit all the high points and have a clear conversation.

"Okay." As Trent moves over me and inside me, I can't manage to think about anything at all.

"Thank you," he says as he presses his forehead to mine and lets go of the tight chains he'd held on his control.

And together we fall over the edge.

It would only be a little later that I wished I had paid more attention to Trent's warnings, but hey, hindsight is twenty-twenty.

"Here's your white chocolate mocha and your bagel," the girl behind the counter says as she hands me my goods.

"Thank you."

I take my bounty of carbs and sugar over to a secluded table in the back. I'm the first one here, so I get to choose the table. I figure they will appreciate this one since Granny must have called this clandestine meeting for a reason.

I wave as Granny and Marla saunter in like the octogenarian badasses that they are. They smile at me before stepping up to the counter to order their coffees and treats. Here's hoping they stick to the menu this time. We haven't been here for a while because we were strongly warned last time that if they brought in hooch hidden in the granny purses one more time, we would be banned.

I let out a sigh. Life with these two is never boring, but for the most part, it's a blast. I hope that when I'm a grandmother, I'm living my best life too—hashtag and all.

They settle into the seats around the table, and we all dig into our treats.

"Where is Daisy?" I ask.

"I don't know," Granny says as her eyebrows pull low over her eyes. Something isn't right. "She's the one who sounded the alarm on the phone tree this morning."

Shit. I hope she's okay. We are no closer to finding the killer than we were a week ago. Now that Daisy is in the wind, I can't help but wonder if she's really okay or if she's the next victim. Although, that would be breaking pattern. Daisy is no longer a prostitute and hasn't been for some time. In fact, she took my old job at the home improvement store, in the custom kitchens and bath department, and she's killing it.

"Do you think she's all right?" I have to voice the thoughts we're all thinking. The ones that have the bagel churning in my stomach.

"Daisy's a smart girl," Marla says after some thought. "She'll be all right."

"Yeah," I echo her thoughts, but I'm not really sure I feel as confident as I sound.

"Let's give her time to get here before we really panic," Granny says wisely, but in my head, I'm dialing Trent's number right now. But I don't. I pick up my paper cup and take a sip.

"So, where do we go from here?" Granny asks just as the front door to the coffee shop swings open with a clang and Daisy storms in.

"It's about time you got here!" Granny says.

"We were worried, darling girl," Marla says to Daisy.

She takes a deep breath before responding. "I know. I'm sorry I made you all worry."

"That's all right," Granny says. "Now what kept you so long?"

And then Daisy says all the words that change the rules of the game. "Alyssa is gone."

"What?" I gasp.

"I went to hang out with her last night and she wasn't home," Daisy explains.

"Could she have just been out?" Marla asks.

"I thought about that." She nods her head. "So I went back this morning, and she still wasn't there."

"Could she have been with a gentleman?" Granny

asks.

"I thought about that too, so I called her while I was standing outside her apartment door," she says. "I pulled my phone out of my substantial cleavage and dialed her number, and I heard it ring on the other side of the door before it went to voicemail. Now, my girl always answers her phone. So I yelled her name real loud and made the neighbors mad."

"Piss on them," Granny says.

"True dat." Daisy holds up her fist to Granny for a knuckle bump. "So I told them to shut up and then I called her phone again. And again I heard it ring."

"So then what did you do?" I ask.

"I went and got the super. I told him we had an emergency in Alyssa's apartment, so I had him unlock the door for me."

"And?" we all shout at the same time.

"And her phone was there, but Alyssa wasn't."

"Maybe she left it behind on accident?" I ask. "I do that all the time."

"Alyssa is a working girl and a boss bee all rolled into one," Daisy explains. "She never leaves home without her phone. When I say Alyssa is gone, she's gone."

I was afraid she was going to say that.

"So what do we do now?" I ask.

"I think we have to split up," Daisy says.

"I'm not so su—" I start to say.

"I think that's a good idea," Marla agrees.

"I'll scope out Alyssa's territory and talk to her girls," Daisy says. "They all know me and will talk to me."

"Okay," Granny says. "Maybe Marla and I should go back to her apartment and see if she shows?"

"That's a great idea. The super gave me a spare key so I could get back in." Daisy hands them the silver key. The same generic type we cut fifty times a day at the home improvement store.

"Shell, you go back to George's," Granny tells me. "Nothing has been happening there, and George will be there if anything happens."

"Are you sure?" I ask.

"Of course," she answers me. "You'll be fine."

"Famous last words," I mumble.

"Don't be such a Debbie Downer," she chastises me.

"You're right," I say as I gather up my trash. "Fortunately, I keep my fake-hooker gear in my bag now."

"That's my girl," Marla cheers, and I can't help but laugh.

"Call Trent if anything goes wrong," I tell them. "He's not on board, but he's here to help. And check in regularly."

"Roger Dodger." Daisy salutes, and I smile at her as I sling my bag over my shoulder and head out the door.

I unlock the doors with my key fob on my little white SUV and climb in, tossing my bag onto the passenger seat. My phone is still on vibrate from this morning, so I don't hear it ring in my bag. Too bad, because answering that call might have saved me from having a few years being scared off my life.

I pull into the parking lot at George's and look around. There are far more cars here on a Sunday afternoon than I ever would have thought imaginable. I grab my bag, step out of the car, and head into the club. I wave to a couple of girls I've met a few times here on my way to the back room. As far as they know, I'm one of Alyssa's girls and she has a deal going with George. Everyone here knows Alyssa since she manages a lot of the girls in the area.

I put my bag on the counter in the back room and take off my clothes. I fold them up and tuck them into my bag before stowing it in a cabinet. I slip on a pair of red satin panties and buckle up a matching corset with black lace ruffles and a big black satin bow along the top. It kind of reminds me of an old-school cancan dancer.

I slip on my black patent leather heels and walk over to the door to flip the light on before heading back into the center of the room. I look at the couch with moderate disgust. I can imagine the ghosts of all the jizz that has touched that sofa and shudder. I hope I don't have to wait long because I do not want to sit down there.

Fortunately, I don't have to wait at all because there is a knock at the door.

"Come in," I call out in my sexy voice as I sashay on my heels over to the stereo to turn it on. I hear the door click open and then snick closed, but I don't hear anything else. The man must be light on his feet. I'm just about to turn around when something crashes over my head. He must have been closer than I had thought.

My last thoughts are that I am probably going to die just like Christina and Stacy, and then everything goes black.

I'm dead meat. Literally. Dead. Meat.

Last month, when Trent and I started up for real after all of our false starts at the beginning of our relationship, I promised him I wouldn't do anything crazy. I wouldn't go off half-cocked. And most importantly, I wouldn't follow our grandmothers down the crazy-assed rabbit hole of Granny Grabbers and Dangerous Dames. And I should have listened.

I blink my eyes again, trying to clear them, but everything is blurry. I let out a groan as the polka band in my head keeps clogging away. I try to move but I can't. I'm handcuffed to something cold . . . metal, maybe? Fuck, I really am going to die.

"Oh, good, you're awake," the voice of a definite blast from my past rings out through the fog. No, it can't be. He wouldn't do this. He wouldn't kill me.

"No." I cough and vomit next to me.

"That's disgusting, Shelby," James gripes. "Let's show a little decorum, shall we?"

"Why?" I ask, feeling my anger grow by the minute. "You're just going to kill me anyway, so I'll puke when I feel like it. Thank you very much."

"Kill you?" he says, sounding shocked. "Why would I kill you?"

"Well, you kidnapped me and handcuffed me to . . . where am I, anyway? It's too dark in here to see," I say, losing my train of thought. Whatever hit me over the head did me dirty.

"My apologies," my ex-boyfriend says as he flicks on some lights. "It's a bathroom sink."

As it turned out, we had allegedly agreed that I wouldn't go on any more capers with my friend Daisy, the retired hooker, and our grandmothers. Sophia was out; she was at some big, fancy figure-skating competition in Chicago. Thank God. Her dad wouldn't just shit a brick if he caught her tangled up in this mess; he'd shit the whole White House. I laugh out loud. That was a good one.

"What's so funny?" James snaps.

"Nothing," I mumble. Maybe it wasn't so funny after all.

"I'm not going to kill you, Shelby," he says and he sounds earnest.

"Then why kidnap me?" I ask.

"Kidnap is such a dirty word."

"James—"

He sighs. "I needed you away from the cop."

"Trent?" I ask.

"If the bloody ape's name is Trent, then yes," he answers. Yeah, that sounds like how James would describe Trent. The difference between the two of them is glaringly obvious. What could I have ever seen in someone like James, anyway?

"What does Trent have to do with anything?" I ask.

"I've been trying to get to you for months now," he says. "He's blocked my every move."

Well, that's news.

"Why?" I ask. I can't see any reason why he would want to get a hold of me.

"Because I want you back!" he shouts, losing his

patience, and I cringe. This is the James I know. This James is dangerous, and I have to tread lightly.

"Why would you want me back?" I ask cautiously. "What about Bella?"

"What about Bella?" he roars just before he slaps the shit out of me.

James always struck out with words or with fists when he didn't get his way. Trent would never hit me.

"I thought you were happy with her, James."

"She's not you," he says, caressing the cheek he had just struck. James could also flip on a dime.

"But I'm with someone else," I tell him, something we both already know.

"Not for long," he grumbles.

"No, James. Trent and I are together for the long haul," I tell him. "Maybe forever."

"Don't be ridiculous, Shelby. I'm tired of your tantrums." James rolls his eyes at me. Anytime I disagreed with him, I was behaving irrationally or childishly. Never could I have had honest feelings that should've been taken into account. So I say the only thing he can't combat or brush away.

"I'm in love with Trent, James. Not you."

"I can't deal with you when you're being this unreasonable!" He throws his hands over his head before heading for the door.

"Wh-where are you going?" I ask. I hate the stutter in my voice. I hate the fear and anxiety that only James can put there.

"I'm trying to be fair, Shelby." He sighs. "I brought your bag and your things. I could take care of you if you'll let me. Or you can sit here dressed like a common whore in a motel bathroom. It's your choice." He shrugs like it's no big deal.

"So my only choice is to go with you and do what you say or stay chained to a motel sink in my underwear?" I ask for clarification.

"Yes. Like I said, you decide. I'll be back in a little bit." And then he walks out of the little bathroom and into the room. I hear the main door click closed behind him.

As much as Trent was right, I shouldn't have started investigating the disappearance of Christina and Stacy. I agreed with him when he said we weren't cops. We didn't know what we were doing. I mean, what kind of trouble could two widowed senior citizens, a retired hooker, and an obituaries columnist for the local paper get into? I mean, really. Lightning doesn't strike twice. It doesn't, right?

And Trent and I had worked out some kinks. He yelled less. I pretended to listen more. And when I didn't, he used his handsome mouth in better ways than yelling, if you catch my drift. We were officially in the love bubble. The honeymoon stage. I wasn't ready to rock the boat for just anything all willy-nilly.

But Daisy, my sweet, fabulous, eccentrically dressed best friend, had a problem and she came to me for help . . . advice . . . I don't really know what. All I know is that that led me to today, as I sit, handcuffed to the pipes of a bathroom sink in a filthy motel just this side of Mexico, dressed like a cheap hooker. Yep, I'm in trouble, folks. Just like I said . . . Dead. Meat.

I close my eyes and let out a tired sigh. I have no idea how long I'm going to be here, and this corset is starting to cut off my air supply. Or maybe that's my mounting panic. I would say that James wouldn't keep me chained up in this bathroom forever, but then I would be lying to myself. The truth is that James is kind of a mean son of a bitch and he always has been.

I should have seen the writing on the wall when we started dating and he asked me to change . . . well . . . everything about me. Unfortunately, I wasted three years of my life on him, changed a bunch of myself that I shouldn't have, and lost a lot of self-respect and confidence, all before I caught him banging my best friend. Needless to say, we're not friends anymore.

That also doesn't mean that I want him back. I was pretty happy with the slow progression of my relationship with Trent before James's dumbass trotted back into my life in his golf slacks and loafers. He says he's giving me a choice, but he's not. This is the same old abusive bullshit he has always been dishing out.

I need to get out of here.

I look around. There's no phone in the bathroom, and I am handcuffed to exposed pipes below a sink. The No Smoking sign is in Spanish. The floral linoleum under my ass is scuffed and stained and looks like the stuff my parents had in their kitchen, from the '80s, before they remodeled last year.

I pull on the cuffs, but . . . nothing. Fuck! Where the hell did James get a pair of real handcuffs? Actually, I don't want to know. I rattle them on the pipes, but it just makes my wrists raw as the bracelets scrape my skin.

I need something to pick this lock. Granny once had us watch a YouTube video on lock picking. This guy's whole channel was devoted to picking locks with different everyday items. I just have to find one, and then I could probably do it. Although, picking the lock on a door is a lot easier than picking the lock on police-issued cuffs.

I look around. Damn that tidy motherfucker! Not that I'm surprised. He used to always criticize my lack of organization. But right now, I could really use a dental floss pick or a bobby pin or something. Wait! I have a couple of bobby pins in my hair.

While my mane is long and heavy, it also has a natural curl that has a mind of its own. I pinned some pieces back from my face to keep them from falling in my eyes and to get some volume for my faux hooker gig this afternoon. Now I just have to get one out without dropping it.

I lean forward, trying to angle my head toward my restrained hands, and *ping*! I must have moved too quickly in my excitement and overestimated my trajectory because I bounced my forehead off of the galvanized metal pipe that my hands are bound to.

"Goddammit!" I grumble. My head was already pounding, but that's going to leave a mark.

I shake off the stars that are circling and the birds that are tweeting around my head and lean in again. It takes a couple of tries because my fingers are on pins and needles from being cuffed for however long, but I manage to grab a bobby pin from my hair and pinch it in my fingertips. I lean in again and grab the hairpin in my mouth to adjust the grip in my hand as I try to feed it into the keyhole on the cuff.

Just as I had thought, the cuff is a tight fit for the

pin and even harder to pick. Great for the crime-fighting cops, not so great for me while I try to escape the evil clutches of my crazy-ass ex. I feel the tears building up inside of me like a tidal wave. My nose stings. I can't get a purchase on this stupid bobby pin, and I can't feel anything but a burning sensation in my fingers. If I don't get this lock popped before James gets back, I'm never getting out of here.

I hear the lock on the door click open. Shit, shit, motherfucking shit! I'm stuck. I'm screwed.

"Shelby?" Trent's voice calls out. "Shelby, where are you?"

"I'm in here," I call out.

Trent races into the bathroom with Kane and several other police officers behind him. I don't care that I'm in my underwear or that my hair is a mess. I don't care that my makeup is smeared from crying. I just care that Trent is here.

"Hang tight, honey," he says softly. "We just have to get some pictures."

"No." I pant. I don't want pictures. I want out of here. "It wasn't the killer. It was James." Trent and Kane's entire demeanor changes with the mention of that one name.

"I'll fucking kill him," Trent growls.

"Me first," Kane says.

"Just get me out of here," I plead.

Kane produces a set of keys from his pocket and unlocks the cuffs, letting me tumble into Trent's waiting arms.

"I was so scared," I admit. "How did you find me?"

"I put a tracker in your purse."

"I'm pretty sure that's not legal," I mumble into the front of his shirt.

"Who cares?" He shrugs. "You're alive."

"Good point," I agree.

"Sorry it took so long," Kane says. "We had another body."

"Oh no. Stacy?" I ask.

"Yeah," Trent says. "I thought you would be safe at the club. I didn't realize this time you would be alone."

"It was a last-minute change of plans," I tell them.

"Why?" Kane and Trent ask at the same time.

"Alyssa is missing."

"What?" they both shout.

"Daisy says she's missing."

"Shit," Trent bites out as Kane pulls his phone from his pocket and makes a call.

chapter SIXTEEN

FUNERALS AND YOGA OR A TYPICAL TUESDAY

One week later . . .

"So does anyone look suspicious?" Granny stage-whispers from beside me. "I left my glasses at home and now I can't see shit."

"Well, why did you leave them at home?" I ask.

"I was in a hurry. I didn't think Stacy's funeral would happen so fast," she explains.

"It's been a week," I remind her. "Plus, it was pretty cut and dried, from what I've heard." Which was absolutely nothing. Trent has been pretty tight-lipped ever since I was kidnapped. It doesn't help matters that my douchey ex is in the wind.

I have been on edge the entire week, afraid that James would pop out of some corner and exact his own punishment again. I can't ask Trent about the case because, while Trent is no longer keeping me from helping Daisy look into the deaths of her friends, he is definitely pissed that James popped out of the abyss to nab me. I had spent the last couple of months thinking that he had finally lost interest in me, but it turns out Trent has been keeping the ghosts of my past at bay—silently protecting me from dangers I didn't know were hiding in the shadows.

But enough is enough. I can't live like that. And I won't be afraid of my own shadow any longer. *Mama didn't raise no chickens here*. So it's back in the saddle again. And by "back in the saddle," I mean back to the funeral home to cover another funeral. Unfortunately, the funeral is that of Daisy's friend Stacy.

Exactly one week ago, Stacy's body had been found abandoned in her car in a parking lot in Balboa Park. She was sitting in the driver's seat with her eyes closed and a knife in her belly—just as Christina had been. The rest of the details were murky. Well, to me they were. Trent is no longer in a sharing mood. That likely has something to do with the fact that I was kidnapped at the same time that the call went out that the body had been found. It took hours for the police to find me in a pay-by-the-hour motel down by the border crossing into Tijuana.

My ex-boyfriend, James, had apparently gotten a little desperate after Trent had thrown up roadblock after roadblock when he tried to see me or speak to me. In all fairness, the last time Trent had seen James with me was when he roughed me up in a back hallway at the home improvement store I used to work at. That probably wouldn't encourage confidence in anyone, least of all the man who wants to be in my life now. So when James saw an opening, meaning me all alone in the private back room at a strip club, he took it by bashing me over the head and spiriting me away to said sketchy motel. Again, he does not encourage confidence.

So here we are now, a week later, wondering when the other shoe is going to drop. I would love to say all is well and magical in the greater San Diego area, but according to the murdered prostitutes and the gnawing pit in my stomach, it is anything but.

"Well . . ." Granny reminds me that she had asked a question, and I didn't answer. Life is a little distracting these days.

"Honestly, we're the most suspicious-looking people here."

"Well, that's both disappointing and not entirely surprising at the same time," she sighs. And she's not wrong. We're kind of a motley crew of ridiculousness. While we are dressed more appropriately than not—although, with Granny squinting at everyone and Daisy alternating between sobbing and blowing her nose loudly—we stand out more than anyone else. Not to mention . . . eek!

"Uh . . . uhh . . ." I stammer.

"Speak up, dear," Marla says.

"Don't mumble," Granny says. "I can't read lips today so spit it out."

"Miss Marla, Big Thunder is . . . uh . . . poking his . . . head . . . uh . . . out of the top of your pocketbook." I clamp my mouth shut to keep from laughing. Laughing out loud would definitely draw attention to us at this funeral.

"Oh dear," she says absentmindedly as she tries to stuff him back down. I snort, losing my hold on the hilarity that has become my life lately. I mean, I was bound to snap sometime. Apparently, that time is now, so pass the funny jackets and horse tranquilizers and point me toward the happy room, please.

"Stop laughing!" Daisy orders, but even she's laughing. "Shit. I needed that."

I wipe a stray tear from my eye. "I think we all did."

"We better get out of here," Daisy says, looking around the room. "Everyone is looking this way."

"I guess we're not incognito anymore," I agree. "Shall we, ladies?"

"I'd rather go to yoga class anyway," Granny says, and I can't help the groan that tries to escape my mouth.

"I haven't been to a yoga class in ages!" Daisy says excitedly. "I could use me some zen."

"You should see how limber my Harold has gotten," Marla preens.

"You know what I always say?" Daisy asks, and I know that I really, really don't want to know.

"What's that, dear?" Marla asks as we push through the glass doors and out into the parking lot.

"A limber man is worth two in the bush. Get it? Bush!" Daisy responds, and they all throw their heads back and cackle.

"Fuck my life," I mutter to myself.

"What's that, dear?" Granny asks me. "You know I hate it when you mumble."

"Goddammit, Ruth!" Granny shouts after another toot rattles the walls of the yoga room back at Peaceful Sunset.

"It wasn't me!" Ruth cries.

"Fuck me," someone gripes from the other side of the room. "I haven't been gassed this bad since I was a prisoner of the VC."

"You are blades of grass waving in the cool summer breeze," Harmony says.

Fffwwaaaaaaaarrrrpppffttt.

"Maybe grass at one of those stinky dairy farms off the 15," Granny mumbles.

"You know what kind of grass I could go for?" Harold asks and answers before anyone else can. "The kind you roll up and smoke. It's been a long time since I had some good shit."

"It's all about the edibles now, old man," Harmony shares.

"Fucking charlies."

"Those mess me up," Harold says. "I tried some—I got the glaucoma, you know—but that shit made me so paranoid that I found myself hiding in a 7-Eleven down on Front Street, eating an entire aisle of Funyuns."

"Ooohh." Harmony nods. "Bad trips are no joke. You should talk to my man, Hector. He'll hook you up. He runs the dispensary over on Adams."

"I will!" Harold says. "Thanks, Harmony!"

Fwwaaarrrppptthhh.

"For the love of all that's holy," Harmony, the yoga instructor, wails. "Someone start a petition, a Change. org thing, or something. We have to get chili off of the freaking menu!"

"Oooohh," someone says. "I haven't been to a sit-in in years!"

"Yeah, like, fifty years," the same man, who appears to be reliving his time in Vietnam, shouts.

Fwwaaaaaaaaaarrrrrpppp.

"Dear Jesus, not a sit-in," Harmony snaps, and I can't help but laugh.

After we bailed on the funeral, the ladies and I had piled into Harold's baby-blue Caddy and headed back to the senior living high-rise where Granny and Marla live. We all changed into our yoga gear of cropped leggings and matching sports bras, each set in a different color.

We met Marla and Harold at the door.

"Nice leggings," I told Harold when I spotted him in a pair of skintight Nike running pants.

"Thanks." He smiled broadly. "After seeing your young man in a pair, I felt inspired."

"Trust me, Mr. Harold," Daisy said. "After seeing Trent in a pair of those tight pants, we all felt inspired." And she's not wrong.

And then we walked into Harmony's yoga class, where things quickly derailed.

"We should be fine as long as Ruth isn't invited." Granny snickers. "She'd probably just crap her pants anyway."

"That was one time!" Ruth shouts. "I crapped my pants one time!"

"I knew it!" someone shouts from the back.

"It wasn't even my fault," Ruth wails. "Someone spiked my Metamucil."

It was probably Granny and her friends.

"Now, who would do a thing like that?" Granny questions Ruth. I shoot her a wide-eyed look. Oh, fuck me, it was her! I was kidding, joking around. I wasn't serious.

Granny just quietly shrugs.

Sweet Baby Jesus in a flasher trench coat. Granny is going to go up the river for murder one!

"Now move into Warrior One," Harmony instructs.

I take a deep breath and try to re-center myself, but it's no use. There is too much swirling around in my brain, and I can't take it. There is something that's been bugging me, something at the back of my mind, and I just haven't figured it out yet, but the harder I try to access it, the farther away it gets.

"Now, drop your hands into Triangle Pose."

I twist and drop my hand to the mat, feeling my strength from my core out. I have been practicing for years, and because of it, I am able to move smoothly through the movements. Usually, I find peace and enjoyment in this class with my granny and her friends, but not today. I can't stay focused with my mind wandering and my body still feeling a little out of whack after James's mini reign of terror.

Fffffwwaarrrrrrppppttt.

"Jesus Christ," Harmony snaps. "I can't take any more of this shit. Ruth, get your bowels under control."

"It wasn't me!" Ruth whines.

"Class dismissed," Harmony says.

I sigh and roll up my yoga mat. This really is for the best. I slide my feet into my flip-flops and walk over to my friends, who are waiting for me.

"Did you see the look on Ruth's face when Harmony told her to control her bowels?" Granny cackles.

"It. Was. *Awesome*!" Marla cheers. "Maybe she'll learn her lesson about being so awful to other people."

"Doubtful, but it was still fun." Granny laughs.

Missy Elliot sounds from within Daisy's massive tote bag, and she reaches in and pulls out her phone. She looks at the screen and makes a face.

"I must have missed a call," she says as she presses a button and puts the phone to her ear. Whatever Daisy hears is not good. She blanches as she listens further.

"Daisy?" I ask, but she shakes her head. She'll tell me when she's done.

Granny, Marla, Harold, and I stand there and wait for her to finish. I look around at everyone in our small group. Worry is etched on all of our faces.

"Well?" Granny asks when Daisy hangs up the phone.

"Don't keep us waiting, girl," Marla says.

"That was Alyssa," Daisy answers quietly.

"What?" we all shout at the same time.

"Where is she?" Granny asks.

"Where was she?" Marla questions.

"Is she okay?" I ask cautiously.

"No," Daisy answers me. "No, she's not okay."

"What happened?"

"She's been kidnapped, just like we thought, and if we don't find her, she's going to die too," Daisy says. I can hear the panic rising up in her voice.

"We don't know that—" I start, but she cuts me off.

"We do. Just listen." She swipes her finger across the screen of her phone to unlock it again. Daisy presses a few buttons to call up her voicemail and puts it on speakerphone so we can all hear it.

"Daisy . . . *crackle* . . ." The connection is bad. "Daisy, I need your help . . . *crackle crackle* . . . I've been kidnapped . . . find me . . . *crackle* . . . before . . . too late . . . *crackle crackle* . . . be careful . . . it's . . ." And then the call ends abruptly.

"Oh no," Marla says.

"I'm so sorry, Daisy," Granny tells her.

"We have to do something!" she shouts. "We have to find her."

"You have to give this to Trent," I tell her. "He has to know about this."

"I'm not going to sit by and wait for the police to figure it out," she says.

"I know that," I say, trying to calm her down. "But we shouldn't prevent them either. The faster that we find her, the better it will be for Alyssa, and for everyone. Okay?"

"Okay." Daisy sighs. "Let me call Trent."

"Good."

She pulls her phone back up and dials Trent's number. After speaking to him in hushed tones for a while, she agrees to meet him to turn over her phone so it can be analyzed by the computer nerds at the police department. He calls them specialists, but, let's be real, they are super crime-fighting nerds.

My own phone chimes in my pocket. I see that I have a text message from an unknown caller. A chill goes up my spine and the hair on the back of my neck stands on end as I swipe across the screen to unlock it.

UNKNOWN CALLER: You should have listened to me.

That was it, nothing else. I panic and hit Delete before Granny can ask me what I was looking at. I don't want her involved in this mess at all. But I know she's already in it up to her pretty neck. I just have to keep her away from it as much as possible.

"I have to run and meet Trent to hand over my phone, so you won't be able to get ahold of me for a while," Daisy says as she rejoins our group.

"No worries," I tell her. "Whatever comes up, we'll handle it."

"Thanks, Shelby," she says, surprising me with a fierce hug. "You're a good friend. The best."

"So are you," I tell her. And she is. I love her to pieces.

"Trent said you'll be hearing from him," she tells me, and I just roll my eyes.

"Of course I will," I droll.

"He worries because he cares," she says sagely.

"I know," I agree.

Daisy stuffs her phone back into the tote bag and slings it over her shoulder before hurrying out the door. Just then my phone chimes again.

TRENT: Don't do anything stupid.

ME: I assure you that I am never stupid.

TRENT: ...

ME: I'm not!

TRENT: I never said you were.

ME: You were thinking it.

TRENT: I never think you're stupid. I think you're wild and reckless and eventually I'm either going to have to arrest you or bury you, and the thought of either both breaks my heart and is actively turning all my fucking hair gray.

ME: Your hair isn't gray.

TRENT: You're not looking closely enough.

ME: Just saying…

TRENT: Nice save.

ME: Thank you. I thought it was rather uninspired.

TRENT: Try not to get yourself killed, please.

ME: I like that you said please.

TRENT: It would piss me right the

```
hell off if you died.

ME: Annnndd you ruined it.

TRENT: Gotta go. Talk to you later.

ME: Talk to you later.
```

"Well," Granny says. "There's really only one thing left to do." I definitely don't like the way she says that, but at the same time, I know she's right.

I let out a weary sigh and agree. "I know."

I DID NOT SEE THAT COMING

"I'm . . . I'm not sure how this works," I say as I admit defeat in the new bikini that Granny ordered for me off the internet.

"Now, you know I think you're beautiful and I love you," Granny starts, and I know that what comes next is going to be awful. "But you look kind of like a busted can of biscuits."

"I know!" I wail. "But I don't know how to get either in it all the way or out of it."

The top of the bikini has all of these gold straps that crisscross all over my cleavage, and it seemed simple enough, but now I'm strung up like a squirrel in a trap.

"Yeah," Marla says, scratching her head. "I don't really know either. It's kind of like a Rubik's Cube of boobies."

"Guys!" I shout as I start to panic. "I need help here!"

"Well, don't start to panic now!" Granny takes

command of the situation. "We'll get you out of this . . . or in it. I'm not rightly sure which, but we'll figure it out!"

"Granny?" I whisper, feeling a little scared.

"Yeah, Shell?"

"I can't feel my nipple."

"Well, shit," she barks out. "Marla, work faster!"

After Daisy left to meet Trent at the police station, Granny, Marla, and I had all piled back into the Caddy and headed down to George Washington's club again, hoping against hope that we would find the answers we needed.

With our bags of glitter and stripper heels in tow, we all raced into the club, through the main room, and down the hall to the back room. Granny looked as cool as you please and not the slightest bit out of breath, while I had huffed and puffed to blow the house down. She reached into the bowels of her granny purse and procured a gold metallic bikini with deep push-up cups like a regular bra and all the little crisscrossing straps for days. The bottoms looked like teeny-tiny metallic gold briefs. It had seemed straightforward enough, but when I took off all of my clothes and tried to put it on, things went a little sideways on me.

Now, I'm standing here wearing nothing but the top, and that's a pretty loose definition of the term *wearing,* and in danger of losing my right nipple, as it might have fallen off and I just haven't realized it yet.

"Almost got it," she grunts as she pulls really hard.

Something pops, and all of a sudden, the feeling rushes back into my nipple. I scream out loud as searing pain rips through my tender flesh, and I almost black out.

"Whoa there," Granny says as they try to steady me on my feet. "You all right there?"

"I'm fine," I say for my benefit as much as theirs. Maybe more. "I'm fine."

I stagger a bit until I get my feet underneath me once and for all. Who knew an epic purple nurple could drop you to your knees? I pull on the bathing suit bottoms and step into my heels before wiping the back of my hand across my brow.

"Whew, that was a workout." I laugh. "But I think I'm ready now."

"Um, Shelby?" Marla asks me.

"Yes, Miss Marla?"

"Is now a bad time to tell you that we forgot to put pasties on you before you got that top on?" she asks hesitantly.

"Motherfucker!" I grumble. "You have got to be shitting me."

"No, dear, we're not . . . um . . . shitting you," she answers.

"Shelby, do calm down." Granny rolls her eyes. "It'll be fine."

"What's going to be fine?" I yell. "Ripping off my other nipple? More emotional and/or physical scarring? It's not going to be fine!"

"Well," Marla hedges. "Maybe she doesn't need them."

"Maybe she doesn't need nipples either!" I snark.

"There is no room for that attitude in this investigation, Shelby!" Granny snaps at me. "Don't make me spank you."

"You wouldn't dare," I huff.

"Wouldn't I?" Granny asks with her chin held high. "Was I fibbing when I busted your butt for stomping in my flower beds after I told you not to?"

"No," I mumble.

"No what?" she says softly. Damn, she's amazing. A true force to be reckoned with.

"No, ma'am."

"That's what I thought. Now, maybe we can access those giant nipples of yours from the bottom instead of the top," she muses.

"They're not that big!" I shout.

"They're like freaking dinner plates right now!" Granny yells back.

"That's because you almost ripped them right the hell off!" I shout back. "I could have died."

"But you didn't. Now, pop those Christmas chargers out and let Marla slap some Forever stamps on them," she orders.

"Fine!" I pout before pulling my breast out of the bottom of the bikini top one at a time, and fuck me if they aren't huge and bright red. My poor nipples might never be the same again. "No slapping!"

"I wouldn't dream of it," Marla says softly before placing a stamp over each abused tip.

"But I would so hurry up," Granny barks.

"What's gotten into you two?" I ask. "I'm not sure if I understand the good cop, bad cop routine here."

Granny turns and looks to me. When her eyes meet mine, there is no more joking around. No more worrying about ruined nipples, because in her eyes, I see the stark fear she has been keeping banked for my benefit.

This isn't a joke or a game. Women are dying, and we don't know where they're being taken or why.

"I'm sorry," I whisper.

"I know, darling girl," Granny says before wrapping me up in her strong arms.

"I'm scared," I admit.

"Me too, but we'll be okay. Whitmore girls always come on top." She winks at me.

"Don't you mean 'Whitmore girls always come *out* on top'?" I ask.

"No." She laughs. "We always come on top, but we'll survive this too."

"You're terrible," I say with a laugh. We needed the tension broken before we fought each other instead of the real villain.

There's a knock at the door.

"Quick!" I whisper. "You better hide." Shit, we didn't have time to hide any weapons or get my two favorite octogenarians into their cramped hiding spots.

I am just reaching for the On switch on the stereo when the door to the room bangs open.

"Don't bother," a voice I was hoping to never hear again says after the door clicks closed behind him.

"And what, pray tell, brings you here?" I ask my very own personal mobster when I turn around to face him.

"A warning." He says nothing else. He just stands there with his back to the door and his arms crossed in front of his chest.

"That's it?" I ask incredulously. "You just say 'warning' and don't actually give a warning?"

"Someone's watching you," he says into the silent

room.

"You, I'm sure," I huff. Today has not been my day. I'm not sure how it's ever going to turn around. Trent is scared that James is lying in wait, I'm frustrated that we don't know who is killing these women, and Alyssa may be lost forever. There really isn't any way to turn that kind of day around. And now I have Mr. Silent and Deadly staring me down while I'm practically naked and my nipple is still smarting.

"No," he answers.

"Then who?" I force myself not to rub my nipple wound while it still stings.

"I don't know," he says.

"Then what are you doing here?" I ask again.

"Like I said, a warning." He opens his mouth like he wants to say more and then snaps his jaw closed, obviously thinking better of it. "Just watch your back."

And with that parting shot, he turns and storms out the same way he came in.

"Good talk," I say to no one at all.

"What the hell was that all about?" Marla asks the room at large.

"I don't know," Granny says, rubbing her arms as if she's suddenly cold. "But I don't like it."

And neither do I.

I'm not sure how long we stand there while we collectively worry about what a warning from our friendly, neighborhood mob boss could mean. Actually, I'm pretty positive it doesn't mean anything good. Let's just hope it doesn't mean my impending doom because I stuck my neck out to help Daisy find the girls.

A loud crash sounds in the main room, followed by

a scream.

"What the fuck was that?" Granny shouts. Granted, she was a field nurse during wartimes, so she's pretty unflappable, even in her eighties.

"I don't know," Marla says.

I'm secretly wondering if it's a marker of the apocalypse.

The door bangs open again, and George Washington himself sticks his head inside.

"George!" Marla shouts. "What happened?"

"I had a girl fall and split her leg right open," he explains. "Bone showing and everything."

"Oh, gross," I mumble. I'll be the first to admit I am not good with blood and guts.

"I heard you gals were back here again," George says. "I could really use some help keeping her settled until the ambulance gets here."

"Of course," Granny says before taking charge of the situation. "Let's go, ladies."

"Uh . . . I'll just stay here," I say.

"Shelby—" Marla starts, but she takes one look at my ashen face and knows that I can't. "She'll be fine, Verna. Let's go."

"You sure you're going to be all right?" Granny asks me.

"I'm fine," I reassure her. "My nipple hardly hurts at all anymore."

"Very funny." She rolls her eyes. "We'll be right back."

"All right."

I watch as Marla and Granny file out the door to go help the poor girl with the broken leg until the ambulance gets here. What a mess. I shudder. One time in college, we were prepping the room for a rush party and two girls were tasked with hanging stars from the classroom ceiling. They were too short to reach while standing on a chair, so they decided that one would sit in the chair to hold it down and the other would climb on top of the little writing desk that stuck off of the front of the chair.

Well, when they were done hanging the decorations, the girl standing on the desk announced that the stars were all hung and started to hop down, but before she could get off of the desk, the girl in the chair jumped up, and the chair toppled over, girls and all. The one on the desk had broken her leg so badly that the bone stuck up through the skin. I took one look at it and almost passed out, so I know without a doubt that I would be of no use to them out there right now. Granny and Marla, on the other hand, are made of tougher stuff than I am. I smile at the thought. I hope I'm just as cool as they are when I'm eighty.

I hear the door click closed behind me.

"Well, that was quick," I say as I turn around. "The ambulance must have been right around the corner."

"I'm afraid it's not that quick," the surprise guest in the back room says.

It's not my grandmother who stands right in front of me, but a face I never thought I would see here. I feel my face pull in confusion. This all has to be a misunderstanding. Why would he be here now?

"I see that I have confused you," he says. "I promise I'll explain everything. Just . . . later."

I open my mouth to respond, but he strikes fast like

a snake before I can even react, and I am clubbed over the head for the second time in as many weeks. *I really wish people would stop doing that.* is my very last thought before everything goes black.

chapter EIGHTEEN

WELL, SHIT FIRE AND SAVE MATCHES

My head is pounding in time with my pulse. At least that's what it feels like.

My mouth feels dry, as if it's packed with cotton. I swallow back against it, but it's no use. My eyes are blurry. I have to blink them over and over again to clear them.

"So glad you could finally join me," my old boss from the home improvement store says.

"Bill? Is that you?" I ask.

"Of course." He smirks. "It took you long enough to figure it out."

"I didn't figure it out at all," I say before I think better of it. Clearly, being hit over the head repeatedly is doing wonders for my brain-to-mouth filter. I would roll my eyes at that thought, but my head is pounding so bad that I'm afraid I may puke or pass out.

"I know," Bill says sadly. "And I am so disappointed."

"I-I'm sorry," I stammer. My brain is playing a deadly game of catch-up. If I can't get it together, there is no way I'm going to make it out of here alive.

He sighs. "I guess it's all right. I mean, I do have you, after all." And the way he smiles at me makes my skin crawl.

"What do you mean, you have me now?" I ask. I have to swallow back against the bile to force the words out.

"Well, this is all for you, silly." Bill smiles at me indulgently. "I did everything for you."

What the actual fuck?

"What?" I ask. My voice sounds small and breathy, and I hate that. I hate feeling small and powerless and scared.

"Well, not all for you," Bill says offhandly. And one, thank fuck he's not killing hookers for me, because that would be terrible; two, I don't know what two is, but this is really fucking creepy; and three, I really need him to keep talking until I can figure all of this shit out.

"What do you mean?" I ask him. I mean, really, how can he be killing for me? I haven't worked at that store in over a year. I haven't seen him or thought about him in anything other than passing while visiting my friend Hilde at the store.

"I always wanted you when you worked for me," he says calmly, like this is a fucking walk in the park, when, no, sir, it is not! "You had to have noticed me watching you. Didn't you?"

"Yes," I answer. I mean, of course I noticed the creepy looks he gave me over the years. Not to mention all the accidental boob grazes and butt touches when he was trying to show me something. I thought I had a case for sexual harassment in the workplace, not a fucking murderer on my hands!

Jesus H. Christ. If I get out of here alive, I'm going to need a fucking drink. And an ibuprofen the size of Alaska. My head is killing me. I'm pretty sure I have a concussion.

"I would have married you years ago," he says, and thank God for those unanswered prayers. Holy shit, I could have been dead years ago. And never had the carnal knowledge that comes with a round of orgasms provided by Trent Foyle. Now, that's a sad thought. "But Mama did not approve of you."

"What?" I say before I can think better of it. "What do you mean? Everyone loves me!" Maybe I shouldn't talk anymore. Maybe the less I say, the better, and then good old, crazy fucking Bill can talk all he wants and not kill me.

"Mama always said that red hair was the stamp of the devil," he explains.

"Well, it's not like I could help that," I mumble to myself.

"That's what I thought too, but she said, 'Fire on the head must be fire in the bed,' and she was sure that you were a whore of the worst sort," he says. "Personally, I always wondered about the 'fire in bed' part. I think about that often at night and when I'm alone." Well, now that's icky. I could have done without that knowledge.

"Oh . . . um . . . thanks." I can barely choke out the words. I want to barf, but I know that wouldn't go over well. I need to be smart here, but with my bell having been rung so many times in the last week or so, I'm not sure I can be. I only know that I need to tread lightly now.

"And then James stole you away from me," he says, and the anger that sweeps across Bill's face chills me to my very bones. "That did not make me happy, Shelby."

"I-I'm sorry." My palms are clammy and my upper lip is sweaty. This is all pretty gross, but I'm so nervous I can't help it. At least I haven't tooted yet.

"You're lucky you cut him loose," Bill growls. "If you hadn't gotten rid of him when you did, I might have been forced to take action regardless of what Mama said to do or not to do."

Well, I don't like the sound of that!

"Oh . . . well . . . good." I don't think at all, but at the same time, I feel like it doesn't behoove me to make Bill even madder.

"But then you took up with the detective with all the muscles," he snaps. Well, he's got me there; I did do that. And the cop with all the muscles. I did him too. Gladly. Apparently, the bump on the noggin and being this close to death is making me a little kooky. My bad.

"I'm sorry." I'm not, actually. I'm not sorry at all. The only thing I'm sorry about right now is letting this crazy ass get the drop on me.

"It's all right," he purrs, his mood flipping on a dime. Shit! Someone's off their meds today. "What matters is you're here now."

"Oh, okay." Shit, fuck, damn. What do I do now? My eyes are still a little blurry, and I blink them again, making them water.

"Don't cry, my darling," Bill coos. I hate that he thinks I'm worried about him. I'm not. I'm worried about me! And my head hurts. "I was with other women. Well, I tried to be. But it wasn't like I sat around and pined for you all the time while you whored around with half of the greater San Diego area."

"Uh . . . thanks," I say. This guy is not making it easy to look past his shit and feel bad for his being crazy and all that. I kind of want to punch him in the face, but my arms aren't working real well right now.

I look down at my lap and realize that my arms aren't working because my wrists are handcuffed in my lap. And what is with these assholes getting their hands on handcuffs? Don't they know this shit chafes?

"It's your fault, really," Bill explains. "I wanted you so bad that no one else would do. I could only get hard for you."

"Awesome," I say, but really, this is not awesome. I'm not real wild about my psycho ex-boss only being able to pop a boner over me.

"I tried to date the women Mama chose for me, but I could barely manage a twitch, let alone an erection." He lets out a heavy sigh. "So they had to go." Jesus, I hope he means that he just didn't call them back and not that he killed them like he did Christina and Stacy and probably Alyssa. How many bodies has this guy buried?

"I'm sorry." Not sorry. Not sorry at freaking all. Holy shit, I hope this guy rots in hell.

"So I started visiting hookers," he explains, and suddenly all the dots are starting to line up. "It was okay for a while, but Mama hated it. She beat me when she caught me with a hooker in a red wig." That is alarming on so many levels that I can't even describe it. In fact, I don't want to.

"I'm sorry. That must have been awful for you," I say softly and infuse my words with false compassion so that I sound like I care. Fuck, I hope that was believable. I hope it works. Really, I'm wondering how I can kill him or, at the very least, incapacitate him. I need to get out of here, but I don't want to jump the gun and make him mad. I don't want to die.

"You know what they say?" He shrugs.

"No," I respond. "What?"

"'What doesn't kill you makes you stronger.' And besides, after Mama and I had it out, I couldn't complete the act with anyone but you, and now I have you," he says with triumph shining in his eyes. Well, shit fire and save matches. That's not good.

"Oh . . . okay," I mumble, but inside, I am screaming that this is not okay. Nothing about this is okay. And nothing about this is ever going to be okay. Oh God, does he want to have sex, like, right now? I feel the bile rise up in my throat. I force it back down. I am probably as good as dead if I puke on his face right now at the thought of banging him. But I also can't bang him. Ever. He's crazy. And I'm in love with Trent.

"Don't worry, pet," he says as he tenderly brushes some of the hair that's fallen in my face, and the action surprises me. "I want you clean and beautiful when you come to me. I will not take you until then."

Thank God. I won't wash for a year if it keeps his hands off of my person. And then it's as if he hears my thoughts—maybe he did because the head injury has me acting a little funny—because, as if he wasn't capable of being sweet and gentle as he was a moment ago, Bill slaps the shit out of me so hard that my teeth rattle.

"That was for the cop," he says through gritted teeth before grabbing me by my upper arm and hauling me to my feet. I stumble a bit, but after he struck me so fiercely, I don't want to do anything to anger him more. "But this is perfect. I have been waiting for ages to get my hands on you, and now you've practically fallen into my lap."

"Oh . . . good." Said no woman ever where this man is concerned.

"I know I'll be able to keep it up for you," he says seriously. "Those other whores weren't the right ones to keep me hard, but I know you'll be up to the task. I've been watching you with the cop, so I know you're willing to go the distance." That's unfortunate.

Oh, gross. Well, that is disgusting. If I get out of here alive, I'm going to have to talk to Trent about heavier curtains in the bedroom.

Bill hauls me through a door that I didn't see because it was behind me and tosses me onto the floor of what has to be a storage room seeing as it has cold, hard floors. With my hands still bound, there's no way to break my fall, and my head cracks against the hard floor before everything goes black.

WE'RE NOT DOWN AND OUT YET

"**H**ey!" someone whisper-shouts just before they slap me. "Hey, you gotta wake up."

I blink my eyes open, and when they clear, I look up into Alyssa's concerned face.

"Holy shit!" I practically shout. "You're alive!"

"I am. Now keep it down!" she shushes me.

"I'm sorry," I say softly. "Where are we?"

"We're in some kind of storage room in a house or building of some kind," she explains. "We have to get out of here, or he's going to kill us. Stacy was alive when I got here, but not for long."

"Shit," I mumble to myself, but she obviously hears it.

" 'Shit' is right. Can you move? Is anything broken?" she asks me.

"Only my head," I groan as I try to sit up. "I really wish people would stop hitting me over the head this week. I think it's done permanent damage."

"Probably." She shrugs. "We need to get out of here."

"How?" I ask.

"I don't know," she tells me. "Can you get out of those?" She points to my cuffed wrists.

"No, can you?" I ask, feeling hopeful.

"Of course." She winks at me and pulls a hairpin from her shoulder-length brown hair before working it into the lock on the cuffs. The minute they spring free, I rub the sting out of my wrists.

I look around the room and take stock of our surroundings. I see small bags of concrete or grout maybe and a metal folding table and chairs set just like the one my great-grandma used to host her canasta group every third Wednesday of the month.

"Have you tried the door?" I ask her, looking to the one door in the room.

"Yeah, it's always locked," Alyssa says. "You can try it, but don't be frustrated if it doesn't work."

"Okay," I agree as I make my way over to the door. I put my hand on the cold metal of the doorknob and turn it in my hand. And it doesn't budge. I let out a frustrated sigh.

"I told you so," Alyssa says, and, I'm not gonna lie, she kind of irritates me right now with her negative attitude.

"I know that," I snap.

"Look, don't be pissed at me," she says, and I know she's right. "Be pissed at the crazy killer dude who's obsessed with you."

"His name is Bill," I tell her.

"What?" she asks.

"His name is Bill, and he was the general manager at the home improvement store I used to work at, in the custom kitchens and bath department," I explain.

"Huh," she says in thought. "Was he always batshit crazy?"

"Not that I could tell." I shrug. "I mean, he was always kind of a lecher, but he never gave off the psychotic-murderer vibes before."

"Weird, I wonder what changed," she muses, and I also wonder what could have changed until it dawns on me what it could be.

"He was talking a lot about his mom not approving of his romantic interests," I tell her. "When he had me in the other room. I think she died last month. Maybe that's when he snapped."

"Maybe," Alyssa agrees. "I've seen dudes with mommy issues do some weird shit."

"True dat," I agree and hold up my fist for a knuckle bump, and she taps hers to mine.

"I think our best bet is to take him by surprise when he comes in here next," she says after some thought.

"Okay," I agree. "That sounds good. Do you have a plan?"

chapter TWENTY

BIG PLANS AND CHIPOTLE

"**A**re you going to be okay?" she asks me when I lean against the wall and close my eyes to catch my breath.

"I have to be," I answer without opening my eyes. I just need this minute to regroup, and to get the room to stop spinning. That would also be both great and highly effective.

"We can wait if you're not ready right now," Alyssa says softly. "I don't want to push you too far."

"And what happens if he comes and we're not ready?" I snap my eyes open to meet her stare as I ask the question we both know the answer to.

"We don't know that he's going to kill me next," she says. "Or at all."

"Yes, we do," I push. "And I won't risk it."

"I just don't want you to get hurt, or worse, because of me," she says, showing her soft side for a moment.

"Look at me." I hold my arms wide and laugh without humor. "I'm already hurt. I've been hit over the head this week more times than I can count. I'm pretty sure I look like a panda right now."

"That's because you do," she agrees readily.

"You're not supposed to agree!" I snap. "You're supposed to tell me that I am beautiful and magnificent."

Alyssa laughs her soft, tinkling laugh. "You are beautiful and magnificent. You also look like you went a few rounds with Ronda Rousey and lost. Big-time."

"Thank you . . . I think," I say after I think better on it.

"Anytime," she says. Alyssa is silent and contemplative for a minute before she speaks again, and when she does, her voice is quiet and small, and I hate it. No one should be made to feel that way. "I'm scared."

"I know," I admit. "I am too, but we're going to get out of here together."

"Thank you," Alyssa says after another quiet moment. "I needed to hear that."

"Anytime."

"You should get some rest," she tells me.

"I don't want to leave you alone," I admit. "What if he comes back?"

"I'll wake you. I promise." She takes a deep breath. "Why don't you drink some of that water and eat a PowerBar or two—there's, like, a billion of them—and then get some shut-eye. Now that I know you're not going to keel over and die, you can get some healing rest. I'll wake you in a few hours to take the next watch."

"That sounds like a plan," I agree. "I'll just eat a bit

and then hit the hay."

"Good."

I grab a water bottle and a PowerBar from the cupboard that Alyssa pointed out. It's like a prepper's pantry full of dry goods and water. I wonder what else is in here and look around a bit but don't want to waste my precious nap time. I don't know how much time I will actually get before Bill comes back for one of us. There seems to be a medium-sized cast-iron pan, some rope, tons of water, and food. Not to mention sleeping bags all rolled up, batteries, and a storm radio.

"Hey, look at this," I call out when I pick up the radio.

"Quit playing around," she barks softly. "I don't want to call his attention to us when we're exhausted and unprepared."

"That's true," I admit. "I don't want to call his attention either. My uncle, Sal, has a radio similar to this one. I used to play with it as a kid."

"And?" she asks. "What's so exciting about an old radio?"

"Well, the one Uncle Sal had could both receive and transmit," I say proudly. "I wonder if it can get a message out for us."

"Yeah, but who would we call?" she asks. "It was a great idea, but now we're back to square one."

"Not exactly," I tell her. "All local law enforcement use the same channels, and it is illegal for anyone else to use them."

"So we're screwed," she says sadly. I hate this defeated look on Alyssa's face. We're down but we're not out yet!

"Not at all." I smile at this strong but sweet woman whom I haven't known for very long, but I know with all of my heart that she is now part of the tribe. Whether she likes it or not, she's a Dangerous Dame now. No take-backs. "I think that is a great way for them to find us. And that they will understand why we broke the rules."

"Do you know what channels to try?" she asks me, and I can see that she's getting excited over the idea.

"Of course." I wink at her. "You stand guard while I try to get this old girl going again."

"Okay. I'll let you know if I hear anything."

I set the radio on the folding table and turn down the dial for the volume so if it does come on, we don't alert Bill to our plan before we have a chance to get it off the ground. I turn the dial for the frequency that I know most officers use and start turning the old crank handle. It's hard to get moving at first, but then I really get it going, and the lights start to flicker and light up on the old radio.

"Yes!" I quietly pump my fist in the air.

"Did you get it?" Alyssa asks excitedly.

"Yes!" I whisper, not wanting to jinx it just yet. "Let's test her out."

I turn the volume up slightly and hear familiar voices. We must still be in San Diego County. Thank God. Alyssa and I needed a break, and this may just be it. I pick up the handset and click it a couple of times.

"This is a law enforcement channel. Please change frequencies," a local dispatcher that I know says.

"Cora, it's Shelby," I say quickly. "I need your help."

"Shelby, everyone is looking for you," she says. "Where are you?"

"I don't know," I say quickly. "I was kidnapped by Bill Carmichael. He was my old boss."

"What else can you tell me about where you're being held?" Cora asks me.

"I don't know. We're in a storage closet of some kind. Cement floors, but otherwise I was unconscious when I came in," I tell her before I think about what I just said. "Do me a favor and don't tell Trent that part. He gets a little upset when people render me unconscious."

"Shelby, I switched this to broadcast, so he's hearing it right now," she says, peeing all over my parade. "They can all hear it."

"Well, damn," I utter before I can think of anything else to say. "I guess I'm in a bit of a pickle. Could you help me out?"

"We'll find you," she promises me.

"Thanks."

"Keep this line open," Cora tells me. "You won't be able to hear me, but we'll be able to hear you. Just know that the cavalry is on their way."

"Thank you."

I hurry back into the cabinet and grab some duct tape and tape the buttons on the hand mic down so that they will continue to transmit.

"I think he's coming," Alyssa says.

"Shit," I mumble. "Okay, it's okay. Just grab what you can."

"Okay," she says as she picks up the cast-iron pan.

I grab one of the folding chairs from the table and

close it. I hold it up so I'll be ready to swing when he opens the door and steps inside.

Alyssa and I are as quiet as can be. I think we even hold our breath; I know that I am. You can hear the key scrape in the lock before the doorknob slowly turns. Bill pushes the door open, and it swings on squeaky hinges into the room.

"Shelby? Alyssa?" he calls out, but we don't answer.

Bill steps into the room, clearing the doorjamb. He doesn't see that I am right behind him yet.

"Now!" Alyssa shouts, and I swing my metal folding chair hard enough to make a professional wrestler proud. My swing catches Bill off guard, and he doubles forward but doesn't lose his balance as he stumbles.

Alyssa jumps down from her perch and swings her cast-iron frying pan. But I guess it's heavier than she anticipated because she misses the mark. Bill stumbles back and loses his balance in the process.

"Run!" I shout, and we both drop our makeshift weapons. Alyssa and I head for the door, with me in the lead. When we get into the main part of the house, it's clear that there is no obvious direction to get out.

"This way!" she says, and we head down the hallway and find a dead end.

"Maybe it's this way!" I call out, and we turn in another direction.

I find stairs that I'm sure will lead to the main floor of the house. We race down the stairs, and I can see porch lights streaming through the glass windows on dual antique front doors. Shit! We're really going to make it. Alyssa and I are actually going to survive this.

But I should have known better than counting my chickens before they've had a chance to hatch. Granny would be so disappointed.

I stop in my tracks, and my blood runs cold when I hear Alyssa scream. Slowly, I turn around. Bill has her arms pinned to her sides under his and a very sharp-looking knife held firmly under her chin.

"Don't. Move," Bill orders. "Or your friend will die."

"Don't listen to him, Shelby," Alyssa says. "I'm dead anyway."

"Don't say that!" I cry.

"We both know it's true," she says as tears run down her cheeks. "So run, be safe, bang the hot cop for me."

"There has to be another way," I tell her.

"There isn't," Alyssa says with her pleading eyes locked on mine. I can't leave her here. I refuse to, so we're locked in this deadly stalemate with a crazed killer.

"Hi-yaaaa!" Granny shouts as she jumps out of the shadows and slams Big Thunder down over Bill's head. "There's always another way, dear."

The blow doesn't knock Bill out, but it does make him loosen his hold on Alyssa. Daisy jumps out and grabs her, pulling her friend into her arms.

"It's all going to be all right now," Daisy says to comfort her friend.

"There's still the little problem of the psycho killer to deal with," I say to the room at large as Bill starts to charge.

And then the room explodes.

Okay, it doesn't explode; it just sounds like it. I shake my head like an Etch A Sketch to clear my mind. After all the head trauma, the gunshot kind of shook things up a bit. Wait a minute . . .

Gunshot!

I look behind me and see Marla holding a massive, nickel-plated Desert Eagle pointed toward Bill, who is now on the ground, in her shaking hands. I would think that she's killed him, but he appears to be rolling around on the floor, writhing in pain.

"My knee!" he screams like a little girl. "She shot off my fucking kneecap!"

"Well, that's unfortunate." She shrugs. "I was aiming for his balls. Fucking arthritis."

"Should we tie him up?" Daisy asks as we all stand around staring at him.

"Maybe we should call him an ambulance?" I ask.

"Nah," Alyssa adds. "He seems fine. He can wait for a minute."

"So, how did you find us, anyway?" I ask.

"After you disappeared, George and I looked at the tapes and this guy was seen in the hallways, but then he disappeared," Granny explains.

"Daisy came down to the club after she met with Trent," Marla adds.

"I had heard something in the background on Alyssa's voicemail message that I couldn't place. When the old ladies showed me the tapes, I realized the voice I couldn't place was Bill's. I knew he had taken you."

"So we called Trent," Granny says.

"But he had already heard your call go out to Cora at dispatch," Marla chimes in. "It was already being traced."

"But we couldn't wait for all those hot cops to pull their thumbs out of their asses," Granny says. "So we headed out on our own."

"And got here just in the nick of time." I smile at my girl tribe. "Besides, I thought Trent got rid of the Eagle."

"Oh, what Trent doesn't know won't hurt him." Marla winks at me.

"Is anyone going to help me?" Bill wails.

"No," Daisy says firmly.

"But it fucking hurts!" he cries.

"Just think, this is better than what you did to Stacy and Christina," she says quietly.

We all turn and look over our shoulders as the front door bangs open and Trent and Kane storm in with a sea of uniformed police officers behind them.

"Police! Freeze!" Kane shouts. "Oh, well, it looks like you guys have this covered."

"Always a bridesmaid, huh, Kane?" I laugh.

"Don't you know it." He chuckles. "So . . . Chipotle, anyone?"

And then we all went and had burritos.

epilogue

ALL SETTLED IN

"**P**izza should be here any minute," Kane calls out as Jones and Trent move the sofa for the eleventy billionth time.

All morning the gang has been unloading a moving van containing all of the worldly possessions of Daisy and Alyssa into the condo they are renting to own. And it just so happens to be two doors down from my own condo.

"So tell me what happened again?" Sophia asks. "I can't believe I missed all the fun."

"I'm not so sure I would call it 'fun,' babe," Kane says as he drops a kiss on her lips. "I'm fucking over the moon that you missed it all, even though I did miss you."

"Awwwwww!" Granny and Marla coo at the same time before breaking into another round of giggles. They have been heckling Kane and Sophia ever since she reemerged this morning after returning from the mystery tryout in Chicago.

As it turns out, Bill had always been a little off his rocker, but once his abusive mother passed away, it was as if the floodgates had opened up. Somewhere along the way, he had decided that he could have me if he just took me. Christina and Stacy, and almost Alyssa too, were to be my punishment for not seeing that he was a prince among men all of those years ago and for not fighting for our love.

What a crock of bullshit, right?

Back when I was in college, my mom had set me up on a date with a guy who helped install the new windows on my parents' house. He was pretty cute, with blond hair and a nice body, so I said yes right away. I mean, he seemed nice enough.

It wasn't until we were at dinner at a little Italian fast-food place by the movie theater that his crazy really began to show when he told me about how he used to bite the heads off of live birds with a friend when they were kids.

I saw the serial-killer writing on the bathroom wall then and never called him back after that first date. Actually, I wonder where he is now. I should look him up on Facebook when I get a free moment. But I digress. That guy was the craziest I had ever known until I met Bill, and I had no idea.

That turns my stomach. I will always hate that it's sort of my fault that Stacy and Christina died. Daisy said I can't blame myself, but I know I always will, if just a little bit. If Bill hadn't set his sights on me, they might still be alive today.

All I know is that I need to change the subject, and

fast, before this blue mood takes me down a darker path than I am willing to travel.

"Yeah, we don't want to talk about what you missed." I wink at Kane. "It was absolutely boring without you. Now, tell us all about Chicago."

"Chicago was awesome!" She practically beams sunshine and rainbows as she tells us all about her magical tryout. "I get to go to the Olympics!"

"What? I thought you were disqualified?" I ask.

"Oh, I was," she says, smiling her usual sunny smile. "In ladies' singles. But the female partner in a pairs team that did qualify has to fade into the shadows for some undisclosed reason, and her partner needed a new one to take her place. Isn't that awesome? Well, not the part about her going into hiding, but the part about his picking me!"

"It is!" I agree. I'm pretty sure Kane had said something about this before but it's been a pretty crazy time lately. "Congratulations. He would have been an idiot not to have picked you."

"Thanks, Shelby," she says, squeezing my hand in hers for a second.

"So who is the lucky guy?" Kane asks, and Sophie grows visibly nervous.

"Oh, you know, just an old hockey player turned pairs skater," she says with false brightness.

"Anyone I know?" he asks when Jones walks past us with an armload of pizza boxes heads toward the kitchen.

"He said you guys might know each other," she says softly.

"Oh, what's his name?"

"Luc."

"Luc." Kane seems to think for second before every muscle in his body tenses. "Luc Saucier? No. Fucking. Way."

"It's already been decided, Kane," she says quietly. "There's no going back now."

"Of course there's going back," Kane practically roars. "You are not going anywhere near that womanizing asshole, and that's that."

"This is my dream, Kane. My one dream. And you, or any other man, will not take that from me. You do not get a say here, because this is my life, not yours, and if you can't understand that, then you can see your way out of my life."

You could hear a pin drop in the condo. Poor Sophie. Why are men such douchenozzles? I will never understand.

"Congrats on the new house, ladies," Sophie says politely before walking out the door.

"Sophie, wait!" Kane calls out before racing after her. Sophie doesn't look back once.

"Why are men such douchenozzles?" Granny gives voice to my earlier thoughts.

"It's the age-old question," Marla answers. "That one should know better, though. I am a little disappointed."

"Aw, they'll work it all out," Trent says as he comes up behind me, handing me a paper plate with enough pizza on it to feed an army.

"Leave any for the others?" I ask.

"I thought we could share," he says as he wraps his arms around me from behind.

"Sounds good to me." I settle in for the rest of the afternoon with my people. I think of Kane and Sophia. *Well, most of my people.*

"So, what are your plans now?" Trent asks Daisy and Alyssa.

"Man, you do not want to know," Jones says from the other side of the room, and Trent's muscles tense around me.

"What do you mean?" he asks.

"Well, you know I got a big settlement from the home improvement store chain," I tell Trent.

"Yeah . . . ," he says cautiously.

"Well, Daisy got one as well," I explain.

"It was really more of a mutual parting of the ways," she chimes in. "I didn't want to be reminded of Bill, and they didn't want to be reminded of what Bill did to everyone. They said it would detract from the sales of home shit like keys and pipes and plants."

"Okay . . . ," Trent says. "I'm still not following."

"Well, the idea to go undercover to find the girls was my idea," Daisy explains.

"And you almost got Shelby killed," Trent growls.

"Semantics." She waves his comments off. "And I found Shelby and Alyssa before you did."

"I'm not so sure I like where this conversation is going," Trent says. "Please tell me you are not going to go for your P. I. license."

Spoiler alert: the girls totally already have their P. I. licenses and are setting up shop here in this very condo.

Jones lets out a full belly laugh and Trent groans.

"Just as long as you don't go along with them," he growls. "I like you all in one piece, and I haven't fully recovered from this last adventure."

"Aww, that's sweet," I tell him as I place my palm on his cheek and press my mouth to his. "I'm off of the adventure market, at least for a little while."

Spoiler alert: I totally want a P. I. license, but even I know when not to push my luck.

"Good," he says. "I'm looking forward to a little break in the excitement.

Famous last words . . .

THE END

(For Now)

Stay Tuned for a Sneak Peek of the next Dangerous Dames novel, Layback . . .

PLAYLIST

Vandalizer—Sam Hunt

Dead and Gone—T.I. featuring Justin Timberlake

Reputation—Taylor Swift

Any Man of Mine—Shania Twain

California Gurls—Katy Perry

Come Over—Sam Hunt

Party in the U.S.A.—Miley Cyrus

Cop Car—Sam Hunt

Fancy—Reba McEntire

Rose Garden—Martina McBride

Lose It—Kane Brown

Every Breath You Take—The Police

It Ain't My Fault—Brothers Osborne

Out of the Woods—Taylor Swift

Murder on Ice Series

lay BACK

IT'S NOT WHAT YOU THINK

"**S**weet Kristi Yamaguchi's daisy dress," I whisper more to myself than anyone else. "You have got to be kidding me."

"This is not what you think," Luc says and there is a note of panic in his voice that makes me backup a step.

"Really?" I ask as my anger rises up to the surface. What kind of bubble headed moron does he think I am? I wasn't born yesterday. "Because it looks to me like you are standing over the dead body of our competitor."

"Okay," Luc says hesitantly. "It is what it looks like."

"Darn it, Luc!" I snap. "How could you?"

"What?" he says surprised. "You can't possibly think that I did this?"

"Well, I don't really know what to think right now,

now do I?" I bite back.

"Sophie, please," he pleads. "You've got to believe me."

"This looks bad, Luc," I tell him. "Really, really bad."

"I know." He lets out a frustrated sigh and pushes a hand through his thick hair.

Luc and I stand there, facing each other off, with Layla's body sprawled over a chair between us. I'm not sure which is more disconcerting, the ropes tied around her nude body or the ones tied around her neck.

"Please don't run from me. I'm not going to hurt you."

"I'm not going to lie, Luc, this scares me," I admit.

"I know. Me too."

He sighs again and pulls his hand through his hair. The silence between us speaks volumes. This was supposed to be my second chance at the Games. My last one as a singles competitor was taken from me by my Stepmonster and her evil henchman when they broke my leg. But when the opportunity to replace half of a pairs team came up, I jumped on it. Now, it seems like I should have paid more attention to the fine print.

"You have to believe me," he pleads with those big, brown puppy dog eyes, the ones that have probably gotten him out of more scrapes than he deserves.

I let out a sigh and admit, "I do."

"Thank fuck," Luc blurts out. "But what are we going to do now?"

I wish like heck that I knew myself. This is more than a little complication.

"I don't know." What I do know is that my mostly

on again boyfriend, former professional hockey player and current San Diego PD homicide detective, Kane Fucking Green, is not going to be thrilled when he hears what happened.

Kane is going to be pissed. *Excuse my french.*

My name is Sophia Eleanore Dubois, daughter of a United States Senator, still an Olympic hopeful figure skater, and holy mother of Dorothy Hamill, my life is still complicated . . .

ABOUT JENNIFER

Jennifer is a thirty something lover of words, all words: the written, the spoken, the sung (*even poorly*), the sweet, the funny, and even the four letter variety. She is a native of San Diego, California where she grew up reading the Brownings and Rebecca with her mother and Clifford and the Dog who Glowed in the Dark with her dad, much to her mother's dismay.

Jennifer is a graduate of California State University San Marcos where she studied Criminology and Justice Studies. She is also a member of Alpha Xi Delta.

13 years ago, she was swept off her feet by her very own sailor. Today, they are happily married and the parents of a 10 year old and 8 year old twins. She lives in East Texas where she can often be found on the soccer fields, drawing with her children, or reading. Jennifer is convinced that if she puts her fitbit on one of the dogs, she might finally make her step goals.

She loves a great romance, an alpha hero, and lots and lots of laughter.

STALK ME . . .

www.JenniferRebeccaAuthor.com
Facebook.com/JenniferRebeccaAuthor
Twitter: @JenniRLreads
Instagram @JenniRLreads
Pintrest: @Jennigrl83
SnapChat @JennyRLreads

MORE BOOKS BY JENNIFER

FUNERALS AND OBITUARIES SERIES
I Met a Girl (A Funerals Prequel)**,** FREE on Wattpad
Dead and Buried
Dead and Gone
Dead and Deceived, Coming Late Summer 2019

MURDERS ON ICE
Attack Zone
Layback, Coming May 13, 2019
Hat Trick, Coming Late 2019

THE CLAIRE GOODNITE SERIES
Tell Me a Story
Tuck Me in Tight
Say a Sweet Prayer
Kiss Me Goodnight

THE SOUTHERN HEARTBEAT SERIES
Stand
Whiskey Lullabye
Mercy, FREE on Wattpad

For an complete updated list visit:
www.jenniferrebeccaauthor.com/books

ACKNOWLEDGMENTS

O. M. G. Thank you all so much for hanging with me this last year and patiently waiting for Shelby and the gang to come back to town. I can't even explain how much your excitement of this series means to me. I first had the idea of Shelby after my grandfather's funeral and I was sad and needed to laugh. This fun group of women and their silly yet sexy men helped heal my heart. There is so much of my real family in these books. From the bottom of my heart, thank you for loving them the way that I do.

Thank you to Nazarea Andrews of InkSlinger PR. She busts her ass on every cover reveal and release to make them as successful as possible and it shows. She knocks it out of the park every time and I would be lost without her.

Thank you to Bethany Pennypacker of Outthink Editing. I'm pretty sure I never told her how dyslexic I really am, if at all, and yet she makes me look good every time.

Thank you to Reggie Deanching of R+M Photography and BT Urruela for the awesome cover image. It's perfect.

Thank you to Alyssa Garcia of Uplifting Designs. She always makes my books look good. She's talented and hard working and she's my bestie. If it all went away tomorrow she would still be my ride or die and that means more to me than anything.

Thank you to Stacy Garcia of Graphics by Stacy for making everything else beautiful. She is so talented and creative on her own but somehow manages to make graphics that seamlessly blend with the cover design and branding.

Thank you to my parents who still think this is so cool and tell all of their friends that they have to read my books. And for encouraging me to put all of our family awkwards into a book.

And last, thank you to my husband, Sean, for showing me that there really are great guys out there. They are not perfect, they leave their underwear on the towel rack, they have a mildly unhealthy relationship with magic cards, and have more love to give than anyone could ever deserve. Thank you for being the rock that holds us all up when we can't do it alone. It was only ever you.

Made in the USA
San Bernardino, CA
11 August 2019